PARENTAL

An Ice Knights Novel

GUIDANCE

D1473877

PARENTAL

An Ice Knights Novel

GUIDANCE

AVERY FLYNN

Preview of *Awk-weird* © 2019 by Avery Flynn

Entangled Publishing, LLC
2614 South Timberline Road
Suite 105, PMB 159
Fort Collins, CO 80525
rights@entangledpublishing.com

Amara is an imprint of Entangled Publishing, LLC.

Edited by Liz Pelletier
Cover illustrated by Elizabeth Turner Stokes
Background image by Oxy_gen/Shutterstock

Manufactured in the United States of America

First Edition June 2019

To the readers. Thank you.

Chapter One

Just when Caleb Stuckey thought it couldn't get any worse, his mom walked in.

Now, some people might think getting an ass-chewing by the Ice Knights' coach, Winston Peppers, and the team's oh-my-God-our-players-fucked-up-again public relations guru, Lucy Kavanagh, was about as bad as it could get. They would be wrong. Having his mom join the ass-chewing party in Lucy's office on the fifty-sixth floor of Harbor City's Carlyle Building brought the entire shitstorm to a whole new level of misery.

Britany Stuckey—AKA Brit the Ballbuster, according to some of her players—wasn't just a state champion high school boys' hockey coach and one of the handful of female boys' hockey coaches in the country, she was also the Stuckey family titleholder for taking absolutely, 100 percent no shit from anyone. The anyone, in this case, being him. And the fact that he was a grown man and a professional hockey player with the Harbor City Ice Knights meant nothing. He would, as she often told him, forever be her little Caleb

Cutie—a nickname that proved a mother's love blinded her to her offspring's physical flaws—and she would probably treat him as such until the day one of them got hit by the number six crosstown bus.

He turned to Peppers, a man he thought would have his back despite the video-recorded smack talk that had been blown all out of proportion. "You called my mom?"

"Yes," Peppers asserted, not bothering to slow his pace as he marched from one end of the room to the other as if he were still in the locker room giving his team a what-for in between periods. "Because she is a crucial part of this rehabilitation plan to fix your fuckup."

Caleb slouched down in his chair. "It wasn't that bad."

"Really?" Lucy asked from her seat behind her desk, snark dripping from her voice. "Do I need to play the video again? I can, because every media site on the face of the earth has posted it. Bad Lip Reading even did a mockery of it."

Yeah, and he would have laughed his ass off at anyone else who'd been caught running his mouth like an idiot. Objectively, it was funny. It wasn't every day almost the entire first line of a hockey team got caught bitching and moaning about the team, their playing, the coaches, and the quality of puck bunnies they banged. They'd sounded like spoiled assholes, which he totally admitted wasn't 100 percent not the truth.

Fuck, the next words out of his mouth were going to hurt.

"Okay," he said, avoiding eye contact with every person in the room. "It was dumb. I should have shut it down sooner."

"Dumb?" his mom said, how-in-the-hell-did-I-birth-this-idiot thick in her voice. "You were the most senior player in that car, and you let the younger guys trash their own team!"

He flinched. Yeah, that was not a good look. Still… "I'd had some beers, and they were letting off steam. And it should be noted that I did the right thing by taking an Uber instead of driving."

His mom rolled her eyes. "That's called doing the bare minimum to adult properly."

The room went silent except for the mental buzz saw revving in his ears so realistically that he could smell the diesel fumes. He clenched his teeth hard enough that his jaw ached so he wouldn't snap off a nasty retort at his mom. That wouldn't get him anywhere. She hadn't gotten where she was because she backed down from fights. He'd inherited the trait, but he'd learned that sometimes the best way to win was to appear like he wasn't fighting at all. Guerrilla warfare. Psyops. Subterfuge. When it came to winning a war with his mom, those were the only ways to go.

Never mind that he was an adult with a mortgage, a retirement plan, and a degree in sports management. Sure, he'd had a lot of help from a tutor to earn his degree, but he'd still use it to open his own company when it came time to hang up his skates for good. To his mom, though, he would forever and always be Caleb Cutie who'd fucked up again. And again. And again.

It was fucking exhausting trying to meet Britany Stuckey's expectations.

Lucy, who'd been uncharacteristically watching the goings-on with her mouth shut, broke the tense silence. "Here's what it comes down to, Stuckey. You embarrassed yourself by not stopping the smack talk. You embarrassed the team. You embarrassed Harbor City. This has to be fixed. You are going to have to change the narrative and give everyone something else to talk about besides what dickheads you all are—that is, if you want to keep playing for the Ice Knights." She gave him a second to digest that bit of *yes, it's been confirmed you're an asshole, and if you don't fix it, you'll be playing in the reindeer league at the North Pole.* "And that's why you're going to give the media a story they won't be able to stop talking about.

You're going to let your mom be in charge of your dating profile on Bramble, and you're going to tell her about each date so she can film video segments that the company will use in ads that will begin running immediately."

He couldn't breathe, and a throbbing started in his head right behind his eyes. "That's not gonna happen. I didn't even say anything about the puck bunnies. Why do I have to be part of a date PR nightmare?"

"Because you didn't tell your teammates to shut the fuck up, either," Lucy said. "And because you were the senior player in the car, and you have to set the example or pay the price, whichever the public decides needs to be done for the team as a whole to move past this."

She wasn't wrong. His silence had spoken just as loudly as if he'd made any of the dumb-ass comments.

Still, there was nothing in the world they could say that would make him give in to this bizarre plan. Him? The center of all that attention? No fucking way. Even the idea of it had his stomach doing a triple spin.

"If you don't," Lucy said, "they're going to trade Petrov to reshuffle the first line. This isn't just the possibility of you earning a spot as the Ice Knights' assistant captain on the line."

One of those silences fell that was so heavy, there was no way the news Lucy had just delivered wasn't true. Reshuffle? It had taken two seasons for the team to really gel with their current lineup. Sure, Petrov was coming back from injury, but he would only miss a few of the new season games, and they needed him. He wasn't a player who scored a lot, but he was the glue for the first line. Without him? The team would be fucked. Damn, why was the front office such a bag of dicks?

"They can trade him, and for a guy just off his peak and a couple of early-round draft picks," Peppers said. "I'm not for it, but it's the GM's call."

Guilt squeezing his throat and expanding his lungs, Caleb turned back to Lucy. The look on her face wasn't recrimination so much as an ice-cold warning that actions have consequences—and not just on the person doing the acting.

Okay, so Caleb had heard the rumblings about Petrov—but that had all been before they'd turned the last season around. Then he'd gotten injured. Training camp was a week away, then it was preseason games and the new season. Petrov was at the gym rehabbing every day to get back for it.

The Ice Knights were going to be unstoppable this season. And people would realize that if the Harbor City sports media would focus on the team instead of his viral fuckup. He sank down in his chair as the old familiar you're-failing-again gut punch landed with a solid thud against his solar plexus.

Way to go, fuckhead.

Lucy let out a sigh and shook her head. "Here's what we need to know. Do you want to make the perception problem that you're a team full of privileged rich whiners go away so you can earn the A and the front office will stop eyeballing your boy Petrov?"

Caleb pinched the bridge of his nose, hoping it would stave off the ache making him think his head might explode, and nodded. "Yes."

"Then this publicity stunt is gonna happen," Lucy said. "Lucky for you, Bramble is totally on board with using you to promote their dating app. As the founder told me yesterday, if they can make you datable, then anyone is game."

Ouch.

"So here's how it works," she continued. "Bramble requires a five-date commitment so that everyone really gets a chance to know each other. However, each party must reconfirm their interest on the app after each date. Bramble will set up the first two dates, and after that it's up to you, your date, and your parents."

His headache was only getting worse. "Five dates?"

"Stop whining, Caleb." His mom gave him the look. "What's that in comparison to being able to reach your goal?"

"Got it," he muttered. "Five dates."

"After each date, you'll do a little here's-how-the-date-went chat with your mom. Bramble will interview her and your date's mom. That footage will be used in their latest ad campaign to show that anyone can meet their match using the app."

Oh God. Would this nightmare ever end?

"And I already filled out most of your profile for you," his mom added, handing him an iPad with the Bramble app open on it.

God's answer? *No. It's only gonna get worse. Enjoy your time visiting hell, sucker.*

He didn't want to, but he looked down at the screen anyway. Just like they had for as long as he could remember, the words bunched together on the screen, overlapping and squashing in on one another as the letters jumped. It wasn't a quick scan—but then again, it never was when it came to reading—but he managed to get through what was on the screen.

The backs of his eyeballs were aching by the time he got done, and the anxious fear that someone would realize how slow he was going twisted his gut as per usual. A quick glance around Lucy's office confirmed that either it hadn't taken him as long to read as his clammy palms testified or the others were working hard to pretend they hadn't noticed. The uncertainty had him chewing the inside of his cheek, but it was better than the mocking looks and full-on taunts of "hey, stupid" he'd gotten in school. He'd take a puck to the face before living through that ever again.

"Do we have to add a picture?" he asked.

"Nope." Lucy shook her head. "They don't have photos in an effort to eliminate unconscious bias in dating, on the theory that users will be more open to the person on the inside that way."

And what was inside him? A fuckup dating a chick as a publicity stunt. Yeah, he was a real catch. The whole thing just kept getting more and more messed up.

"So how do they match people?" he asked.

The grin on his mom's face should have warned him of a fresh, new level of hell. "So glad you asked."

She reached over and clicked on a question mark icon. A new tab opened filled with—he scrolled down and down and down—at least a billion questions. Yeah. This was Brit the Ballbuster, not Mom right now. She knew his weakness and had been convinced since forever that all he needed was to push harder, and by some sort of miracle all the letters would stay in the right order when he looked at them.

Kill me now.

"You fill out those, the app will match you with a few possibilities," his mom said. "Then I'll pick out your new girl."

That buzz saw in his ears? It turned into mortar fire, deafeningly loud and almost certain to fuck up his world. He looked at Lucy and Coach Peppers, desperate for another option that wouldn't include him having to get the letters on the screen to stop moving the fuck around when they shouldn't or putting his mom in charge of his dating life. When Lucy and Coach met his gaze without blinking, he turned back to the woman way too happy to have her control-freak fingers all up in his life.

"Whoever you pick, I'm not going out with her past date five," he said. "This is a publicity stunt only. Nothing more."

"No one is saying you have to or that you should," Lucy said. "The point of those little exercises is to change the narrative and clean up your image. What is more wholesome than a boy's mother helping him pick out a date?"

Had he fallen into a parallel universe where it was the total opposite of reality? His mom in charge of his love life? "That's not wholesome. It's creepy and wrong."

"Well, unless you have a better plan to fix this disaster so you have a chance at a leadership position within the team and Petrov isn't sent packing," Peppers said from his spot across the room, "then you're stuck with it."

Having his balls dipped in battery acid sounded like a better idea to Caleb at the moment, but he had no real alternate plan to offer. This parental-guidance-type date looked like the best option.

His toes itched as badly as that time when he'd skipped using his shower shoes at hockey camp when he was in middle school, and his headache went from rumba-throb to death-metal hammering.

He turned to Lucy. "And you're behind this plan? Really?"

"You dating a woman your mom picked out is a story that will grab the media's attention away from that stupid viral video of you and your teammates being jackasses. This is a plan that will work—for everyone," Lucy said.

Translation: *You are so screwed...so very screwed.*

He couldn't agree more.

. . .

Zara Ambrose was neck-deep in one-twelfth-size alligators, and all of them looked like shit. Okay, to someone who didn't spend their life devoted to the care and creation of miniatures, the alligators probably looked normal. Cute, even. To her, though, they were an abomination.

"I'm gonna have to toss them all and start again," she said, accepting the shot of sympathy tequila her bestie, Gemma MacNamara, handed her. "There's something wrong with their eyes. They just don't look right."

"No, there is something wrong with your work-life balance," Gemma said, tapping her paper Dixie cup against Zara's. "And it's time you do something about it."

It was the same line she'd been feeding Zara for the past two years—basically ever since her friend had met and fallen for the accountant next door. Yesterday, he'd proposed. Tonight, Gemma had shown up at Zara's apartment with a bottle of tequila and a smile that sparkled almost as much as the diamond on her left ring finger. They were holed up in Zara's miniatures studio, otherwise known as her loft apartment, supposedly celebrating Gemma's impending wedding. Too bad, with that last comment, this was starting to feel like a well-laid trap.

"What is this, the Gemma MacNamara version of an intervention?" she asked.

"Yes," Gemma said without hesitation.

She took a sniff of the liquid in her little paper cup, and her eyelashes nearly melted off. "Isn't Patrón the wrong thing to be serving at one of those?"

"Not for you." Gemma shot back her tequila like it was Dr Pepper and eyeballed Zara's shot. "Girl, you need to loosen up and stop working like your life depends on it."

Her tequila days were long gone—her dad always said she was the oldest twenty-eight-year-old he'd ever met—but that didn't mean a little revisiting of the old days wasn't warranted. Zara could let loose. She went out gambling. So what if it was bingo night with her grandma? She went out for girls' night dinners with Gemma. That still counted even if she was back home at eight so she could curl up with a book while her Great Dane, Anchovy, snuggled up next to her on the couch. Then there was... Her mind went blank. She really couldn't think of anything else she did on a regular basis that didn't involve work. Fuck. She didn't want to have to admit that to Gemma—as if her bestie didn't already know. Bringing the cup up to her lips, she threw back the shot, the alcohol burning its way down her throat in the best possible way.

"Well, my life does depend on my ability to work hard if I want a roof over my head and food in the fridge."

"Okay, I'll give you that." Gemma nodded in agreement. "You're one of the best miniatures artisans in Harbor City. It's gonna happen for you. I know you're going to break out."

"I love you for thinking that, but you're the only one who does."

She poured another shot for both of them. "Then the rest are idiots."

They drank to that. Then they drank to true love—well, Gemma did. Zara drank to her good luck to never have that particular curse befall her. Then they drank to Gemma's brand-spanking-new engagement. Within the hour, they were giggling like they always had together.

"Oh my God, you won't believe what my dad's latest get-rich-quick scheme is." Her dad was a legend in their neighborhood for being the greatest guy with a million plans, none of which ever panned out. She loved the man almost as much as she hated seeing him go off on another quixotic adventure to line his pockets. Growing up as Jasper Ambrose's daughter would have been amazing if it hadn't been for the fact that their rent money always seemed to disappear in a multilevel marketing scheme, or drinks for all at the neighborhood pub when his pony came in first, or training for a job that was going to be huge in the future like becoming a pig whisperer. "He's decided that he's going to be a character actor. The fact that he has no experience? A minor molehill. The real problem is that he needs to get on TV to earn his Screen Actors Guild card, and—get this—he wants me to do this online dating reality TV thing where parents pick out their kid's date and then offer advice about finding true love. Can you imagine? I need another shot."

"It's not a bad idea."

"More tequila?" She poured them both a half shot. "I agree."

"No, the dating thing," Gemma said. "You should totally do it."

Zara snort-giggled. "Not gonna happen."

"This is a total win-win here." Gemma tossed back her shot. "Your dad will get his SAG card, and you'll get to go out on five fabulous dates with a somewhat normal human being."

"We both know I don't have that kind of luck. He'd probably be some distracted dreamer just like my dad." She took her shot, the tequila burning its way down to her belly. "Hard pass."

"I can get you in the same room with Helene Carlyle." Gemma did a little shimmy dance move across the living room with Anchovy, obviously thinking this was a fun new game, following close behind with an oversize tennis ball in his mouth. "I have tickets to the Harbor City Friends of the Library charity gala, and you can be my plus-one, but only if you agree your dating life needs help and do your dad a solid."

And then, the next thing Zara knew, Gemma had her phone and was downloading the Bramble dating app. When she tried to grab her phone back, her friend easily held it out of reach. That was the problem with being barely five feet tall and being besties with an Amazon.

"Gimme my phone," she said, stretching up and reaching for it. "I don't want to date. Anyone. Ever. I like being in full and complete control of my life."

Gemma held the phone high and shot her a questioning

look, the tequila-induced haze in her eyes giving her a comical look. "Don't you want to meet someone like Hank and fall in love?"

She shook her head. "No."

"What do you want, then?"

She didn't even have to think about it. "To have Helene Carlyle fall in love with my work."

In addition to being one of the richest women in Harbor City, Helene Carlyle was also the metro area's biggest collector of miniatures. If she signed off on someone's work, then the entire art world paid attention. And that meant showings in galleries and private commissions. That, in turn, meant she would be able to create her art, which she knew full well wasn't paying the bills as opposed to creating the commercial miniatures that she sold in her Etsy shop which is what kept a roof over her head now, and use the resulting cash to turn her single Etsy shop into a miniatures-making empire. If everything went according to plan—and she'd make damn sure it would—then she could finally put to bed the nagging worry that it was only a matter of time before she'd miss a payment and the debt collectors would be at her door.

"Zara, I love you, but you are going to put yourself in an early grave if you don't allow yourself to have a little fun every once in a while." Gemma sat down beside her, put the phone on the coffee table, and draped an arm around her shoulders. "I'm seriously worried about you."

"You don't understand what it's like. If you grew up the way I did, you'd be all about work, too."

To make sure the lights stayed on. To guarantee eviction notices didn't appear on the door. To not open the fridge and find only a few ketchup packets. Jasper Ambrose might have been the life of the party and the entire neighborhood's favorite charming dreamer with a million ideas for how to make a billion, but that hadn't made living with him any easier. She loved him—everyone did—but she couldn't shake that feeling even now that the debt collectors would come knocking at any moment and she'd lose everything.

"I know your dad pulled a number on you. I was there to watch a lot of it," Gemma said, her voice wavering with emotion and probably tequila. "However, you can't let your past rule your future. You're an amazing person, and no, you don't need a man to complete you, but you also can't look to work to be the only thing that defines you." She shifted on the couch, turning Zara's shoulders so she had to look her friend straight in the eyes. "You, Zara Ambrose, are so much more than teeny tiny alligators—even if they're the best teeny tiny alligators in the whole wide world. Go out there, meet people, maybe get laid for the first time in forever, and let yourself have fun for once. It doesn't have to be for the rest of eternity, just five dates."

Tomorrow she'd probably be blaming the tequila, but at this moment, Gemma's outrageous plan made sense. "You're killing me, Smalls."

Gemma smiled at the use of her grade-school nickname. "But you know I'm right, Biggie. Your dad's a mess, but he's a good guy. You can help him out, and who knows, this just might be the dream that comes true. Plus, you'll get to meet Helene Carlyle and maybe even have some fun of the orgasmic variety."

Yeah, that wasn't going to happen. Orgasms that she didn't make happen herself—with or without a partner present—never happened. Literally. She had the world's most shy clit ever that never responded to anything but her own fingers and vibe. Still, if she knew going in that it wouldn't be love or climaxes, she'd at least be prepared. Plus, she was getting two things she really wanted: meeting Helene Carlyle and helping her dad get his SAG card.

"Fine." Zara held out her hand, palm upward, knowing she'd been beat. "My phone."

Dating was so far down her priority list that it came after cleaning the dust bunnies under her dresser and defrosting the freezer. However, if going out on five dates could get her what she really wanted and could make her dad happy and got her in to see Helene Carlyle? She'd suffer through listening to some guy ramble on and on about himself over never-ending breadsticks.

Gemma swiped the phone off the coffee table and gave it to her. Since she'd already filled out most of the personal information, all that was really up to Zara was to finish the introductory part. Thumbs hovering over the screen, she tried to figure out what to say. She wasn't looking for love. She had no interest in finding forever. Gemma wasn't wrong about the getting-laid part, though—it had been too long. Waaaaaaaaay too long.

However, the last thing she wanted was to play games or deal with someone who really was looking for Miss Right. She might be a workaholic, but she wasn't a bitch, and she wouldn't do that to someone. How in the world was she supposed to finesse that into an introduction?

And that's when inspiration flicked her on the nose. If she was going to do this, she was going to be 100 percent honest.

Assholes Need Not Apply

I don't believe fairy tales of happily ever after, but are a few not-self-made orgasms with a guy who makes my heart race and isn't a total asshole really just a pipe dream??? I work hard and hardly play. Now I'm ready for a little—really, a lot of—fun with the kind of guy who isn't a total lost cause and can clear out the cobwebs in my vagina. Too honest? Too bad. Life is too short for jerks who don't know their way around a lady garden. Forget being Miss Right. I just want to be Miss Right for Five Dates.

She handed her phone over to Gemma, whose eyebrows went higher the more she read until they were completely hidden behind her bangs.

"If no one answers, Gemma"—and who would respond to that kind of ad—"you still have to take me as your plus-one."

Her best friend nodded. "Deal."

They sealed their agreement with a pinkie shake and another shot of tequila. And by the time Zara curled up in bed hours later, she had almost convinced herself she hadn't just made a huge mistake.

Chapter Two

Tequila was dead to Zara. So was Anchovy. Okay, not really on that second one, but her Great Dane really needed to find a new favorite game that didn't involve hiding one—and only one—of her shoes somewhere in the apartment.

"I buy you the good dog food and this is the thanks I get?"

The dog woofed, tilted his head, and—she'd swear to it on a Bible—grinned at her.

"This stupid date isn't my idea of fun, either, but I gotta go, which means I need two shoes and you have to go get your leash."

At that last word, Anchovy galloped past the couch, around the large kitchen island, and to the entryway hall tree, where he stuffed his face in the basket sitting on its bench seat and came out with his leash between his teeth. Then, as if the beast knew exactly what needed to happen next, he trotted over to the island, raised himself up on his hind legs, planted his front paws on the counter, and looked down into the sink.

"Of course." Zara did the one-foot-in-a-four-inch-heel-and-one-not off-kilter walk to the island and grabbed her other shoe out of the sink. "Hiding my shoes is no way to deal with your separation anxiety, Anchovy."

He just wagged his uncropped tail hard enough that the thump of it against her ass was like being spanked by a tree limb. The vet had warned her about Great Danes' "happy tail" when she'd shown up at his office with Anchovy as an abandoned puppy, but she hadn't been able to bring herself to have the vet cut it short. That made her penchant for minimalist decorating at home even better because otherwise any knickknacks three feet off the ground would get whacked off the shelves.

"Come on, baby," Zara said as she slipped her bare foot into her shoe. Her toes slid past a patch of wet. *Ewwwwwww.* Maybe she would be lucky for once and that was the result of a dripping faucet and not dog slobber. She glanced over at the sink, where there wasn't a drop of water to be found. Gross. "You're going to Aunty Gemma's."

More excited tail wagging that grew into full-body wiggles while she was trying to clip the leash to his collar. It took a few seconds, but she finally got it on. Then she and Anchovy were hustling out the door, into the building's elevator, and out onto the sidewalk of her busy neighborhood. Gemma lived two blocks down in an apartment above a coffee shop. She met Zara and Anchovy at the side door that led to the stairwell to her place. Damn. Zara had been hoping to do a little gossip delay. That wasn't going to happen, based on the do-not-fuck-with-the-timeline look on her bestie's face.

Anchovy gave a happy woof as Gemma took possession of his leash. "Go, you are late."

"You're bossy," Zara said, but she was already turning away.

"Takes one to know one," Gemma said with a laugh. "Go."

Without any other choice, she did. She hurried down Eighteenth Avenue, zipping past the tourists who insisted on slow rolling down the sidewalk. The Harbor City fall humidity—that always had a tinge of urine scent to it—had frizzed out her hair already. Not that she cared what her date thought of her, but getting a brush through it after it reached a certain level would be a nightmare. Determined not to let that happen, she wrapped her hair up in a bun, securing it with the elastic band always around her wrist, as she speed-walked through the ever-thickening crowd.

She was a half block away from her own personal Mt. Doom, AKA The Hummingbird Café, when she tried to pass a pair of tourists and her heel sank between the narrow slats of a metal grate. There was a half second of *oh shit* before she went down, her knees banging against the metal. Thank God she'd decided to go with the jeans she'd already been wearing or her knees would have been aching more than her twisted ankle.

"Oh my God, are you okay, honey?" one of the slow-moving tourists asked, her voice concerned.

Sucking in a deep breath, Zara blinked back the pain and started to get up. "I'm good."

"Those shoes almost killed you," said the other tourist, who going by his body language was married to the slow mover number one. "How y'all walk around in those things is beyond me."

"I've been known to run in them."

"Good for you, honey." The woman reached out and offered her arm to help steady Zara as she stood on one foot and reached down to yank the embedded heel out of the grate. "Don't listen to Steve. He's been known to wear Crocs."

It took the mother of all tugs, but Zara freed her shoe. "Thank you."

"No worries," the woman said. "Are you gonna be able to walk in that? It looks a little worse for wear."

The stranger wasn't wrong. The sides of the heel were all scratched up, but everything looked to still be attached.

Finally, the fates might not be completely fucking with her.

"I appreciate it, but I'll be fine." She slid the shoe on, making sure to stand on the sidewalk proper instead of the grate before letting go of the woman's arm. "I'm meeting someone in the café."

"Oh good, this city is too big to be alone in," the woman said as she slipped her arm through the crook of her husband's, and they turned and strolled down the block as the early evening pedestrian traffic swerved around them.

Even though her ankle ached as she limped toward the café, her mood almost improved with the knowledge that delicious carbs were only a block away. Her expectations for this date were lower than a Chihuahua's stomach, but her excitement at a basket of never-ending breadsticks was at peak levels. A woman had to have priorities.

Once inside, she made a beeline to the hostess stand— well, as much as she could with her current injury. She scanned the restaurant. Lots of guys who looked like they used too much cologne and spent half their paychecks on hair products.

"Just one?" the hostess asked as she picked up a menu.

"I'm meeting someone," Zara said, heat rising in her cheeks at having to say the words out loud. "His name's Caleb."

"Oh yeah." The hostess fanned her face. "He's already here, and let me tell you, you're a lucky woman. He's right"— the hostess pointed across the restaurant to a table in the back—"over there."

Zara followed the woman's direction and froze.

Her date definitely fell into the broad-shouldered, muscular, giant category but was saved from being too damn perfect by a nose that looked like it had decided to go in one direction and then had changed its mind at the last minute. However, there was no denying it. Her date was hot, not in a male-model way but in a superhero movie villain way—like

Loki if he had a gym membership and actually used it.

The water she'd downed before leaving the house sloshed around in her stomach. There was no turning around in the middle of her holy-shit-what-was-I-thinking panic. "Are you sure?"

The hostess nodded. "Said his name was Caleb and he was meeting a date."

Why was she doing this? Zara pressed her hand to her stomach in a vain attempt to calm herself and grabbed ahold of her sense of self-control with both hands. Sure, it was a white-knuckle grip, but she had a plan. The fact that her date was hot didn't change anything. She was in it for the invite and her dad's SAG card. She could do this.

Like a brave but tragic movie heroine about to get her head whacked off by a guillotine, Zara lifted her chin, stood up, and braced her shoulders.

"Hey, Caleb," the hostess hollered across the small restaurant. "What's your date's name?"

A flash of embarrassed heat blasted up from Zara's toes, strong enough that she was surprised flames didn't engulf every individual freckle on her face (and there were enough of them that if someone squinted, she'd look like she actually had a tan for the first time in her life). And just when it seemed like it couldn't get any worse, her date stood up and crossed the café. What would have taken her a minute with her beyond-short legs, he cleared in all of about five strides. He stopped near the hostess stand, and his gaze went lower and lower until it finally dropped enough to be level with her face. His smile faltered and then flattened before he seemed to recover with an upward curl of his lips that looked as practiced as it was insincere.

"Zara?" he asked, sounding like he'd just been told the horrible news that his broccoli wasn't going to be covered in delicious cheese sauce. "I'm Caleb."

She shifted her stance, wishing she could grow about five inches in five seconds. The move put more weight on her bum ankle, the sharp jolt of pain knocking her off-balance and right into the unyielding chest of her date.

. . .

Caleb was used to two-hundred-and-thirty-pound men on skates slamming him against the boards—when they were lucky enough not to be on the receiving end of one of his solid hits—so having a redhead who was small enough to fit in his hockey bag with room to spare fall into him didn't even rock him back on his heels.

He wrapped his fingers around her upper arms to help steady her as she regained her balance. "You okay?"

"Fine, thank you." Her chin went up and the color in her cheeks nearly matched the twenty bazillion peach freckles covering her face. "My heel got caught in a grate on the walk over."

But she wasn't fine. There was no missing the way she favored her right leg by repositioning so most of her weight was on her left.

"You sure?" he asked as he released her and took a step back to give her some space. "Here, let me look. I've got experience with messed-up ankles."

Okay, that experience mainly centered on the health of his ankles rather than anything he could do to fix them, but still, personal experience had to count for something. He squatted down and visually checked her ankle for bruising or swelling, telltale signs of a sprained ankle. There wasn't any, but she was obviously in discomfort. The fact that she was continuing to wear shoes that had to be four inches high definitely didn't help. He was a smart enough man not to make that observation out loud—having sisters growing up had definitely taught him a thing or twenty about how not to get kneed in the nut sack.

"Do you mind if I take a look?"

She sighed, her breath a bit shaky, and nodded. "Go ahead."

He ran the pad of his thumb over and around her ankle, watching her face for signs he'd hit a sensitive spot. Beyond a tightness around her mouth in a few areas, she didn't show any reaction. How many times had a trainer or a coach checked him for injury? Too many to count. This was different, though, and he couldn't quite define how except that it made the hairs on his arms stand up.

He cleared his throat, shaking off the uncomfortable feeling. "How would you rank the pain on a ten-point scale?"

Her brown eyes narrowed as she sized him up, her gaze combing over him like he was a used car she wasn't sure was worth the price but she was considering kicking the tires just for fun. "It's fine. I'll manage."

Message received, he stood up. "Does your ankle hurt enough that you want some help walking?"

"I can manage on my own," she said, the inflection in how she said "own" giving her away as a Harbor City native. "Let's just get this over with."

He and the hostess exchanged what-the-fuck looks over his salty date's head, and he followed her back to the table where he'd been sitting. He noticed two things as they made their way through the café. One, she was definitely limping. Two, her ass in those jeans was phenomenal. The limp he could maybe do something to help with if she was open to an ankle massage—which didn't seem likely. The ass he needed to forget before he messed up this wack-a-doo plan to redeem himself.

The reality was, his mouth, hands, and dick were going to stay untouched by his date tonight.

He gave himself a mental high five. Hell yeah!

That moment of joy faded fast, though. Why? Because this was what his life had come to—a mental fist pump that he would be going home alone to spend solitary quality time with his right hand and would continue to do so until he had five Bramble dates in the win column.

As soon as they sat down at the table, a weird what-in-the-hell-do-we-do-now moment came rushing at him full force. He should have read Zara's dating profile when his mom offered the other day. He could have used the audible read-text option on the iPad, but he hadn't wanted to do that in front of everyone in Lucy's office. Instead, he'd gone onto the dating ice only to find he had no game plan.

"So," he said, picking up his menu. Okay, he wasn't a big dater—he did have this face, after all—but he wasn't a noob, either. He knew how to do this. "Have you eaten here before?"

"No," she said, tucking her bright-red hair behind one ear, her gaze locked on her menu. "I'm more of a street hot dog kind of girl."

"Really?" Was it wrong that he liked her a little for that answer? 98 percent of the time he was on a pretty regimented nutrition plan, but on cheat days? He could eat his weight in street dogs and stadium nachos. "With or without relish?"

She looked up and wrinkled her freckle-covered nose. "What kind of horrible person skips the relish?"

Okay. Maybe this wouldn't be a total shitshow.

"So," Caleb said after the waiter dropped off a bread basket. "What do you do?"

She lay the menu down on the table and lifted her chin as if she was expecting a blow. "I'm a miniatures artisan."

Okay, the jokes here just wrote themselves, and it was killing him to keep his mouth shut. Asshole? Him? Maybe.

"Go ahead and say it," Zara said with a sigh. "I've heard them all."

There was nothing "poor me" in the tone of her voice. Instead, it was more of a weary, *hit me with what you've got, I can take it* that landed like a dirty joke at a Bible study group, sucking out all the immature humor of the moment. Despite it—or maybe because of it—he edged a little closer to appreciating his mom's choice in his Bramble date.

"What do you mean?" he asked, because admitting he'd been thinking exactly along those lines felt shitty.

"Good thing I found a job my size. It must be so much easier to build the doll furniture when you can fit inside the doll's house," she said with a carefully neutral delivery that instead of hiding her hurt just highlighted it. "I've heard both of those a million times. You got a new one?"

That would be a big no. He shook his head.

"How about you?" she asked. "What do you do?"

"I'm a defenseman for the Ice Knights."

Her eyes widened. "The hockey team?"

He nodded. Not being one of the handful of players on the team with endorsement deals who were tailed constantly by the media meant he sometimes had to convince folks that he wasn't kidding about his job. It was a trade-off he'd take every day and twice on Sunday.

"Then why are you on Bramble?" she asked. "Isn't there some ultraexclusive rich-athlete dating app?"

"I have my reasons." Yeah, and those would be because he'd been a total asshole in public. Now wasn't that just the perfect first date talking point. Lucy would definitely not approve.

Lucky for him, the waiter picked that moment to stop by the table to take their drink order before Caleb could say anything stupid, like the truth. He ordered a water while she got a milkshake, the lift of her eyebrow just daring him to make a comment about it. Yeah, that wasn't going to happen.

The waiter left, leaving Caleb still trying to figure out

how to answer her question. Sure, he could come up with some cover story, but that didn't feel right. He might usually let his mouth run faster than his brain, but he was trying not to do that this time. If he was going to make this Bramble date thing work, he couldn't be that kid who stood in front of the class and fumbled for words. Really, there was only one call to make.

"I take it you don't follow the hockey media," he said after the waiter left.

She tucked her hair behind her ears again, revealing a tattoo of three tiny stars at the spot where her neck met her shoulder. "Not even a little bit."

"I got videoed with a group of my teammates who were saying stupid shit, I didn't tell them to cut it out, and the video went viral." That was one way to explain it.

"What kind of stupid shit?" she asked as she tore apart a roll and slathered butter all over it.

Would it be weird to ask if he could smell the white-flour, nutritionally empty carbs? Sure, he ate a three- to four-thousand-calorie diet most of the year, but he wasn't expending in-season calories right now. That meant he was up to his eyeballs in high-quality whole-grain carbs, lean protein, steamed veggies, and fresh fruit.

Too distracted by the sight of her eating the roll to think before he spoke, the truth tumbled out. "They were running off at the mouth about puck bunnies."

"Ohhhh," she said before letting out a snort of disbelief. "And now you're having to do this as some kind of punishment, or is it to look like you're less of an ass?"

"Little of both." He'd argue it if he could, but she wasn't wrong. "So why are you on Bramble?"

She took another small bite from her roll before answering. "My best friend is blackmailing me, and my dad wants a SAG card."

That was definitely not the answer he'd been expecting. "And I thought my reasoning was twisted."

"I'm sure it all makes sense in Gemma's head," Zara said. "She thinks I work too much and need to loosen up. She'll let me be her plus-one to go meet a collector if I do the Bramble five dates thing. And my dad? Well, let's just say he's never met an unlikely plan he didn't think he could pull off."

All the possibilities this created sped around inside his head until one broke free like a perfect fast break late in the third period when the game was on the line. All he had to do was put the biscuit in the net.

"So neither of us really wants to be here," he said. "We're each other's solution to getting back to our regular lives as soon as possible."

It was fucking perfect. Petrov's job with the team would be safe for another season—well, as safe as he could be, considering he didn't have a no-trade deal in his contract.

Zara, though, didn't seem to be seeing the genius of it, going by the suspicious look she gave him as she took another bite of her roll. Instead of giving him a straight-up no, though, she started eating. The words—okay, begging pleas—were bubbling up inside him, but for once, he kept it on lockdown. He wasn't about to rush this play, no matter how it had every nerve in his body jinglejangling.

Finally, she used her napkin to wipe the corners of her mouth, straightened her spine, and looked him dead in the eye. "We'd have to have ground rules."

"Sure. Whatever you want." Ice Knights season tickets? He'd make that happen. A photo op with her dad's favorite player? Done. Whatever it took, he'd do it.

"This isn't a real or fake relationship, it's a temporary alliance," she said without an ounce of humor in her tone. "I'm not pretending to be your girlfriend or the random chick you're banging this week."

"Agreed." All of that sounded like it would cause more problems than it would solve anyway. "I've got a condition. Dressing up is not required. I'm not putting on a suit."

The best thing about the off-season was not having to strangle himself with a tie multiple times a week just for a bus ride to the rink or a plane trip to another city. Coach Peppers was old-fashioned about doing things the original way.

"Fine." Zara held up three fingers. "The third stipulation is that I'm not putting on a good attitude. If it's been a crappy day, I don't have to pretend to be a manic pixie dream girl."

He snorted. "No one who's met you would believe that. You're a little salty." That was putting it mildly based on her attitude when she showed up for their date.

"I have my reasons." She added another finger, so she was holding up four. "Oh, and no making love. Sex?" She paused and looked him over quickly. "Maybe. Emotional, heartfelt, staring-each-other-in-the-eyes making love? Not gonna happen. No offense, but you're not my type."

What the hell? Not her type? He was a professional athlete making millions. He'd been led to believe he was everyone's type.

"Not a problem, since I don't think we could see eye to eye while having sex unless you magically grew a foot," he said.

"You're not into being creative?" Zara rolled her eyes. "I guess that's expected for someone who has probably had women throwing themselves at him for years. You haven't ever had to work for it."

Caleb had no idea what to say to that. He'd been punched square in the face by the most feared goons in hockey and it hadn't knocked him as senseless as this little five-foot-nothing of a snarky woman had done with a few choice words.

"I have one more rule," she said, reaching for another roll. "Five dates and we're done. Period. Do we have a deal?"

Chapter Three

Zara's stomach was folding in on itself she was so hungry. She really had to set alarms or something so she'd remember to eat instead of getting lost in work and missing out on lunch. Her low blood sugar was probably the only reason why she was agreeing to this madness. Hangry plus not wanting to be on this date had combined to make bad decisions sound like good ideas.

The waiter returned with her milkshake and Caleb's water. "Are you folks ready to order?"

"Absolutely." She was half a second from marrying the waiter, she was that grateful. "I'll go with a cheeseburger and seasoned waffle fries, please."

"Which vegetable option would you like?" he asked.

"Can I go with a side order of the mashed potatoes instead of a veggie?" Yes, she was having the dinner of a ten-year-old out without parental supervision, but she was stress eating thanks to this date, and when it came to that, no veggies needed to apply.

"Of course," the waiter said before turning to Caleb.

"And you, sir?"

"I'll go with the spiced grilled chicken and a triple order of steamed mixed vegetables." He handed his menu to the waiter. "You can hold the side order of mashed potatoes that comes with it, thanks."

Zara tried to wrap her brain around the whole no-mashed-potatoes thing while the waiter took her menu and then headed off to the kitchen. No potatoes? That was just wrong.

"Who turns down mashed potatoes?" she asked.

"Who ignores the fact that food is fuel and says 'no thank you' to vegetables?"

"The woman who barely had time for breakfast and totally missed lunch. You're lucking I'm just eating the rolls right now and not the bread basket itself," she said, a little zip of a thrill skimming across her skin at the prospect of debating someone other than Anchovy. A bit of fussy give-and-take always got her blood pumping. "Anyway, don't you burn a million calories a day, so you can eat whatever you want? What's a few carbs to someone like you?"

"Four thousand calories in doughnuts has a totally different impact on how well I do my job compared to a healthy diet of chicken and veggies. Playing well isn't a joke to me. I have to do whatever it takes to play at the top of my game or someone else will take me out." Caleb shrugged as he rolled up the sleeves of his button-up shirt, seemingly slowing down and drawing the process out the longer and harder she watched. "It's not like mashed potatoes are really all that good for you."

Oh, he was good, but that wasn't how this was going to work. She was made of sterner stuff than to back down at the flash of some drool-worthy arm porn.

"You're kidding, right?" Her gaze dipped down to his muscular forearms, not because she was checking him out but because of the movement. Really. And the fact that her heart started to beat a little faster with each sinewy inch he revealed? Totally an accident. "It is the creamiest, yummiest, best food ever."

"The box kind is easy to make, I'll give you that," he said, sitting back in his chair, not even a hint that he was joking about his horrible food hot take. "And you can always add in some food coloring and veggies to vary it up."

"Please tell me you're joking, because all of what you just said was wrong." And not a little. It was really, really wrong.

He shrugged his broad shoulders, cocky arrogance coming off him in waves. "Well, you eat what you want, and I'll eat what I want, and we can take comfort in the fact that we aren't compatible in the least and don't have to worry about ever breaking rule number one."

"Oh yeah, a real relationship is definitely off the table now." Not that it was ever on the table—and not just because hers would always have mashed potatoes on it. She exhaled a melodramatic sigh as if any of this talk meant anything more than more mashed potatoes in the world for her. "I don't know if I can do this for four more dates."

"Too late." He shot a self-satisfied smirk her way. "You already agreed."

She might have reconsidered if she'd known about the mashed-potatoes thing first.

• • •

Lying about mashed potatoes was like dancing with your dog. It was possible to do, but it was weird, seriously weird. However, watching Zara's reaction when he'd sang the praises of boxed mashed potatoes was pure gold. The woman definitely had firm opinions, which—since he'd been raised by a woman who had her own thoughts on everything and never minded airing them—he could appreciate. Okay, so he was poking the pint-size bear, but it was that much fun watching a fierce scrapper like her in the middle of a smack fight.

"You probably have a ton of trash food opinions," he teased, pushing her just a little bit more.

She let out a you-asked-for-it chuckle. "Oh, so we're just going to let it hang out there, huh?"

"Might as well." It wasn't like any of this mattered in the long run.

Neither of them was trying to impress the other. This was the lowest of low-key dates, because whether or not she liked him or he liked her didn't matter. They were badly matched compatriots on a doomed dating cruise.

Zara steepled her fingers and tapped the tip of her nose, looking up at the ceiling as if she was some kind of cartoon villain plotting his demise and giving him the perfect opportunity to check her out. Her bright-red hair, freckles, and height were the first things he'd noticed, followed by her perfect ass when they'd walked to the table. What he hadn't noticed until she started busting his balls about his food choices was how her eyes sparked like she wasn't gonna start a fight but she'd end it if necessary. If the circumstances had been different between them, he might even have asked her out for real. As it was, though, this was just fun.

Finally, she dropped her gaze back down to his face. "Pizza is overrated."

Whoa.

He thought he'd crossed the line with the mashed potatoes, but now she'd gone and destroyed the idea of there ever being a line. Pizza was sacred. There were no jokes to be made about the pie.

"You have obviously not gotten it from Zito's," he said and left it at that, because once someone went to the "pizza is overrated" side of the street, there was no bringing them back. "Peanut butter cookie or oatmeal raisin?"

"Peanut butter with the fork marks on the top. You vote oatmeal raisin?" When he nodded, she rolled her eyes. "Figures."

Before the next round of bad food hot takes could happen, the waiter showed up with their plates. He took one look at his plate and sent up a thank-you to the chef because he was going to demolish his food. His grilled chicken smelled like heaven, and the veggies were steamed perfectly. The team nutritionist had done a whole series of workshops about how eating better could improve a player's on-ice showing and that he wasn't giving up on flavor by doing so. She'd converted him on the spot to a regimented preseason and during-season diet, and this chicken was his reward. Damn, it smelled delicious.

"Are you sniffing my mashed potatoes?" Zara asked as she scooped some up.

Yes. Please. Why couldn't it be the off-season? "Absolutely not."

"Whatever you say." She lifted her fork, a garlic-butter mountain of starch heaven on it. "Sure you don't want a bite?"

Fuck, he was tempted. Garlic mashed potatoes were happiness in food form, everyone knew that. He was balancing on the tightrope when Zara bent forward over the table, confirming that her freckles did go all the way down until they disappeared beneath the deep V of her shirt, and held out her fork.

"You're the worst," he said, giving in. "Just one to see if it's as awful as every other kind."

He should have taken the fork from her, but he didn't. Instead, guided by whatever instinct always got him from point A to point B on the ice before an opposing player had the puck passed to him, he leaned toward her and let her feed him. Her eyes widened for a fraction of an instant before she gave him a wicked grin. The woman was 100 percent trouble and more tempting than the delicious buttery bomb in his mouth.

"Wasn't that worth breaking your rule?" she asked, as smug a know-it-all as could be.

He shrugged. "It's okay."

"You," she said, pointing at him with her fork, "are the world's worst liar."

That probably wasn't wrong, which was why he needed to get away from mashed potato talk before he ratted himself out. So he steered the conversation to the basic first-date topics of work (work was pretty much the only thing both of them did for fun) and living in Harbor City (tourists were the worst). By the time the waiter came by to clear their plates, he had convinced himself that this whole Bramble date plan wasn't going to blow up in his face. One date almost down, four more to go, and then it was back to life as usual. Thank God.

"Do you have any chocolate cake?" she asked the waiter, who nodded. Then she turned to Caleb and winked at him. "One slice of the double fudge chocolate cake with two forks, please—just in case."

The waiter didn't bother to hide his grin as he walked away.

"You're bossy."

She ran a fingertip over her tiny tattoo and gave a one-shouldered shrug. "I'm right."

Uh-huh. He wasn't about to lose this face-off.

"Okay, Miss Right, how about we figure out what we're going to say during these post-date interviews." He paused for effect. "I'm thinking I'm madly in love with you at first sight."

Her jaw nearly hit the table and rattled their glasses. Oh yeah, years on the ice had taught Caleb exactly how to deliver a check. Timing was everything.

He couldn't wait to see her interview about *him*... There was no telling what this snarky pixie would put out there.

Chapter Four

The next day, Caleb picked up his already quick pace as soon as he spotted Zara's distinctive bright-red, almost orange hair outside of Harris Tower. It wasn't like he meant to, but it just sort of happened. If his mom noticed, she didn't say anything, just increased her speed as people swerved out of their way. They were half a block away from the front door of Harris Tower, which housed the TV studio, when Zara noticed them. He knew the exact moment because one minute she was chatting with an older guy who looked too much like her to be anyone other than her dad, then the guy jerked his chin Caleb's way, and a blush turned her cheeks pink.

"Is that her?" his mom asked.

"Yep."

He didn't have to look over at his mom to know she was giving him that tell-me-everything look. Pry? Britany Stuckey? Since the day he was born. So it wasn't that he couldn't look away from Zara so much that he didn't want to have that discussion with his mom—the one where she poked and prodded and coached him through life like he was one of her players.

"She's so tiny," his mom said. "She sounded fiercer in her profile."

"Don't get fooled by appearances." If his mom had seen Zara give him the stink eye and tell him to come on so they could just get their date over with, she would have known that already.

Britany let out a knowing chuckle. "You like her."

"She's a little salty, but yeah, she's all right." She'd agreed to this wild plan, so that was points in her favor.

Another few steps and they were in front of Zara and the man he assumed was her dad. What in the hell did he do now? Did they hug? Did they fist bump? Did they shake hands? Fuck. Welcome to Awkwardville, population Caleb Stuckey.

"Hey, Zara," he said, because it wasn't like his mouth ever waited for his brain to come up with a decent plan.

For once it worked out, though, as he introduced her to his mom and she introduced him to her dad, who did actually give him a fist bump. Then their parents started talking, leaving him and Zara to fill the space between them. But neither spoke. For once, his mouth stayed shut—probably because his eyes were so full of looking at her.

"How's the ankle?" he eventually asked, looking down at her feet and shaking his head because again, she was wearing super-tall fuck-me heels.

"Better," she said. "Thanks."

"That's a relief." His phone vibrated in his jeans pocket as the alarm for the interview went off. "You ready to go make the people of Harbor City think that the totally-not-gonna-happen just might?"

• • •

Zara wasn't ready outside, or during the elevator ride up to the studio standing way too close to Caleb for comfort, or when she walked out into the TV studio. Why in the hell had she ever thought this was a good idea?

The *Harbor City Wake Up* studio looked more impressive on TV. Not that Zara had known what to expect, but when she watched at home, it looked downright expansive with its fake living room on one end where the guests had their little chats with the host, a kitchenette in the middle for demonstrations, and a news desk on the other end where the headlines were announced. Shockingly, the whole set looked like it would fit in her studio apartment. She and her dad were sitting on one couch while Caleb and his mom were sitting on the one next to them. The single oversize chair across from them where Asha would sit was empty.

"It's like the TARDIS on Opposite Day," her dad said as he adjusted the tie he definitely was not used to wearing. "Bigger on the outside."

She couldn't disagree.

Turning, she lowered her voice and asked, "Now, you remember the plan?"

"You say that like I'm not always there for you." He gave her a crooked grin. "You know I will always have my favorite girl's back."

Zara fiddled with the hem of her flowy blue top and clamped her mouth shut so hard, she wasn't sure if her jaw would ever work again. She loved her dad. Without a doubt, he loved her, too. But after Mom left, he kind of melted into being the good-time guy, everyone in the neighborhood's favorite buddy.

He was the guy who bought everyone in the bar a round to celebrate her winning an art contest that he was sure was a sign of amazing things to come. It would have been a sweet gesture if he hadn't bought the drinks with the family rent money. Then there was the time he was supposed to be paying the electric bill in person and in cash because it was late and ended up getting waylaid at the track because his friend had told him about a sure thing. Or the time... She shook her head. The seemingly infinite number of times her dad, the dreamer, had tossed away the good enough in the here and now for the possibility of great in the future only to lose both were legendary.

Her dad wasn't a bad guy. He was actually very kind, funny, and sweet. He just wasn't always in constant contact with the harsh realities of the world—and the man loved to go off script—especially when he was on the high of a sure-to-be-a-winner idea like becoming an actor.

"Dad, I need you to restate the plan for this interview." She held her breath, waiting for his answer with the pent-up anxiety she imagined reality TV dance moms had watching their kids hit the stage.

Her dad shook his head and all but rolled his eyes, but he said it. "We're skeptical of the entire situation. We're not nasty about it but just aren't totally on board with him, but he's got the hots for you."

Zara let out a relieved breath and allowed herself to believe that they might just pull this off.

Four dates. All you have to survive are four more dates to get to what you really want: one step closer to getting face time with Helene Carlyle.

And if to make that happen, she had to sit on a couch with her dad and tell a stranger—and a good chunk of Harbor City—about her dates, then she could suffer through it.

"Don't you want to kind of give yourself permission to have that dream, though, to open yourself up to the possibility of this guy being the one?" her dad asked.

"No, Dad."

"Why not?"

"Because he's not." End of story. She wasn't about to allow anything to disrupt her plans. "I'm here for a reason, and it's not to fall in love with someone I went out with to help you get your SAG card."

He looked like he was about to argue, but the arrival of *Harbor City Wake Up* host Asha Kapoor stopped him. Zara couldn't blame him. It was a little intimidating seeing someone who was usually only seen on a screen or huge billboards. Their sudden gawking didn't seem to bother Asha, though, who breezed into the living room part of the set where they were sitting. Zara, her dad, Caleb, and his mom all stood up.

"You must be Zara. I'm so excited to meet you." Asha reached out and shook Zara's hand before turning to her dad. "And here's Jasper Ambrose, the proud papa. We are going to have a wonderful time. Don't you worry about anything—it'll just be a fun chat." Her mouth tightened with displeasure when she turned her attention to Caleb and his mom. "Shall we do this?"

The word "no" bubbled up inside Zara, but she shoved it back down as everyone started to take their seats. Before they could, though, Asha's producer stopped them, swapping their seating positions so Zara sat with Caleb and her dad sat with Britany. Her couch seemed a lot smaller with Caleb on it, his thigh brushing hers tormenting her already heightened sense of awareness. It was his leg touching hers, for God's sake. It hadn't been *that* long since she'd had sex. Okay, it *had* been that long since she'd had good sex, and there was a difference. Add that to her going-on-TV nerves and, yeah, she was over-aware of *everything*. It had nothing to do with Caleb. It was this whole bizarre situation.

She could do this. After all, how many people watched morning TV?

The flash of surly Asha had sent Caleb's way disappeared, and Asha transformed into the woman people knew on TV:

friendly, open, curious.

"Good morning, Harbor City, it's time to wake up," Asha said. "Today, we're celebrating being the number one morning show in Harbor City, with more viewers than any other morning show anywhere in the nation, and we have something super fun for you. I am so excited to kick off the show this morning with Ice Knights defenseman Caleb Stuckey, his mom—and legendary high school hockey coach—Britany Stuckey, local miniatures artisan Zara Ambrose, and her dad, Jasper Ambrose. They are part of a fun new experiment from the folks at Bramble Dating that combines the technology of online date matching with its many algorithms and the old-fashioned guidance of parental advice. Welcome, all of you!"

"Thank you for having us, Asha. Zara and I just love your show. I watch it every morning at Doodle Bee's Coffee Shop." Her dad made direct eye contact with the camera. "Hey, everyone, I can't wait to see you all there for the tuna plate lunch special later today. It's delicious food at a delicious price."

Oh God. Zara stopped breathing. Her dad had made a side deal.

He never had coffee at Doodle Bee's. He was a Clifford's Diner man all the way. There was no way he'd deliver a plug like that with all the subtlety of someone crunching their way through a bag of chips at a funeral without a paycheck. And if he'd made one deal, her dad had to have made more. What was next, Lucky Louie's Lingerie?

"How lovely, Jasper," Asha said, her tone expressing the exact opposite sentiment. "Now, Zara, what were your first thoughts about Caleb?" Asha leaned forward, as if she couldn't bear to miss a single syllable of the answer.

She gulped, not sure where to start. "My first thought was that he's huge, because he's super tall. He seemed nice enough, but I'm withholding judgment for now."

Uptight? Her? Yes, she totally sounded like she was wrapped tighter than a slice of wedding cake about to be put in the freezer, but she could live with that, and it was part of the plan they'd developed. He would be the all-in admirer—all the better to help his image—and she'd be the yeah-not-gonna-happen person based in reality because come on, it was not gonna happen. The man professed to hate mashed potatoes while she'd never met a starch she didn't immediately love. He was an über-rich athlete while she was busting ass with her Etsy miniatures store to make ends meet. He was big, imposing, and cocky. She was... Well, she was short, freckled, and sarcastic. Anyway, she had things she wanted to do with her life, and a six-two hockey player wasn't one of them.

Asha gave her a come-on-it's-just-us-girls look. "Did you think he was cute?"

Heat smacked Zara in both cheeks. Having this conversation while sitting next to the person in question wasn't awkward *at all*. Resisting the urge to look up and double-check that he was still there, since he'd been keeping his mouth shut after they'd walked in, she took a deep breath and tried to think of something to say.

"'Cute' wouldn't be the word I would use." Overwhelming? Solid? Teasing? The perfect amount of unusually attractive because his smirk and crooked nose edged him from the land of cute and into oh-my-yes territory? "But there's something about him that makes you take notice."

"Are you kidding?" Britany let out a loud scoff. "He's a professional athlete in his prime. Of course she thought he was handsome."

Jasper stiffened and responded in a tone of high offense. "I'm pretty sure my girl knows what she means." He turned to face the camera. "After all, she did attend the Ryerson's

Academy for Learning, which offers all sorts of courses on a wide variety of subjects for the curious student at a reasonable price."

Next to her, Caleb tried to cover his laugh with a cough. She glared up at him. This was not funny. Her "date," however, seemed to disagree. He had his lips pressed together, and not a sound escaped, but his shoulder shaking gave him away. They made eye contact, and despite her better judgment of the direness of the situation, her mouth twitched.

She fought it, but the longer she looked at him while her dad continued to talk about the tutor she'd gone to only once in high school for SAT test prep, the harder it became to ignore the urge to giggle. The whole situation was ridiculous. Pretty soon her dad would be endorsing her former preschool and Anchovy's groomer.

"Not saying she doesn't," Britany continued, her voice drowning out Jasper's #SponCon, "but my Caleb is a total catch for anyone."

"Which is why he, a professional athlete with buckets of money and women throwing themselves at him, has to go on Bramble," Jasper said, bringing the drama that, no doubt, he figured this reality TV needed.

Britany shot Jasper a look that would have sent most of the population running. "He had his reasons."

Caleb froze beside her, laughter draining from him and replaced by a tension that radiated out like the aftershocks of an atom bomb.

"Yes, *those* reasons," Asha said, a gotcha gleam in her eyes as she turned to face Caleb. "Let's chat about those."

Oh. Shit.

· · ·

"So about that viral video," the host said, glancing up from her notes with a decidedly less-than-friendly smile on her face. "Your teammates called women 'puck bunnies' and declared their prowess with them positively impacted their game. You sat silently as they did so. That fact was not taken well by the women of Harbor City."

Caleb's lungs stopped functioning for a second, and cold, clammy beads of sweat made his palms damp. If there was one thing in the world he could do, it would be to take back that moment of trying to fit in with his teammates— make them see him as another one of the guys instead of the weirdo whose lips moved when he read email on the back of the plane during road trips.

"I was an asshole." The declaration came out before his brain had a chance to check it, but it wasn't wrong. "Sorry, forgot about being on TV there for a second. I was a jerk and I should have shut that talk down. I'm sorry."

"Is that what you told your date, Zara, about it?" Asha asked, going in for the kill.

He fought to keep the white noise in his head from getting any louder as his anxiety ratcheted up. His nerves were jumping like popcorn, and it must have been obvious as hell because Zara angled her right leg just enough that it pressed against his, a silent signal that he wasn't alone. It was just enough to slow the spinning whirl inside his head and help him ease back against the couch.

Right as Asha opened her mouth, no doubt to ask a follow-up question, Zara started talking. "I didn't know anything about the video beforehand, but he was up-front with me about it on our first date and I did look it up after I got home." Zara pulled a face, wrinkling her nose in disgust. "It definitely was not a good look."

"Are you concerned, Jasper?" Asha asked, her voice filled with concern that almost sounded heartfelt. "What is your advice to your daughter about dating someone who didn't stop others from saying something like that?"

Jasper paused, pursing his lips together as he looked up at the ceiling, obviously trying to get his thoughts in order. "I think we all make mistakes at some point in our lives, but we should try to judge a person on the totality of what they've said and done." He pivoted so he had a direct line of sight to the cameras. "I know I did when I got into a fender bender. The good folks at Miller's Mechanical fixed me right up, and I made sure not to put myself in a position where I was going to run into someone's bumper again."

Asha cleared her throat, her grip on the index cards she held getting tight enough that they bent. "You certainly seem to have a lot of friends, Jasper."

"He's a walking commercial," Britany said, rolling her eyes.

Jasper shrugged off the insult. "I guess I'm the kind of guy who likes to recognize a job well done and give an encouraging word here and there. I figured that as a coach, you'd appreciate that."

Before Caleb's mom could fire off a retort, Asha broke in. "Coach Stuckey, what made you think taking over your son's dating life was a good idea? Isn't that a little excessive? What's next, calling the Ice Knights' front office to get him out of hot water?"

"Well," Britany said, her voice taking on the tone she used with a player who'd made the same mistake for the hundredth time. "He'd obviously made a mess of it, and as a mom, I wanted to help."

Asha cocked her head to one side. "It didn't seem a little overreaching to you?"

"Like I'm being a helicopter parent on steroids?" Britany let loose with her signature snort-chuckle. "Hell yes it did, but here I am because family is family, even when they mess up."

"So what do you think of his date?" Asha asked. "What

has he told you about how it went?"

"It sounded to me like it went well, and when we saw her outside just now, I gotta say you could tell they're a little taken with each other. It really showed in their body language."

"Who wouldn't be taken with Zara?" Jasper asked. "She's amazing."

Britany crossed her arms and glared at Zara's dad. "No shout-out to her hairdresser?"

He narrowed his eyes. "I don't like what you're implying."

"The place where she gets her high heels?" Caleb's mom continued.

Jasper fiddled with his tie, looking like a rookie who'd just tossed his gloves down before a fight with a veteran and was beginning to realize how much trouble he was in. "You can be snide all you want, but the fact that she's willing to go out on another date with your son really shows how much of a kind person she is, and you can't buy that in a store."

An unnatural silence wrapped around everyone in the studio. Even the people who didn't know Britany seemed to be hanging on the edge of the oh-shit moment.

"Sounds to me, Jasper," Asha said, pulling them all back from the brink, "as if you're not really all that taken with the idea of Zara dating Caleb."

"I have some reservations." Taking a visible gulp, Jasper cut a glance over to Britany before his attention skittered away. "B-b-but I'm trying to keep an open mind."

Britany snorted.

Asha turned to Caleb, her smile cooling by at least twenty degrees. "What about you, Caleb? Are you taken with Zara, or is she just another nameless puck bunny?"

He could feel his breath hitching as what felt like the attention of Harbor City's entire population zoomed in on him. In half a heartbeat, he was that kid standing in front of his class trying to read the daily announcements while the letters moved around on the page. He could feel individual droplets of sweat on the back of his neck, and the urge to get up and leave was almost overwhelming.

"Yeah, I do like her," he said, the words coming out fast and untested. He really should have practiced this bit. *Just remember you're the one who is supposed to be already half in love.* "I knew it the first time I spotted her and she came crashing into me that there would be sparks between us. She owns her own business, she's creative, she speaks her mind, all of which are really attractive, and that's before you even get to the fact that she's totally hot. Zara is the total package. I could totally see myself falling for her."

It sounded almost as stilted as Jasper's commercial pitches, but he had to brazen through it.

"And if I told you she'd said no to going on a second date?" Asha asked.

That metaphorical kick in the balls was enough to make him slam his mouth shut hard enough to rattle his teeth. "Really?"

"Just teasing." Asha laughed, each word sharp as his skate's blades. "She's right here, so let's ask her. Zara, are you going to say yes to a second date or follow the advice of Harbor City's women in our morning flash poll?" She pivoted to look straight into the camera. "While we've been talking, our viewers have been voting. Sixty-eight percent of the ladies voted that Zara should have been one and done. Yes or no to another date, Zara?"

Her knee was jiggling against his, but she answered without hesitation. "Yes."

"Interesting," Asha said, turning the wattage of her smile up to twenty. "I'm sure all of Harbor City will be tuning in after date number two to find out if you or our viewers were right about how it would go. We'll see all of you then on *Harbor City Wake Up.*"

The red light over the camera went dark, Asha got up and started to walk off the set, and everyone in the studio started chattering at once—except for him, Zara, Jasper, and Britany.

Caleb sat there dumbfounded. He got that he was a dipshit. He got that Asha and probably most of Harbor City wanted to give him a public comeuppance, which he could take. What he didn't understand was why he couldn't shake the feeling that this was personal for the TV host.

"I'll be right back," he told Zara before hustling over to where Asha was talking with a guy in a headset who was holding a clipboard. "Thanks for having me."

"You have no idea who I am, do you?" she asked.

Trick question? Maybe, but he was going to play it straight. "You're Asha Kapoor."

Glaring at him, she took a step closer and lowered her voice so only they could hear. "One of your teammates slept with my sister a few months ago, but he wouldn't know who she is because she was just some rando puck bunny, I guess."

Seriously, getting slashed in the face with a stick a hundred times would be worth it if he could go back in time and have another chance to call out his friends for saying such stupid shit. Most of it really was just talk—they weren't bad guys—but they'd acted like it, and that was just as awful.

Guilt twisted his gut. Up until this moment, he hadn't really thought about how the video going viral had impacted the women he and the other Ice Knights had slept with. Yeah, that pretty much confirmed it. He was pond scum. "I'm sorry. I should have said something. I deserve the response I've gotten."

"You do." Asha jabbed her finger into his chest. "And not because of some sex shaming but because these women were human beings, not pussy sleeves for your dicks. They have names."

"You're right." He took a step back and stopped himself. "Please tell your sister I'm sorry."

Asha glared at him, a divot forming between her eyes, but didn't say anything.

Taking the hint, he turned away and walked out of the studio with his mom, Zara, and Jasper. Zara and her dad gave them space, chatting quietly in the corner. From what he could catch, it sounded like Zara was giving her old man the what-for about all the commercial plugs he'd dropped during the interview.

It wasn't until the elevator started going down that his mom pulled him aside and said, "That was rough. You okay?"

"I'll live." He let his head fall back so it thunked against the elevator wall. "Do you think I can come back from this?"

Giving him a considering look, his mom paused, seeming to gather her words. He knew what that meant. Coach Britany was on duty. "Let me ask you this, how would you feel about someone who said what your teammates did about your sisters?"

He didn't even have to think about it. "Like smashing his face in."

"Why?"

"Because it's a shitty, dehumanizing move and they deserve better."

His mom nodded. "So why do I have to make the connection between your sisters and these other women for you to realize the shittiness of this kind of locker room talk, if that's what you want to use as an excuse?"

She shouldn't have to. That was the water his mom was leading him to, and as soon as he was standing over the pond looking down at his reflection, he saw it all. Epic-level dickery.

"So what do I do now?" he asked.

"Act the way you know you should," she said as the elevator doors opened. "Use this opportunity not just to make yourself look better but to be better."

And how exactly he was going to do that, he had to figure out—and soon. A few floors later, he was holding the elevator doors while everyone walked out. His mom and her dad said their goodbyes and walked out, but Zara lingered in the lobby, her fingers wrapped tightly around the strap of her purse as her gaze flicked from one part of the busy lobby to another without ever landing on him.

"You got a minute to chat?" he asked.

This wasn't going to go well. More than likely, she was going to move over to the side of the 68 percent of the city's female population who were ready to kick him to the curb. Who could blame her? Not him. Still, it needed to be done.

"I understand if you want to end this here," he said, walking with her toward the doors. "No hard feelings."

She looked up at him, her gaze wary. "Were you serious up there? Are you really sorry you didn't act or that you got caught?"

"I'm ashamed I didn't say anything." He shoved his fingers through his hair in frustration, mad at himself. "I should have, and I fucked up."

Zara didn't say anything. She didn't even look at him. Instead, she watched the people hustle around them in the lobby. Then she took out her phone and opened the Bramble app. The *yes or no to date number two* confirmation notification popped up immediately.

She tapped *yes*. "Let's see what the Bramble folks have planned for date number two."

Caleb let out the pent-up breath he'd been holding, and they walked out together into the bright Harbor City morning.

Chapter Five

The next day, Caleb was waiting for Zara outside of The Adventure Place, which was housed in a huge warehouse down at the harbor's edge where Bramble had organized an event for matched couples. About twenty people were waiting outside when he got there, each of them pairing off into couples—with the exception of one group of three each wearing "poly proud" T-shirts and looking like they'd all won the Bramble lottery. His date, though, was a no-show.

He checked the Bramble app on his phone for the billionth time. The last message he'd gotten through it informed him that Zara had checked yes for a second date. No updates since then that she'd changed her mind. Shoving his phone in his pocket, he scanned the area, looking for her again.

Finally, just as he was about to give up hope, a small lime-green car turned onto the long drive leading to the warehouse. A Great Dane had his head poking through the open sunroof, the tongue hanging out of its mouth bigger than his mom's Chihuahua.

As soon as the car came to a stop near the entryway, the

passenger door was flung open and Zara scrambled out, her face flush as her gaze darted from one couple to another. When she finally spotted him, she hurried over, making faster time than he thought possible in a pair of sandals that boosted her height by two inches.

"Sorry I'm late." She pulled her hair back into a ponytail as the fall breeze did its best to whip it around her face. "My dog took one of my shoes again."

Caleb took a wild guess. "That horse of a dog?"

"Yep."

A woman opened the glass double doors to the warehouse. "Come on in, Bramble folks. Let's do this."

The *this* in question turned out to be an indoor zip line obstacle course. There were lines that crisscrossed the overhead area of the warehouse with platforms and balance lines along with rolling padded bars that participants had to run across as the bars spun.

The whole thing started with a twenty-foot climbing wall dotted with different-colored holds that stuck out from the surface. The instructor let them know they had to climb up the wall, cross the obstacle course, and then descend the platforms on the other side. As each couple made their way through the course, the leaderboard would show everyone's time.

"The goal is to get across first?" Zara asked as she exchanged her sandals for a pair of climbing shoes provided by their group leader, Charlotte, who'd spent the last five minutes explaining the equipment to everyone in a lecture that included tips about creating harmony with the universe and achieving balance.

"No, it's to learn to communicate and work together," Charlotte said, handing Zara a safety harness. "This is one of those activities that help build connections between couples. You are a team."

Yeah. That sounded like some BS right there. "Is there a course record?" Caleb asked.

Charlotte shook her head, her serene earth-mama expression not shifting in the slightest. "The Adventure Place is about the journey, not the stats."

"And no one knows the course record?" Zara asked.

After letting out a sigh that sounded a lot like a whispered plea for serenity now, Charlotte answered, "Six minutes and twenty-eight seconds. Now if we can move the discussion back to setting your personal intentions for the moment."

Their guide continued on, but Caleb wasn't listening anymore. He and Zara exchanged a look of understanding as they pulled on their harnesses and tightened the straps around their waists while the rest of the Bramble daters seemed to be hanging on Charlotte's every word.

Under the guise of adjusting his climbing shoes, Caleb squatted down beside Zara and kept his voice low. "We're gonna go balls out on this thing, right?"

"Hell yes."

There was no missing the epic level of kick-ass-or-have-your-ass-kicked competitiveness glimmering in her brown eyes. The woman wasn't here to play or get in touch with her inner compass. She was here to dominate.

"You know," he said, grinning at her. "You're all right."

She tipped an imaginary hat at him as they followed Charlotte and the rest of the Bramble daters to the wall. "Let's do this."

They started up the wall. He set the pace slow, taking it easy and reaching for the different colored holds. Everything in him was screaming to go faster, but he wanted to continue the conversation, and his wingspan was probably as long as Zara's entire body. Something bright red flashed in his peripheral vision. It took him a second to realize it was Zara ascending the wall like Spider-Man, her ponytail swaying from side to side along with her heart-shaped ass.

He sped up, catching her quickly. "So, what did you think of my 'already got the hots for her' answer in the interview?"

"It was something." She didn't look his way, just kept her attention focused on picking out the best hold to help leverage her way up. "You were laying it on a little thick, but I suppose you've got to fix your fuckup. Really, what were you guys thinking by saying all of that shit? Did you really have to prove the athlete stereotypes true?"

"That's the thing." He followed a path upward that was parallel to hers, the movements requiring the kind of concentration that was usually taken up by making sure his mouth wasn't going off without his brain. "For some of us, it's not true. I haven't even slept with that many women. It was just talk for some of the guys."

He squeezed his eyes closed for a second and swallowed a groan. Talking and climbing was probably not the best combo for him—too much of the truth spilled out.

"Yeah," she said with a scoff. "Tell that to the women of the world who've been on the receiving end of that kind of 'just talk'—the ones who are made to feel small so guys like you can feel like a big man." She paused, arching back far enough that when she gave him the stink eye, it was without the belay rope in her line of sight. "So how many women have you slept with?"

His grip slipped, along with his ability to keep his mouth shut. "Fifteenish."

"This year?" She shrugged and continued upward. "That's kinda a lot. Not to slut shame you or anything, just to point out that a professional athlete's definition of 'a lot' and a regular person's might be different."

And there it was, the assumption that made the reality stand out that much more. "Not this year," he said, wishing like hell that he could shut up already. "Total."

She paused, considering her next handhold carefully. "Are you a serial monogamist?" she asked without nearly as much judgment as he heard inside his own skull.

He shook his head, embarrassment burning a hole in his stomach lining. "Just shitty with the women."

Zara paused mid-reach for the last hold and turned to look him in the eye. "I don't think you give yourself enough credit."

And with that, she climbed up onto the first platform, unclipped the belay rope, and attached the obstacle course safety line to the carabiner on her harness. He took off after her, but the woman was sprinting across the fifteen-feet-long tightrope over a net. She was across to the platform on the other side before he'd even gotten his new safety line clipped in place.

"Come on," she called out. "You can do it."

Fuck. He flew down the ice on blades three millimeters wide and managed to stay on his feet even when someone slammed into him—well, mostly. So why was a rope nearly four times as thick making his gut clench? A million possibilities of all the ways this could go wrong ran through his head.

Zara tapped on her wrist, her mouth curled in a good-natured, teasing smile. "Clock's ticking, Caleb."

Wiping his palms on the side of his shorts, he started across.

The rope wobbled. His breath caught. He went down, the safety line and net breaking his fall so he bounced, his arms and legs flailing in the air.

As he lay on his back in the middle of the net, he heard Zara yell out, "Don't give up."

Gritting his teeth, he stood and scaled the ladder to the platform. This time he got a running start and tried to sprint his way across. He made it halfway before his shoulders lurched left, the rope went right, and he went down. As he made his way back up the ladder, he could feel Zara's gaze on him, watching and no doubt marking down his every mistake. When he got to the platform and looked across the wire, though, she wasn't giving him that judgmental glare he was expected.

She stood on the opposite platform, one foot in front of the other with her arms straight out. "Keep your arms out like this and your eyes on me. You've got this."

"Highly coachable" had never been one of the descriptors the scouts had given for him—no doubt Freud would say that had something to do with his mom's job. Still, he followed Zara's instructions.

"Make sure to center your weight," she said. "One foot in front of the other. That's it. You're doing great."

She was practically chanting those words over and over again by the time he made it across. Adrenaline pumping, he wrapped an arm around her waist and lifted her up to him in celebration. He hadn't planned on doing that, but once they were face-to-face, her pink mouth only inches from his, the whole thing felt natural—as if he should have done that eons ago. Her hands went to his shoulders, and her lips parted on a soft "oh" that sounded more like a moment of awareness than of surprise.

She didn't fit perfectly against him—with more than a foot height difference, that would never happen—but she still felt right in his arms. Her gaze dropped from his eyes to his mouth, and she lowered her face just enough to let him know that if he didn't stop this now, she was going to kiss him. That was good. That was really damn—bad.

What the hell, Stuckey. Your date is off-limits, remember, asshole? There are rules. You have a goal. Using Zara to get off is not an option. She doesn't even want to be here with you.

Reality driven home, he came back to his senses. He didn't throw Zara down, but he didn't set her gently on her feet, either. Embarrassment chased the confusion right off her face as a deep blush worked its way up from the base of her throat.

"Sorry, I shouldn't have picked you up," he said, shoving a hand through his hair to keep from reaching out for her again. "I got carried away."

She looked everywhere but at him. "Yeah, no worries. We should just—" And then she sprinted off the platform and onto the padded, spinning bars, making it to the third out of five before she went flying.

• • •

What had she been thinking? Kissing Caleb Stuckey? No, that was bad. Really bad. Almost as bad as face planting on the trampoline-like net under the spinning bars of hell.

The idea of laying here looking like she had permanently biffed it sounded pretty good at the moment, but Zara couldn't do it. She had to get up, conquer this obstacle course, and mark date number two off her to-do list before she embarrassed herself any further.

"Are you okay?" Caleb asked.

She rolled over onto her back. He was on the platform, staring down at her. His dark hair was tousled, and the Ice Knights T-shirt he wore showed off his broad shoulders and biceps to perfection.

"I'm good." Good at being an idiot who'd wanted to kiss her very-much-non-date.

Worse. She hadn't just wanted to kiss him. She'd wanted to help him clear his cobwebs. It had been easy to blow off how hot he was when she thought he was another oversexed pro athlete. But fifteen women? His entire life? Sure, for some people that would be a big number, but she figured he'd be in triple digits. The fact that his number was closer to hers than an average pop star's had her discombobulated to the point that she didn't even think before she'd rushed across the tight rope. And then when he'd lifted her up and he smelled so good and her entire body was tuned in to his and everything was just so—

"Do you need help getting off?" Caleb asked.

Help getting off? Oh, if only that was possible in the no-orgasms-with-others zone. She shook her head. She couldn't have heard him right. "Excuse me?"

"Do you need help getting back up here?" he asked, this time making his voice loud enough that the people just starting the rock wall probably heard him.

"I'm good." If imagining what he'd do to help her get off was good, which—to be clear—it was not. "I'll be right there."

She made her way back up the ladder to the platform. The tiny platform. The teeny tiny itty-bitty platform. It was hard to figure out where to stand so she wouldn't be touching him. He was definitely a no-touch zone.

"Are you sure you're okay?" He tucked some hair that had gotten loose in her fall behind her ear. "We don't have to finish this."

"I'm not the kind of person who gives up." Even if the leaderboard had them hovering near last now.

He grinned. "Then it's game time."

High on adrenaline and needing to get away before she did something stupid—again—Zara leaped onto the first of the padded spinning bars and, by the grace of God, finally made it across to the next platform. Her breaths came in hard pants as she watched Caleb rush across the spinning bars. Thanks to the fact that he was wearing loose-fitting shorts, she got some glorious views of his thighs working overtime as he did so.

Stop noticing that.

The distraction had hit the level that she didn't move out of the way in time, and he nearly pounced on her in his final leap to the platform. She let out a squeak of alarm and stumbled back, nearly tumbling off the platform.

"Whoa," Caleb called out, reaching for her and dragging her back from the edge.

That she ended up with her face pressed into his chest—thank you, height difference—at least worked to her advantage to cover up the fact that she took a deep inhale of his scent. God. What was wrong with her? He hated mashed potatoes. Only sociopaths hated mashed potatoes. It was a sign on top of all the other ways they were total and complete opposites that made this whole thing crazy.

"Thanks," she said, her words muffled by the wall of muscle he called his chest, and took a half step back while hoping the extra few inches would clear her head.

It did. Sorta. She was aware enough to read the sign explaining the rules for the next obstacle, at least.

Zara tapped the part of the rules written in bold. "We're skipping that part, right?"

His jaw tightened as his attention moved over to the sign and he narrowed his eyes, everything about him going from loose and easy to hard and tense with the added bonus of uncomfortable silence. She was trying to work out the reason for the change—shit, had she accidentally kneed him in the balls when he'd pulled her back from the brink?—when he let out a harsh breath.

"Rules are rules," he said. "We've got to swing over to the next platform together."

They both looked at the single heavy rope hanging next to the platform. According to the directions, they were to each put a foot in one of the loops made for that purpose, hold on to each other, and swing in a wide arc to the next, lower platform. Then, do it again to a platform closer to the floor and again on a platform only a few feet above the padded mat until they were back on the ground, the course completed.

Caleb grabbed the rope, steadying it. "You get on first."

"This is going to be a disaster," she said as she put her foot in the loop and wrapped her hands around the rope, the fibers scratching her palms.

"What's the worst that could happen?" He jiggled the rope a little, chuckling when she shot him the evil eye in return. "We land face-first on the net. Again."

Looking around, she noticed that most of the Bramble daters were already done and watching the slowpokes still on the course. Some even had their phones out, no doubt to get a shot of Caleb to put up on social media. Great.

"Public humiliation while swinging on a rope with an optimist," she said, wrinkling her nose at the last word. "Just what a woman loves on a second date."

"What can I say, I'm the total package." He put a foot in the hold and shoved off with the other one. "Let's do this."

They swung through the air in a long, sweeping half circle that made the tail of her bedraggled ponytail fly and her heart speed up. It was an amazingly free rush and, as they sailed by the second platform, she reached out for the pole without even worrying if it was possible. Somehow she just knew it would work.

It did not.

The metal pole in the middle of the platform was too slick to grip, and her fingers slid across it without stopping. That happened later after they drifted by the platform again, only now with their momentum shot, they were too far away to reach it. So they held on to the rope as it swayed in slower and slower circles until it finally came to a complete dead stop.

"We officially suck at this," she said, wriggling to try to get some momentum back, a move that had absolutely no

effect.

"Oh well, plan B. Time to play it by instinct and just go for it." The words were barely out of Caleb's mouth before he let go and fell into the safety net below them.

Looking down at the net and then over at the platform, her type-A personality protested, but she had to admit that Caleb had the right idea. Just like them dating, this obstacle course was only a game, so they might as well let go and have fun with it. She unwound her fingers from her death grip on the rope and did a very ungraceful back flop onto the net below.

They didn't even come close to beating the course record; they didn't even beat any of the other Bramble daters—not that anyone else seemed to realize it had been a competition.

By the time they were sitting side by side on a bench by the lockers putting their regular shoes back on, the awkwardness of earlier had faded and she could actually look at Caleb without wanting to crawl into a hole and hide—or climbing him and doing things to him.

"So, are you going to tell Asha all about my severely lacking balance skills?" he asked, scooting closer to her.

Nodding, she leaned down and buckled the strap of her high wedge sandals. "Without a doubt."

"After what happened the other day with you going down hard on the sidewalks of our fair city, do you really think it's a great idea to be wearing shoes like that?"

She sat up and glared at him. "That was a freak accident caused by slow-walking tourists. I can run in these."

"Really?" One side of his mouth curled up in an ornery grin.

Was he teasing her? Yeah, more than likely, but she couldn't let doubt like that stand. "Watch me."

And she did it. She ran the small track beneath the safety nets accompanied by the cheers of encouragement of her

fellow Bramble folks still putting on their shoes and chatting with their dates. Yeah, it may have been more to smooth her wounded ego after he'd given her the heave-ho when she'd started to make a move to kiss him, but a woman had to have her pride, and hers was pretty dinged up. That was all behind her, though—right up until she came to a stop directly in front of him.

There was something about how he stood there, his arms crossed over his wide chest, a crooked smile beneath his equally crooked nose that got her smack-dab in the middle of the overlapping circles in the he's-so-hot and the this-is-a-bad-idea-but-I'm-thinking-it-anyway Venn diagram.

"I'm suitably impressed," he said, falling in beside her as she walked toward the front door. "There's no way I could do that."

"I could give you lessons." No. No, she couldn't. That definitely did not fit into the five-dates-and-done plan.

"I might take you up on that." He held open the door and moved to the side so she could go through first.

They walked out together into the bright sunshine of early September. Neither of them moved toward the parking lot. Trying not to notice how her body was on awareness DEFCON 1 being near him like this, she scanned the parking lot, looking for a sports car or ridiculously expensive luxury vehicle that he probably drove. Nothing fit the bill, and she was about to ask him which car was his when Gemma pulled up, stopping in front of them. Anchovy, with his sassy new doggie bandanna tied around his neck from his trip to the groomer, stuck his head out of the sunroof and gave her a happy hello bark.

"That's my ride," she said, willing her feet to move, which they did not. "Gemma was a lifesaver and took my dog to his grooming appointment while I was here."

Another bark from Anchovy, who was looking between

her and Caleb as if he was trying to figure out if he needed to intervene or jump out to get pets from a stranger.

"I can give you a ride next time." He reached out, hand relaxed, so the dog could sniff his knuckles, which Anchovy did before using his snout to toss Caleb's hand up and onto the top of his furry head for a good pet. "This guy would definitely fit in my truck."

"Maybe," Zara said, a fizzy awareness making her skin tingle as she got into the car.

Gemma didn't say anything, but the raised eyebrow, oh-honey look she gave Zara promised there would be an interrogation later. As it was, Zara was rescued by Anchovy's enthusiastic greeting when Gemma pulled the car into traffic. Zara tried to figure out what in the world she was going to tell her friend about date two when she had no idea what had just happened—because it sure felt like something.

And dear God, she didn't even want to think about what might happen on date three.

Chapter Six

"Tell me everything or there's no way we can be friends," Gemma demanded as they walked into Zara's apartment.

Anchovy galloped inside, rushing around looking for his oversize tennis ball that was the size of a mini basketball. Like the smart women they were, they stayed out of the dog's way. No one wanted to stand between Anchovy and his most prized possession.

"What's there to tell?" She patted Anchovy on the head and scratched behind his ears when he came over, ball in mouth. "It was an obstacle course. We should go sometime; it was actually pretty fun."

Gemma took a sip from her double espresso soy latte with half a shot of hazelnut. "The course was or the date was, because from what I saw when I picked you up, it looked like the second one."

"We were just standing there." Closely, so much so that Zara could feel him even though he wasn't touching her. "You have an overactive imagination."

Her bestie just gave her the you're-full-of-it-but-I-love-you-anyway scoff as she walked to the corner of Zara's apartment that was filled with gorgeous natural light and, therefore, had been designated as her art studio.

"What are you working on now?" Gemma asked, her hand hovering over the unassembled dolls but not touching them.

"It's a piece for the Friends of the Library charity auction." Zara crossed to stand next to Gemma. "It's gonna be a house filled with influential female authors reading one another's books."

By the time she was done, the two-story dollhouse would be filled with twenty-five handmade and hand-painted dolls, dressed in custom-made costumes, reading at the kitchen table, in the bathtub, on a couch, gathered by the fireplace, and tucked into bed. All the books on the shelves would have individual pages, and the covers would be one-twelfth-size replicas of first editions of the authors' books. Her Etsy store of individual miniatures other people used was making bank instead of her own artistic scenes, but it was pieces like this that she really wanted to do. Miniatures art wasn't the most popular or sought after, but there was something that made her soul feel lighter when she created a piece of art showcasing a one-twelfth-size world that she'd love to live in.

"Your work really is amazing." Gemma pivoted, the teasing upturn of her mouth gone, replaced by a tight concern. "You know I would have taken you to the charity ball as my plus-one anyway, right? I would never really stand between you and your dreams. I just really am worried about you."

"I get it." She did, sorta. They'd been friends for too long to get annoyed at her bestie's pushy ways. "We both know what a softie you are."

"It seems like the Bramble dates are going well, though." Gemma picked up Jane Austen's acrylic head.

"Let's just say that Caleb and I have an understanding."

One with rules and structure.

"I hope that understanding involves orgasms."

"It doesn't."

"Not yet, anyway. I saw the way he was looking at you. The man wants to carry you off and do the best kind of wicked things to your body." Gemma put down Jane's head and held out her hand. "I bet you that by date five, you're banging him so good that your lady cobwebs will be knocked forever loose."

Zara clamped her lips together before she did something she'd regret—like agree—and started futzing around with the mail on the counter.

"Our agreement didn't preclude sex, but I'll still take that bet," she said, shaking her friend's hand. "He is not the kind of guy for me."

"Because he's too oh-my-God-I-tripped-and-landed-on-your-big-cock hot?" Gemma tapped the tip of her nose with her finger as if she'd hit on the answer. "Yep, that's totally it. You're right. He's totally not bangable."

Zara fought to keep both the smile off her face and thoughts of a naked Caleb out of her head. She did not need to go there. Cobwebs or not, sleeping with a guy like Caleb who, according to his own words, hung out with people who couldn't remember all the women they'd fucked was not something she was going to do. Ever.

"Very funny," she said, trying to put into words the oh-honey-no alarms that went off around Caleb. "I mean, he's hot and all, but he reminds me too much of my dad."

Gemma let out a spluttering cough and almost dropped the coffee she'd been sipping. "Okay, that definitely went into ew territory."

"That's not what I meant." She flipped off her friend. "He's got this whole 'let's go for it' vibe about him. I clocked it as soon as he threw this whole dating plan at me and today at the obstacle course when he let go of the rope and just went with the flow." And he'd done both with a whole devil-may-care gleam in his eyes. If that didn't scream out "run, you're in danger," she didn't know what would. "You know how much I need predictability. Someone who runs on instinct is the last person I need in my life or between my legs."

"You've thought a lot about Caleb Stuckey," Gemma said.

Zara shrugged, not wanting to admit the truth of that statement. "Okay, a little."

"You know, I think you just might be misjudging him. He could surprise you. What won't surprise me is when I win this bet, because you are so gonna sleep with him." Gemma strode to the door. "And now I have to trek all the way over to Waterbury to meet with that wedding planner everyone at work raved about."

A quick hug and she was out the door. Then it was just Zara and Anchovy, which was how everything usually was. Normally, she'd do one of three things: binge-watch old episodes of *Law & Order*, fall into the latest urban fantasy romance she'd grabbed at the store down the street, or work. Okay, the last one was what she did nine times out of ten.

Shit. Maybe Gemma was right. Maybe it was time she shook things up a little bit in her life.

Slipping out of her strappy sandals, she put on her Keds. "Leash?"

Anchovy dropped his slobbery mess of a ball at her feet and sprinted off to go get his leash out of the basket by the door.

Her phone dinged, and she glanced down to see a notification from Bramble come through. Caleb had accepted date three. Oh boy.

• • •

The next morning, the Ice Knights weight room was nearly deserted when Caleb walked in for a preseason workout session with the other guys on the first line. Along with the line's other defenseman, Zach Blackburn, he and forward Alex Christensen, center Ian Petrov, and forward Cole Phillips had settled into an unofficial off-season workout schedule.

Today, though, the team gym somehow magically managed to smell like melted chocolate and warm vanilla instead of sweat and funk. There was only one explanation for that. Petrov.

"Why does it smell like cookies?" Caleb asked the forward, who was obviously on another one of his weird kicks in his efforts to get off the injured list faster than the team doctor expected, even though the dude was pretty much unofficially healed already.

Sure, his methods were bizarre, but Caleb was starting to think the man was on to something, because Petrov was ready to get out on the ice in time for the season way before he was supposed to. All he needed was the team doc to sign off on him.

Sweat ran down the other man's forehead as he stood with a fifty-pound dumbbell held close to the center of a weight vest that Caleb knew from personal experience clocked in at forty-five pounds. "It's this new thing." Petrov lifted one leg off the ground and executed a single leg squat. "I can't eat them according to the nutritionist, so smelling them pisses me off."

Caleb moved his head from side to side, stretching his neck and then rolling his shoulders, waiting for Petrov to explain what in the hell that had to do with anything. When he didn't, Caleb prompted, "And..."

Petrov cut a glare his way while Smitty, the team trainer, laughed as he set up the agility ropes on the Astroturf across the gym.

"That means," Petrov said, his voice coming out strained as he did another single leg squat, "I lift harder and longer when I'm mad."

What did it say about him that Petrov's latest theory kind of made sense? Nothing good. "Why can't you just have one cookie instead of a dozen?"

"I have to do whatever it takes to get back on the ice. Anyway, who can stop at just one cookie?" Petrov asked as he switched legs.

Caleb raised his hand, holding it aloft and smirking at his line mate as he walked over to the elliptical to warm up.

"Fuck you, Stuckey."

He blew the other man a kiss and cranked up the incline on the elliptical. This part of the near-daily routine he didn't have to think about. Smitty varied up the rest of the off-season training so it wasn't the same every day, but it was always some form of weight lifting, agility training, stretching, and biometrics.

Unlike athletes in other sports, they couldn't afford to show up to training camp at anything other than tip-top shape. Their camp only lasted a few days, with rookies going in two days early for athletic testing and on-ice skills. After that, the returning lineup had two days that followed the same pattern. Then the team went straight into seven preseason games spread out over two weeks before the puck dropped for real.

When it came to hockey, there really was no off-season—just a slower one, which made the fact that it was just him, Petrov, and Smitty in the gym that much weirder. Sure, it wasn't official, but it was usually the entire Ice Knights first line here at the crack-ass of ten in the morning.

"Where are the rest of the guys?" he asked as he jogged.

Petrov put the dumbbell away on the rack and then took

off his weight vest. "Blackburn is doing some charity gig with Fallon, Christensen just left a little bit ago, and Phillips is buying enough flowers for a funeral to try to get back on Marti's good side."

"I thought they were done for real this time?" Of course, he'd thought that every one of the sixty billion times the coach's daughter and the star forward had broken up.

Petrov shrugged. "Give it a couple of weeks; it'll change."

"So much for our regular preseason workout today." He was supposed to be running agility races with Christensen, which was pretty much an advanced course in getting his ass kicked, but he wasn't about to give up until he won.

"You feeling lonely, Stuckey?" Petrov moved over to Smitty, who had his stopwatch ready and was standing next to a metal sled loaded up with close to five hundred pounds of weight plates. "Need me to set you up with a hot date?"

Caleb hit the stop button on the elliptical with more force than necessary, got off, and made his way over to the free weights. "You'd be better than my mom."

"How's the lovely Britany?" Petrov asked, just like he did every time his mom got mentioned.

"Shut up, asshole." Now it was his turn to flip off his line mate as he strapped on his own weight vest and picked up a dumbbell to do a round of single leg squats. "She's my mom."

Petrov shrugged and got set behind the sled, readying to push it the forty-eight yards down the turf. "Your mom is hot, deal."

"She's also in control of my dating life in the world's stupidest play for public redemption."

As soon as the words were out of his mouth, he regretted it. Petrov had been with him in the Uber that night, but he'd been smart enough to not run his mouth insulting the female half of Harbor City's population when the video none of them knew about was rolling. Neither had Phillips. It had just been a couple of rookies acting like asshole players, but that didn't matter. In the player hierarchy of the team, it had been his responsibility to set the rookies straight. It had been up to him to set the example for the other players to follow. He was the one who wanted to be a leader on the team, to get that A for assistant captain on his jersey. To make that happen, he had to act like a leader—a good one.

And he'd fucked up like a dumb-ass. Maybe his middle school teacher had been right. Maybe without hockey, he wouldn't be able to be anything more than what that asshole voice in his head had decided was: a barely literate loser.

"Better you than me." Petrov snorted. "I'm trying to imagine who my mom would pick out, and it scares the shit out of me." He got set again behind the sled. "But I also don't spill a metric shit-ton of BS."

Then Petrov started pushing the sled, grunting with effort and bitching about "motherfucking cookies" with each agonizing step, effectively ending the conversation, which was fine with Caleb. It wasn't like he wanted his current dating hellscape analyzed. He was here for the muscle burn and to sweat out the memory of yesterday's almost-kiss with Zara.

Tomorrow, he'd be back at the TV station for the date number two recap video. He'd get to do a play-by-play breakdown for his mom then. Only a root canal could be any better than that.

He was halfway through the first round of right leg squat reps when Coach Peppers and a short guy in an expensive suit walked through. It took a second to place the other guy— what with never seeing him outside of a very limited number of team meet and greets—but once he made the connection, he didn't have a single doubt. Herbie Dawson, principal owner of the Ice Knights, stood, scowling, just inside the doorway in what had to be a custom-made suit. He didn't have a single close-cropped white hair out of place. Peppers, on the other hand, was in Ice Knights workout gear and his black hair was going every which way. Whatever the two had been discussing, it must have sucked balls, because Peppers had been through the wringer.

"Stuckey," Dawson said, his trademark wheezy voice doing nothing to soften his harsh tone as he strode across the gym to where Caleb stood. "I understand your situation is being handled."

A cold sweat broke out at the base of Caleb's neck, and his heart rate picked up enough to get a little beep notification from his smart watch. "Yes, sir, Mr. Dawson."

"And we're not going to have to deal with any more problems on your watch?" Dawson asked, his gaze as sharp as the blades on Caleb's skates.

His grip tightened on the weight he was still holding to his chest like an asshole. "No, sir."

"The Ice Knights have a code, Stuckey." Dawson had to tilt his chin up to look Caleb in the eye. "We don't make fools of ourselves or one another. We do not embarrass the team. Ever."

For half a heartbeat, he was back in sixth grade, standing at the front of the class, the piece of paper shaking in his clammy grip as everyone stared at him, their whispers sounding like shouts to his heated ears. Then he was back, staring down at the pissed-off man who was telling him in no uncertain terms that he was fucked if he didn't make this Bramble thing work.

"I understand, sir."

"Good." He paused, just eye-stabbing Caleb for a few eternity-lasting seconds before turning and leaving the gym.

Caleb's breath came out in a whoosh, and he slammed the fifty-pound weight down onto the rack. This wasn't supposed to happen anymore. He'd worked too long to freeze in those moments, to fall back into shitty habits now. If he locked up on the ice, forget a viral video that made him—and the team—look like a bag of dicks, he'd never lace up again.

"What the hell, Coach?" he snarled at the one person in the room who had just as much on the line as he did.

"Don't start with me, Stuckey," Coach grumbled as he marched to the treadmill and began punching in an incline level before starting to run at a fast pace. "Just make this PR fix Lucy came up with work. Whatever it takes. Do not fuck this up."

• • •

Zara had finally slid under the covers for the night after finishing up the costume for Maya Angelou for her current art piece when her phone buzzed on the bed. Anchovy laid his head on top of it, obviously casting his vote that it was too late for texts.

"You're so bossy, dog," she said as she slid her hand under his heavy head and retrieved her phone.

Caleb: *So about tomorrow's interview…*

Zara: *Wondering which neighborhood businesses my dad's gonna be shilling for this time?*

The three dots of a typing box appeared, disappeared, and reappeared several times before the message came through.

Caleb: *He can do that the entire time if it keeps everyone's attention on him.*

Yeah, she could see that after Asha had put him on blast last time.

Zara: *Worried about more blowback from the video?*

Caleb: *A little of that, but more that I'd rather get a root canal than have everyone in the room staring at me.*

Okay, she'd credited his tension during the interview to the video, but maybe there was more to it.

Zara: *You do realize your job involves having people stare at your every move and judge you the entire time, right?*

Caleb: *I never notice when I'm out on the ice. Too busy making plays and winning games.*

Zara: *Don't worry, I'm sure my dad will have a whole slew of friends' businesses to plug. At least there are only four more interviews to go.*

Caleb: *You sure you're still in for four more?*

She had considered running for the dating hills after she'd seen the video of him in the Uber with his hockey buddies. The Bramble app allowed for an emergency out from the five-date rule if needed but tried to get everyone to give each person they matched with five dates. She hadn't been able to do it, though, and it hadn't just been because she needed to be Gemma's plus-one or because her dad was hilariously and somewhat bizarrely working to get his acting chops recognized. There was just something about Caleb that made her feel like there was more to the story than what the Uber driver had posted.

Zara: *We made a deal. I'm sticking to my side of it.*

Caleb: *It is in the rules.*

ZARA: *Exactly.*

Caleb: *Any idea what the setup is for the interview tomorrow?*

Zara: *All I know is that it's you, me, and our parents all together again. What could possibly go wrong? Don't answer. I can come up with enough nightmare scenarios on my own.*

Caleb: *So what are you doing tonight?*

Zara: *Cuddled up with my dog, Anchovy.*

Caleb: *Anchovy??? How could you name him that?*

Zara: *I rescued him as a puppy, and he must have rolled in something nasty before I found him in the alley, because he smelled bad.*

She gave her guy a good head rub, and he answered with one of his signature talky growls that almost sounded like words—and in this case a complaint that they weren't both asleep by now.

Caleb: *What kind of dog is he anyway?*

Zara: *Part Great Dane, part shoe thief.*

Caleb: *I need a full pic. I only saw his head before.*

She scrolled through her phone, found one where he was standing with his front paws on the island holding one of her shoes in his mouth, and hit send. Obviously annoyed at her, Anchovy jumped down from the bed and padded over to the light switch. She knew what was coming next.

"Anchovy, don't—"

Too late. He reached up and turned the light off before coming back to bed.

"You are such a pain in my butt, dog."

Anchovy's only answer was a talky growl as he flopped down next to her.

Caleb: *That's a horse, not a dog.*

Zara: *Yeah, one that just turned out the light. I think he's trying to send a message. See you tomorrow.*

Caleb: *Night.*

After making sure she'd set her alarm, she plugged in her phone and put it down on the nightstand. Then she closed her eyes. And opened them. And closed them. And tossed. And turned. And opened her eyes. And yeah, it was gonna be a long-ass night, because she knew that tonight was going to be just like last night. Her subconscious was going to play a game called Let's Have Sexy Times With Caleb, and in her dreams she'd have the best toe-curling orgasm ever—because that's the only place where all her orgasms with other people happened.

She never should have made that bet with Gemma. All it had done was rouse the oh-yeah-that's-what-you-think part of her brain, and it had doubled down on images of shirtless Caleb that she may or may not have found while doing Google searches for purely scientific reasons.

Sticking her foot out from underneath the covers, she inhaled a deep breath and gave in to the mental image of Caleb's bare chest with its dusting of dark hair across his hard pecs, his chiseled abs, and those V lines that drew a person's gaze to the bottom edge of the picture. That was okay. She had all night to imagine everything below where the photo had been cropped.

And hope like hell her dreams didn't make her turn fifty shades of red for the cameras when she saw him tomorrow.

Chapter Seven

"Why are we here so early?" Britany asked as soon as they stepped off the elevator.

Caleb looked around the *Harbor City Wake Up* studio where they were set to pre-tape their interview, scanning for a flash of distinctive red hair. "No reason."

There were fewer people now than during the live show last time, and it should have been easy to spot Zara even if she was so much shorter than probably everyone here. It didn't take long, though, to confirm his first impression that she wasn't here.

"So," his mom said, giving him a pointed look. "It has nothing to do with the fact that Zara is going to be here?"

Okay, this was definitely not a conversation he wanted to have with his mom ever—let alone in public and especially not when he'd woken up an hour early and the only thought in his head was that he was going to get to see Zara. Yeah, he'd rather get cross-checked by an elephant than tell his mom that. Having her in control of his dating life was bad enough without adding in that she'd made a decent choice.

"Weren't you the one who taught me that being on time was being late?" he asked in a verbal deke.

She lifted an eyebrow. "You can blame eight years in the military for that one, and I'm not buying it."

Well, it had been worth a try. That's when he spotted Asha striding across the set with her producer. He braced for a laser beam look of hate that would sizzle him until he resembled a burned fry, but she ignored him.

"Well, I also have some business to take care of before our interview." Then he made a fast break away from his mom and hustled over to Asha by the fake living room set.

The producer stopped mid-word, but Asha refused to look over at Caleb. The urge to take the hint and get the fuck out of there was making his toes itch, but he hadn't been the kind of guy who ran when things got hard before, so he wasn't about to start now.

"Asha, I was an asshole."

"No shit." Asha crossed her arms and lowered her voice. "You know, my sister wasn't expecting a proposal. She went in knowing it was a one-night stand and was totally cool with that, but for him to act like he couldn't remember her name? That's just a real dick move. How many women out there spent days after that video came out feeling like they hadn't had some mutual fun but instead had just been a nameless, replaceable woman? This isn't about relationships or old-timey bullshit family values or anything like that—it's about respect."

It was like his ultimate dumb-ass jerk move he'd pulled was an onion—every time he peeled back a layer of obnoxiousness, he revealed a fresh, biting layer of how he'd inadvertently hurt someone and shown shit-ass leadership skills. He should have been better than that, and he hadn't been.

He nodded. "You're right."

Asha's rigid posture relaxed, but her glare remained in place. "I still don't like you."

"That's fair." Really, it was probably more than he could have hoped for.

The left side of her mouth twitched upward but never made it all the way. "Fine." She started walking toward the set. "Let's go get this farce of an interview started."

Caleb let out the breath he'd been holding in preparation for getting his ass chewed on TV again and looked over at his mom as he followed Asha. Britany was already on one love seat sitting next to Zara's dad, and they were talking animatedly about God knew what, but at least they weren't ready to throw down like last time.

Zara was alone on the other love seat. When she looked up and spotted him as he was stepping onto the set, he tripped over his own feet and went flying forward. He flung his arms out to catch himself and landed, splayed out like he was about to get a spanking, on Zara's lap.

• • •

It was chaos around them as people gasped and gave warning shouts as time seemed to stand still while Caleb sailed through the air right at her. His mom and her dad leaped up from their love seat. The producer hurried forward, arms outstretched. The makeup artist, who'd just finished with a light dusting on her dad's cheeks, ducked to get out of the way.

Her instincts? Well, they pretty much all got distracted by a flying Caleb, and he landed on her lap with a thump that knocked time back into motion but didn't hurt because the love seat cushions eased the blow. And then she couldn't look away from Caleb's ass as he lay across her lap. His butt was round and firm and still covered in denim, but she could just imagine—okay, she had imagined all night long—what it looked like without the jeans. A heated flush swept up her body, which was weird because she was frozen to the spot, squashed between Caleb on her lap and the couch.

"Shit." Caleb scrambled off her lap and sat down next to her, his forehead crinkled with concern. "I'm so sorry. Are you okay?"

"I'm fine." Just a little tingly all over in ways that she should very much not be. "Are you hurt?"

He gave her a sheepish smile. "Only my ego."

"Lucky break," Caleb's mom said as she let out a relieved sigh and sat back down. "Could you imagine if you'd broken something? The season is about to start."

"And my daughter could have been crushed. She's half his size!" her dad exclaimed, his words coming out almost in tandem with Britany's. "You okay, Button?"

"I'm fine," she and Caleb said at the same time.

Embarrassment had her slumping back in her seat. Button? That hated nickname was not one she wanted to be said in public pretty much ever.

Both parents looked like they were about to continue when the show's producer sidled up to the love seat with a clipboard and a pen. "I'm gonna need you to sign this release saying so. Just a formality, you understand, but our lawyers insist anytime something goes awry on set."

She took the clipboard, gave the incident report a quick read, and signed her name on the line before handing it off to Caleb. He mouthed *sorry* as he took it from her, squinted down at the words on the paper—his jaw tightening.

"Did you want me to take a look?" his mom asked, half rising from her love seat.

"No," he said, the words coming out between gritted teeth. "It looks fine."

"It just says he tripped and landed on me but that we're both unhurt," Zara said, looking between the two of them and not quite understanding where all the gritted-teeth frustration was coming from.

Maybe it was just because he was used to having lots of people look at legal stuff before he had to sign? It made sense but still felt off, especially when Britany muttered something under her breath that sounded a lot like "stubborn boy" as she sat back down. Caleb glanced down at the form and then scrawled his signature under hers.

After they handed the clipboard back to the producers, Asha sat down in the chair opposite the love seats, a short stack of index cards in her hand; the cameraman counted down from five; and the interview began.

"We're back with Ice Knights defenseman Caleb Stuckey and miniatures artist Zara Ambrose along with Caleb's mom, Britany, and Zara's dad, Jasper, who are going to offer some dating parental guidance. So, Britany, tell us a little bit about what it was about Zara's profile that jumped out at you?"

Zara blindly reached for Caleb's hand between them and squeezed as panic zoomed through her. The last thing she needed was for her dad and the whole of Harbor City to hear about her vagina cobwebs.

Kill. Me. Now.

"I admired how forthright she was," Britany said. "She didn't seem like someone who'd be thrown by unexpected events."

"Not my Zara," her dad answered. "She's always been a rock, which she proved at Little Bloomers Preschool on Forty-Eighth Street. As a single parent, it was such a relief for me to know Ms. McGee and her staff were looking out for my little Button, and I highly recommend them."

Caleb squeezed her hand back and managed to morph his chuckle into an extended clearing of his throat. Really, they should have set up some sort of drinking game. One shot for every business her dad plugged on the air. Two shots if Asha finally lost her cool and smacked Jasper with her notecards.

Of course, he was probably utterly sincere in his praise. That was what kept her from losing patience with his ridiculous get-rich schemes or the instances where he'd give away more than they could afford—like the time he'd come home from a night out with his friends and confided in her that their rent money was going to be a little short because Jessie the bartender was about to have her baby and all the fellas took up a collection to leave her a big tip to help carry her through. Even when he was being ridiculous, he meant it with all his heart, and she, like just about everyone in the neighborhood, couldn't help but love him.

"Jasper, what kind of dating advice did you offer to Zara before date one?" Asha asked, bringing the interview back to the task at hand.

Her dad dragged his fingers through his hair, which was only a few shades less orange than her own, and for half a second, something that looked a lot like regret crossed his face before it was replaced with his usual charming mask. "I wasn't involved in that one—we didn't talk about all of this until after they'd had their first dinner."

Asha cocked her head to one side, definitely not buying his act. "But you've given her other dating advice?"

Jasper pivoted in his seat so he faced Zara, and he gave her that warm look of love that had given her faith as a child that everything would work out, in the end, no matter what crazy get-rich scheme her dad had embarked on or his ever-changing stories about why her mom had left. It sucked all the air out of her lungs, and in an instant, she was back to being that girl who believed again. She must have made a noise or flinched or something because Caleb ran his thumb over the top of her hand in a slow, calming line.

"Advice?" Her dad chuckled. "Just to believe what her heart is telling her but not to leave out her brain entirely."

"Excellent advice for all of us singles," Asha said in that breezy, we're-all-the-best-of-friends voice morning TV hosts all seemed to have. "And, Britany, what have you told Caleb?"

Britany didn't hesitate. "To be smart about things and to always wrap it up."

Next to her, Caleb groaned and his thumb stopped moving. In the shocked silence that fell after that ode to safe sex, the sound of the producer dropping her clipboard boomed through the studio.

As for Zara, she just wanted to sink into a hole. So much for parental guidance. Her dad was using the opportunity to audition, and his mom was making sure to let the world know her precious son shouldn't knock up his date. Oh God. Did it get worse? She shouldn't even wonder, because that was just tempting fate, and there had been enough proof already that fate was up to the challenge.

No doubt wondering why in the hell she'd agreed to do these interviews, Asha, her eyes wide, turned to Caleb and asked in a shakier tone, "How have the dates been going? Did your mom pick well?"

"She most definitely did." He nodded and squeezed Zara's hand. "I really wasn't excited for her to take over my profile, because who in their right mind would want their mom picking out their dates? But Zara is pretty amazing."

Okay, this was awkward—nothing like having people talk about her when she was sitting right there.

Asha, back on her game, leaned forward, as if the conversation was taking place over drinks at a pub and not in front of cameras. "Tell us more about that."

"She's smart, funny, and she isn't scared to try anything. She's got this weird shoe-addiction thing. And according to the photos of her work that I've seen online, she's really talented." He lifted their joined hands and winked at her before brushing his lips across the back of her hand. "My mom picked a really amazing woman, and I'm damn lucky."

"Wow. That's not a bad impression for two dates." Asha glanced down at Zara's fingers interlaced with Caleb's. "Are you equally smitten?"

Put on the spot by both of them and not liking it even one little bit, Zara could feel her pulse beating in her earlobes as she slid her hand free. "He seems nice."

"Ouch there, Caleb." Asha laughed. "That's not quite a ringing endorsement."

He didn't seem fazed, just relaxed against the love seat and draped his arm across the back of it, not touching Zara but coming close enough that she could feel his presence.

"I've got three more dates to convince her," he said. "Hopefully I'll be able to before the final buzzer goes off."

It was annoying and sexy and weird and a total turn-on for reasons that made no sense. She really needed to go home, have an orgasm, and get her brain straight. Also, she really needed to not say any of that out loud, which was why when Asha made eye contact, Zara gave a subtle shake of her head.

Smooth and cool again, Asha turned to the occupants of the other love seat. "Jasper and Britany, any last words of advice?"

"Give him a chance," her dad said, the soft look in his eyes showing just how much of a romantic dreamer he was even after all these years. "You never know what you'll discover about people when you do."

"That's excellent advice for all of us," Asha said as she turned to face the camera. "Now, as all of Harbor City's Ice Knights fans know, non-rookie training camp starts tomorrow, and then it's straight into the first preseason game, so we'll all be on the edge of our seats waiting for at least a week until these two can meet up again for date three and we can find out if there really is something to Bramble's parent-involved dating algorithms."

A week?

Zara's stomach clenched—obviously because she wanted to get these dates knocked out as quickly as possible and *not* because she had already kinda gotten used to seeing him on a regular basis and now she wouldn't.

"From all of us at *Harbor City Wake Up*, this is Asha Kapoor wishing you a great rest of your day. We'll see you back here tomorrow!"

Asha held her friendly smile for a count of three, and then the camera light blinked off while Zara was still trying to figure out why in the hell she was so annoyed.

• • •

Caleb had spent his formative years around women. He'd learned early on to recognize the it's-fine expression on Zara's face and know that it meant his ass was about to be mowed down. He had to fix whatever he'd done to fuck this up and fast. He hustled after her to the elevator, where she was already pressing the down button repeatedly while looking straight ahead.

"Hey," he said, coming to a stop next to her. "Can we grab some coffee real quick?"

"Why?" She took out her phone and started scrolling through email. "It can't be an official Bramble date unless we schedule it through the app."

Oh yeah, she was pissed, and he had no clue why. Everything had seemed fine when they'd gotten there. The interview had been awkward as hell, but he'd been figuring on that. The only thing unexpected had been when Asha had brought up training camp and— He nearly smacked himself on the forehead. Zara didn't follow hockey. She had no idea about the schedule, that even preseason was crazy busy. Once again, he was an asshole.

The elevator doors opened right as his mom and Jasper joined them. He let everyone get on the elevator before him and then made sure to get a spot next to Zara. She hit the lobby button and kept her attention focused on the little TV screen above the buttons.

"I'm sorry I didn't explain about training camp and the preseason games," he said, keeping his voice quiet. "I know that slows us down for knocking out the five dates. Let me make it up to you with coffee, and we'll figure out how we can still get through the dates as fast as possible."

"It's fine, really, just a surprise. But I'm not ever gonna turn down coffee." Zara turned to look at their parents, who were standing really close together for an elevator that had plenty of room in it. "Dad, do you have time for coffee before I take you home?"

"Actually," Jasper said as the elevator slowed and announced they were at the lobby level. "I was going to go have lunch with Britany."

"We want to talk about you two when there aren't cameras around," his mom said.

He automatically held his hand in front of the elevator's open doors so everyone could get out. "What's there to talk about?"

"Caleb Cutie, there is so much to discuss." She kissed him on the cheek, gave Zara a wave goodbye, and walked out of the elevator with Jasper, the two of them disappearing into the crowded lobby.

Shaking her head, Zara let out a deep sigh. "Nothing good will come from that."

She wasn't wrong. His mom was trouble when she was on her own. He couldn't imagine how bad her interfering disguised as coaching would be if she had a sidekick. "Does your dad think this whole parent-guided dating thing is nuts?"

She rolled her eyes. "He and my friend Gemma, who was

the one who got me to sign up for Bramble, think it's hilarious and exactly what I need to get out of my work-only rut."

All the possible shit outcomes from their parents ganging up to take this from a dating agreement to really dating—because that's exactly what his mom would do—ran through his head as he held the door for Zara. "We are in so much shit."

She nodded as they walked outside into the bright sunshine. She looked like she was about to say something else when her phone started beeping. Shooting him an apologetic look, she took it out of her purse.

"Oh shit." Zara's head fell back and let out a groan. "I'm sorry, but I gotta ago. Anchovy just set off my apartment's security alarm."

"You sure it wasn't someone breaking in?" His own phone was out of his pocket, and he was ready to call 911 before the words were even out of his mouth.

She turned her phone around. Her screen had a huge diagonal crack, but he could still see the live-streaming feed of a mountain of a dog doing high-speed laps around the studio apartment, stopping at the alarm pad to lick the camera and then taking off again while howling along to the siren.

"He has separation anxiety, and this is his latest trick to get me back home."

Caleb laughed; he couldn't help it. The dog was an evil genius. "That's pretty smart."

"And expensive." Zara clicked out of the livestream and started to scroll through her contacts list. "If I don't call off the security company, they'll charge me a fine that I cannot afford. Sorry to skip out on coffee, but I gotta take care of this." She made it a few steps before turning around, her headphones in her hand. "And I'm sorry for how I acted before. I'm not mad about the preseason stuff. I was just caught unaware of things, which is pretty much my most hated thing ever."

"So, no surprise parties?" Not that they would know each other long enough for either of them to throw a party for the other.

Zara scoffed and put in one earbud. "Only under penalty of death."

"Duly noted."

"Okay, I gotta go." She popped in the other earbud and hit the call button on her phone. "Good luck with whatever it is that happens at training camp."

Then she was gone, talking to her security company as she weaved through the crowded Harbor City sidewalk like a pint-size forward zipping around defensemen on her way to the goal, leaving him alone and wondering why he was so disappointed.

And when he'd get to see her again.

Chapter Eight

Zara's latest favorite song filled her apartment, Anchovy slept under her workbench, and she had the cover of a one-twelfth-size copy of *Murder on the Orient Express* clenched between the tongs of her best work tweezers. This was the moment of truth, and it got her nervous every time.

She'd already created the inside of the book by cutting paper into tiny little pages, adding in small text across the center spread and the other visible pages. Then, she'd arranged the pages so they aligned and painted the edges so it looked as if they had gold edging. After that, she'd used a paper clamp and a layer of glue to form the spine before applying more glue to the outside pages. Now, holding her breath, she lowered the hand-painted cover, making sure corners lined up and the spine was straight. Her heart was going a bazillion miles a minute, but her hands were steady. Still, it wasn't until she'd smoothed the brilliant blue cover and set the book down to dry that she let out a relieved breath.

One book down, only thirty or so more to go. Her shoulders slumped, and she let out a puff of air that sent the hair around her face flying. And to think, she could have gone into something less stressful, like air traffic control.

All the nerve-racking work would be worth it, though, when she finished and there was a one-twelfth-size Ursula K. Le Guin curled up on an overstuffed chair by the fire with the Christie mystery in one hand and a cup of tea in the other. Plus, the other great authors reading one another's books throughout the house. Her favorite would probably be Georgette Heyer and Barbara Cartland sharing a bottle of champagne as they read *Emma* and *Jane Eyre*.

Zara was just starting to eyeball the *I Know Why The Caged Bird Sings* cover when the intercom sounded three quick buzzes. There was only one person in her life who did that—the man who believed in the power of threes, that his ship would always come in, and that dreams were the stuff that got a person through the hard times. What her dad had never realized was that sometimes those dreams were the cause of those hard times.

Anchovy jiggled her workbench a bit when he got up, but he was already across the room, big paws on either side of the intercom before she could tell him to be careful.

"Yes, I know." She walked over to the intercom and hit the button to unlock the building's front door. "Your Prince Charming has arrived bearing doggie treats and probably a new tennis ball."

Since she was on the third floor and her dad was the kind of person who always took the stairs two at a time, it only took him a couple of minutes to get to her door.

"Hey, Button." He gave her the devil-may-care grin and wink of his that made everyone in every room ever want to be his friend. "You're looking adorable."

"Thanks, Dad. You look pretty nice yourself." In fact, if she didn't know any better, she'd say he looked almost too nice. The man who loved nothing more than a comfy pair of worn jeans and a T-shirt was in new jeans and a button-up. "What are you all dressed up for?"

His gaze flicked down for a second before he gave her a quick kiss on the forehead and then walked inside her apartment. "Because the sun is out, I'm with my favorite daughter, and I have something spectacular for the world's best pooch."

"I'm your only daughter." She gave him a closer look. Besides the upgrade in clothes, he looked pretty much the same from his hair to the scuffed-toe work boots. Still… "What are you up to?"

"What do I always tell you, Button? Life is a banquet…"

"And most poor suckers are starving to death." She finished the line from *Auntie Mame* for him.

Zara sighed. This was their game. He was the Auntie Mame in their relationship, and she was forever the flustered, timid Agnes Gooch.

"Exactly." He pulled a neon-green ball made out of the hard rubber that the manufacturers claimed was indestructible, which Anchovy just took as a challenge. "So I came to rescue you from your tower to take you to lunch at our favorite hot-dog stand."

He flipped the ball up in the air, and the dog caught it and ran off to his favorite chew spot under her worktable.

Of course, watching his progress just reminded her of where she should be right now, and it wasn't chitchatting with her dad. "I'm working."

"When did you start?" he asked, concern darkening his eyes.

"It wasn't that early." She folded under his disbelieving look. "Okay, I've been at it since five."

"It's three in the afternoon." He looped his arm through hers and pivoted them both so they were facing the open door. "Hot dogs and snow cones and sunshine are required."

She looked over her shoulder. "But Anchovy—"

"Has a new toy and is fine to be on his own for an hour. Come on, let your old man show you some fun."

Taking a deep breath, she went through the never-ending to-do list that lived in her brain. Unlike her dad, she'd never been able to block out the nuts-and-bolts part of everyday living. He always managed to get by on charm and a dream, because she'd been there after her mom left to make sure the bills got paid on time and her school field trip permission slips were signed. After doing that for most of her life, it was hard to turn that part of herself off.

"The library fund-raiser is only a month away, though, and I have to finish this piece between the orders for my Etsy store."

Her dad cupped her chin and turned her so she faced him. There was no missing the bittersweet tinged with guilt in his eyes. "It'll be there in an hour, and you can get back to your workaholic ways. Life is a banquet. Don't starve."

Of course, her stomach picked that moment to growl because, per usual, she'd worked through lunch. As if that sound was the victory bell, her dad relaxed back into the incorrigible charmer everyone down at the bar or the track or the job site knew him to be.

"You're not giving me an Agnes Gooch makeover," she said, grabbing her keys from the hook by the door and telling Anchovy to be a good boy (good luck).

He lifted his arms in triumph. "But she lived!"

Laughing, she closed the door behind them and double-checked the locks. She really should still be at her workbench, even if she'd been there for almost ten hours that day, and then followed her dad down the stairs. And maybe, while her dad stood in line at the hot-dog stand, she checked her Bramble app for the twelfth time that day to see if there were any messages from Caleb, but that didn't mean anything.

Nothing at all.

• • •

Caleb submerged himself up to his chest in the cold-water bath at the Ice Knights facility. Even with all the off-season workouts, he needed it after that grueling three-hour, on-ice training camp session. Coach Peppers had them doing goal line to the far blue line sprints, more sprints from center ice to the net and back, enough laps around the ice that his guts tried to climb out of his body, and more. His eyes closed and, the back of his head resting against the tub's edge, he let the frigid water do its work so he wouldn't be walking like an eighty-year-old man tonight.

"Oh my God." The unmistakable voice of star forward, total shit disturber, and one of his best friends, Cole Phillips, blasted through the room. "Are you the guy from *Harbor City Wake Up*? The one whose mommy has to pick out his dates?"

Caleb, not bothering to open his eyes, flipped off Cole.

"Dude, my mom is glued to that shit." Phillips eased into the ice bath next to Caleb's, judging by the sound of the sloshing water and the other man's quick intake of breath. "You do not know how many calls from her I've had to avoid so she won't start in on what a great idea it is again. You have screwed over your gender, man."

Yes, that was exactly what he had been worried about when the choice had been put before him to either do this and take some of the heated attention off Petrov so he wouldn't get traded or make all the men on the globe get uncomfortable with the idea of giving up a little control.

"It wasn't by choice," he grumbled, keeping his eyes closed.

"Yeah, my mom doesn't care. She just wants to find me a

nice girl who isn't so dramatic."

That made Caleb open his eyes and turn to look at Phillips. "You mom isn't Team Marti, huh?"

Marti was Coach Peppers's daughter, all-around amazing woman, and the other half of Phillips's twisted love life.

"She got off that train about six breakups ago." Phillips's jaw tightened, and sure, it could have been because of the fifty-degree water, which didn't sound that frigid until you were easing into it despite the protests of your cold-shrinking junk. "Anyway, we're here talking about your dating life, not mine."

This guy was giving him conversational whiplash. "You're the one who brought up your mom and Marti."

Cole pulled a face and didn't respond to Caleb's valid point—shocker. He shut his eyes again, and they settled into a comfortable silence as other teammates walked through on their way to a post-camp massage or other recovery option.

"You coming to Blackburn's for Xbox and pre–road trip eats tonight?" Phillips asked after about five minutes of silence, which might be a world record for him.

Zach Blackburn was the team captain and complete asshole who'd downgraded to occasional asshole after falling for Fallon Hartigan. Watching that happen in real time had been hilarious because there was none more ill-equipped for that to happen than Blackburn.

"Where else would I be?" Caleb asked as he got out of the tub.

"Getting it on with your teeny tiny redhead."

The middle finger salute he gave the forward went unnoticed because Phillips had his eyes closed. Caleb had enough shit on his plate without that. Watching his parents' marriage fall apart had shown him how much work staying together was, and he had to invest all his energy into hockey. Half-assing it was not how he did things. There'd be time for relationships after he unlaced his skates for the last time. Anyway, he and Zara had agreed to the rules—the number one being no relationship. He might play by instinct on the ice, but off it, he followed the rules, whether it was a diet plan the team nutritionist put together or using his turn signal every time he switched lanes.

"It's not like that," he said. "Neither of us wants to be dating."

Phillips smirked. "And yet you are."

"Only a few more times."

Three dates to be exact, and then he was done and his life could get back to normal, knowing that he'd fixed the fuckup of his viral video, helped keep Petrov on the team, and maybe earned back a chance at being assistant captain. It was all he wanted, but for some reason—maybe the come down after a hard practice? Yeah, that had to be the reason—it didn't feel like enough.

• • •

Just another exciting Friday night at home with her dog, watching TV in her softest pj's and trying to ignore the fact that work was only a few steps away and she could totally finish up painting Agatha Christie's face before she crashed out for the night. If only she hadn't promised Gemma and her dad that she would take the night off. To no one's surprise, Anchovy was loving it. He was curled up on the couch with her while the TV showed two detectives trying to track down who murdered a super-rich couple while searching for the dead couple's daughter's stalker.

She was scrolling through Insta when she got a text message alert that made her drop her phone as soon as she read the name Caleb Stuckey. Damn it. Her screen was already cracked—she couldn't afford to have it go completely just because her means-nothing Bramble partner made her all nervous and champagne fizzy all of a sudden.

Caleb: *What are you doing?*

She shoved the box of Chicken In A Biskit crackers off to the other side of the couch.

Zara: *Watching Law and Order.*

CALEB: Ugh. That show is always the same.

Which was its total brilliance. *Law & Order* didn't come home and tell you it had to figure out how to cover the utility bill because the ponies didn't cross the finish line in the order expected. *Law & Order* did what it said it would do. It investigated the crimes and prosecuted the criminals. Every. Time.

Zara: *I hate surprises, remember?*

Caleb: *You need to allow a little unusual into your life.*

Zara: *I guess that's why I temporarily have you. ;)*

Oh God. Why had she used the winky face? What was wrong with her?

Caleb: *Cable or streaming?*

Zara: *Who has cable?*

Well, probably him, since he made professional athlete bank and lived a lifestyle totally opposite of hers where he didn't worry about things like cable versus streaming.

Caleb: *Okay, episode number.*

Zara: *Episode 12. Season 11. I just started. Why?*

Her phone started buzzing with a notification that Caleb Stuckey wanted to FaceTime. This was so very not part of their agreement. She lingered over the decline button for a second, but Anchovy bumped her elbow and she ended up tapping accept. Really, that was what happened and she'd testify to it in court.

His face took up the whole screen, giving her an up-close-and-personal view she didn't normally get because of the more than a foot height difference between them. Seeing him shouldn't make her straighten up from being slouched against the couch pillows and smooth back the hair that had fallen out of her just-lounging-around-the-apartment topknot.

He rubbed his stubble-covered jaw and grinned at her. "Hey there."

"This isn't part of our agreement." And she was grumpy about it because she believed in following the rules, not because she was happily flustered at seeing him.

"True," he said, nodding. "But it's not against the rules, either. We never said no contact outside of the official dates. You left a loophole."

Okay, he had her there. Really she should have thought of that, but there was no going back to fix it.

What did she do with her phone? Holding it up close to her face was... OMG, she couldn't stop staring at herself in the little box because there just might be—okay there was—Chicken In A Biskit cracker crumbs on her lips. A good dog would have told her. Anchovy had things to answer for, never mind that he couldn't speak.

Determined not to let her awkward show—at least not in zoom—she leaned her phone against the art books on her coffee table and tried to slyly wipe her mouth.

"So, what was with playing up your fake admiration during the interview?" she asked as the detectives on the screen started to question a stalker who turned out to be another cop on a case where all the fraud clues pointed to the not-so-grieving daughter.

"Fake?" He scoffed, the sound drawing Anchovy's attention. "I didn't say anything that wasn't true."

Uh-huh. Yeah. "You were laying it on pretty thick. I know you're the one who needs to fix your shit reputation and all, so you have to play the guy who's open to finding love, but maybe don't layer it on so heavy next time." No one was going to buy it if he kept saying things like he was lucky and she was amazing. Not to mention it made the what-if part of her brain wake up, and she learned a long time ago that dreams weren't worth the mental bandwidth. "So, how was training camp?"

"Good," he said, setting his phone down on something and walking away, giving her a view of his bedroom with not a single dirty sock or crumpled T-shirt in sight. The sound of *Law & Order* was low in the background. "We've got two preseason road games and then one at home this week."

Zara was about to tell him that seemed like a lot when he whipped off his shirt and her brain hiccupped. Caleb's attention was focused on the TV hanging from the wall across from his absolutely humongous bed. Her attention? It was on the muscled expanse of his chest. It was even better than the photo—or twelve—that she'd seen online. And by *seen*, she meant stared at for an embarrassingly long time wondering what it would be like to run her fingertips over the hard ridges and valleys of his six-pack.

"I knew it!" Caleb raised his right arm and did a fist pump. "That woman has murderer written all over her."

Murderer?

Woman?

What?

Holy shit, Zara. Stop eye fucking the off-limits man and try to remember what in the hell this episode had been about so he doesn't know you're definitely going to be breaking out your favorite vibrator tonight because you've obviously lost your damn mind from a lack of regular orgasms.

Desperate to recover, she pulled out a safe observation that any *Law & Order* viewer knew was true. "Well yeah, any time an actor who everyone knows is on the show, they are the murderer."

"Not every time," he said, tossing his shirt into a laundry basket next to the closet and then walking back toward the phone.

"Nine and a half out of ten." The words came out more like a croak. She needed to end this call before she asked him to do push-ups or something.

"Okay, you got me," he said, seemingly oblivious to her discomfort.

That was a blessing, because as he made his way across his bedroom, back to where he'd left his phone, the little barriers she'd erected to block out his hotness started to fall. Okay, they'd already been crumbling like an ice wall under the melting fire of a White Walker's dragon. The miles of muscles, the clueless-about-what-he-was-doing-to-her attitude, the way his been-broken-more-than-once nose shouldn't work to make him look even hotter but somehow did? All of it combined to remind her exactly how long it had been since she'd gotten herself off.

Caleb picked up the phone just as she let out a panic yawn because her body had to let the energy out somehow and why not with an embarrassingly gigantic yawn that probably gave him a good look at her tonsils?

"Am I boring you?" he asked with a chuckle.

"Some of us have been up since five working on an art piece." Okay, that came out super prickly, but her panties were damp, her nipples were hard, and there was nothing she could do about it until she got off this damn call.

He picked up his phone, once again giving her a close-up of his hotness. "I wanna see what you've got."

Welcome to the club, buddy.

Way too grateful that she hadn't actually said that out loud, she floundered for something to say. "You're not really interested."

"Wrong. I checked you out online. Your Etsy shop is the stuff of my sister's dreams, and your art pieces are amazing. I really liked the sky pirates one."

She sat up straight and grabbed her phone from the coffee table. "You really looked me up? That wasn't BS before?"

"You saying you didn't Google me?" He paused, extended his arm so the phone was far away from his face, and then brought it back in fast, as if he were zooming in on the knowing look on his face. "Are you blushing, Zara? You must be, because otherwise all those freckles on your face just turned pink for no reason. You did look me up. What did you find?"

Stupid, stupid, stupid blushing. She got up, hoping walking around her studio apartment would cool her off. "There are some message boards." She gulped, remembering some of the posts about his ass. "And some news reports." Truth? It had been more like watching gifs of snippets of locker room interviews where his shirt was off and he ran his fingers through his wet hair, which really showed off his biceps. "And a few Tumblr fan pages." Those? Oh God, those she couldn't even think about right now.

He raised an eyebrow, no doubt giving her his best The Rock impression. "Is it wrong of me to ask if you liked what you saw?"

"More like it's irrelevant," she said, looking around and realizing she had walked past the bookcase dividers that blocked off her bedroom from the rest of the apartment.

Paging Dr. Freud.

She would have turned right around but Anchovy, who'd been trailing behind her the whole time, did his favorite trick and turned out the lights.

"Is Anchovy telling you to go to bed again?" Caleb asked.

The involuntary thrill of hearing him say the word "bed" should have been negated by the fact that he was talking about her dog. It wasn't. Damn. She seriously needed to get off this call.

"Yeah, he's a pain that way," she said as she scratched Anchovy behind the ears to say thank you.

Caleb, still perfectly lit in his bedroom, sat down on his bed that she could lay down on spread-eagle and not touch the edges. Not that she was thinking about doing that. Not. At. All.

"It'll be crazy over the next few days. We have our first road trip," he said. "But I'll see you for date number three when I get back into town next week. Have a good night's sleep, Zara."

"Night, Caleb."

She ended the call, let her head fall back, and released a half moan/half groan of OMG-what-the-fuck-is-wrong-with-me. A good night's sleep? Yeah, she'd be lucky to get *any* shut-eye tonight.

And the third date? Oh God, she definitely wouldn't be sleeping if she tried to imagine what it would be.

Chapter Nine

Six days and three games later, Caleb finished the short walk from the subway station and looked down at the Bramble app on his phone to confirm he was at the right location. Yep. Fifty-eight Forty-two Rockaway Avenue. This was it. He glanced up at the sign hanging above the opaque glass doors that read HOT THANG REVIEW with a kitty cat strutting above the word "thang." Everything about the place, from the neon sign to the no-neck guy standing with his arms crossed over his massive chest outside the doors, screamed strip club.

What in the hell had Zara been thinking? Her official third date message had come through while he'd been at the morning skate. Just the address, the time, and the note that their parents had sweet-talked the Bramble folks into letting them pick out where date three would take place. That was, without a doubt, the scariest bit of news he'd had since he'd sat down for his ass-chewing in Lucy's office.

He hadn't done any Google searches, just showered, got on the subway, and traveled across Harbor City to make it on time. Now he didn't know what to do. His position with the team was better than before the Bramble stuff started, but getting photographed coming out of a strip club covered in glitter was not going to keep him in Coach Peppers's good graces.

Just when he was about to text Zara, the front door opened and she strolled out. She was in a pair of heels that added at least four inches to her height, a pair of tight jeans, and a low-cut blue T-shirt tied just under her tits. Her skin glowed with a heated flush, as if she'd been running sprints, but there wasn't a sparkle of glitter on her.

This isn't a real date, numbnuts.

Well, it was but it wasn't and it couldn't, so whatever dirty thoughts were screaming through his brain and bad ideas had his cock thickening against his thigh didn't mean anything.

There were rules.

It took a second for the sudden rush of blood from his brain to his dick to even out before he understood. Realization crackled like thunder, loud and ominous. This was not good. Not at all. He'd heard about this from one of the guys on the team who'd gone with his girlfriend.

His mom and her dad had set them up on a learn-to-pole-dance date. Britany, no doubt, was somewhere laughing her ass off.

"Are you going to stand outside all day or come in for your lesson?" Zara asked, opening the door farther.

The guy next to the doorway shot a dirty look her way and then ambled off down the block.

Caleb hustled over to the door, holding it for her but not going inside. "I'm not stripping."

She crossed her arms and exhaled a sigh that perfectly telegraphed how disappointed she was in him. "Well, you know how to suck all the fun out of things."

Shaking her head, she looked away and down. It started small—just an up-down bobbing of her shoulders—before the first giggles broke free and she looked back up at him, a huge smile on her face.

"Oh my God, you are too easy, Caleb. This isn't a strip club. It's a restaurant, and the chef, John Thang, is giving us cooking lessons. Do I look like I'm about to go strip?"

No matter how hot she looked right now, he knew better than to answer that question. Instead, he followed her inside the Hot Thang Review, which turned out to be a pop-up restaurant/cooking school. There were about fifteen people in the dining room, which was decorated with small shadow boxes showing the same family in different domestic scenes. Walking along the back wall, he could follow the progression from scene to scene as the baby in the first one grew up until, in the final shadow box, he wore a chef's toque as his parents and grandparents looked on with proud smiles.

The man standing closest to the kitchen wasn't in a toque, though—he was wearing a chef's jacket and he held out his hand. "You must be Zara's friend Caleb. I'm John. Welcome to class. I hope you two have as much fun as your parents hoped you would when Jasper called to see if I had room for two more today."

Caleb shook the other man's hand. "I have to warn you, my best kitchen skill is making a mean boxed mashed potatoes."

"Well, you're going to walk out of here today knowing a little bit more than that."

The chef gave Zara a hug, and the two chatted like old friends for a few minutes before he moved on to greet the other couples.

Zara leaned in close. "Not quite the den of inequity you were expecting."

"I'm never going to live that down, am I?" What could he say? His brain went a totally different direction than it should when he was around her.

One red eyebrow went up. "Highly doubtful."

Pointing out the scenes with the miniatures, he asked, "So the art is yours, isn't it?"

"Yeah, they're mine." Her cheeks turned a darker shade of pink. "John's grandmother was one of my first customers at my Etsy store. When John made the list of the hottest chefs in Harbor City, she commissioned the dioramas showing his journey."

"It's pretty amazing." The detailing in each scene blew him away, right down to the bowls of pho, the shoes by the door, and the love that seemed to permeate all of it.

"It was the first piece I was ever commissioned to do." She pointed to the scene of two parents bringing home a baby wrapped up in the same pink, blue, and white blanket his sisters had come home from the hospital in. "Up until then, everything was accessories and dolls for others' scenes."

"Why not your own?" The woman was talented beyond belief. She really needed to do more of her own art like these.

She shrugged, letting out a weary sigh before giving him a smile that had a brittle edge to it. "That's a long story, and we're here to make bún bò Huê. It's the best noodle soup you'll ever have. It has pork hocks, beef shanks, cubes of congealed pork blood, a deliciously spicy broth, and a sate chili sauce made with annatto seeds. It's so good."

Judging by the look of foodie bliss on her face, he had to believe her. For the next four hours, they moved around the kitchen, working together as he did with his teammates on the ice.

There was an easy flow between them as they sliced, diced, mixed, and boiled the soup. She teased him about stripping while he pounded the lemongrass stalks to release their oil. He told her about Phillips's on-again, off-again dating drama with Marti, asking for a woman's advice to pass along. She'd snorted and told him that dating advice was not her thing—maybe he should ask his mom.

Then they ate their creation in the dining room, and it was heaven. "You were not lying. This is really good."

"Better than boxed mashed potatoes?" Zara asked, pointedly looking at his empty bowl that he'd practically licked clean.

"Without a doubt." He rubbed his very full stomach. "Now all I want to do is sit on the couch and watch *Law and Order* while I pet a super-smart dog's belly."

She rolled her eyes. "That was oddly specific."

"Oh no, you saw through me." He added a melodramatic gasp for good measure. "What do you say? My place is across the harbor in Waterbury. Let me recuperate for a bit at your place?"

For a moment, she just stared at him, no doubt trying to give him her best evil eye. The bún bò Huê had obviously done its magic, though, and put her in the best of moods, because the corners of her mouth curled upward even as she gave him a minimal stink eye.

"Coming over to watch TV is not in the rules," she said.

"It's not against them, either, because it won't be a date. It's just us watching a show minus FaceTime. Exactly what we've already done."

Another minor stare off before she laughed, the sound even better than the buzzer after a goal.

"I really should have been more specific when we made that list," she said with a chuckle before standing up and pointing at the containers of leftover bún bò Huê. "You're carrying that on the train back to my apartment."

This wasn't the best idea he'd ever had. He had to face it: spending time alone with Zara was just asking for trouble. It was hard enough to keep from picturing her naked when they were in a kitchen full of people and boiling broth. Of course, that wasn't about to stop him from going home with Zara, where he would sit on his end of the couch and she would be on the other and that small horse of a dog of hers would be between them, like a furry chaperone.

Everything would be fine.

. . .

The loud snuffling on the other side of her apartment door followed by a muffled woof meant Zara's arrival home wasn't a surprise. It never was. Anchovy always knew when she was here—and when she had company.

"So, a word of warning." She slid her key into the dead bolt. "Anchovy thinks he's a lapdog and that personal boundaries are a myth."

Caleb nodded, seemingly not worried at all, and she opened the door. Anchovy gave her a hearty bark of a greeting that would no doubt get her a nasty gram from Mr. Tottingham next door. Then he started to do the zoomies around the couch and the kitchen island, occasionally stopping to accept a quick behind-the-ear scratch from both of them.

"Have you been gone for a long time?" Caleb asked when Anchovy ducked his big head under her bed and came back with the already mauled neon-green ball her dad had given him yesterday.

"I could go downstairs and get the mail in the lobby, and this would be my greeting when I walked back in." She took the leftovers from him and put them in her fridge. "I'm already signed in to Prime, so why don't you grab the remote and pick out a *Law and Order* episode."

He shoved his fingers through his thick, dark hair. "It's your place—you should pick."

"You go ahead and choose." She glanced over at the Great Dane. "I have to take Anchovy outside before he explodes."

As soon as she said the word "outside," the dog dropped his new favorite toy and rushed over to the basket holding his leash, using his big snout to push all the other things in there to retrieve it. Caleb didn't look convinced, but judging by the urgency with which Anchovy shoved his leash into her hand, she didn't have time to argue.

She snapped on the dog's leash. "I'll be back. Whatever you go with is fine, just wait for me to start."

Then she was out the door for a quick trip to the park across the street so Anchovy could pee on the same fire hydrant he always did and then sniff every bush along the short path until she said the magic word ("treat") and then trot along next to her back inside the building. When she opened her front door, Caleb was standing close to the TV, his lips moving as he slowly and quietly read the episode descriptions out loud.

She froze, not able to shake the feeling that she was intruding on a private moment. Anchovy, though, took full advantage of her loosening her grip on his leash. Probably thrilled to see his new best friend was still there, he bolted inside, snagged his ball from the ground while galloping toward Caleb, who turned to face them just in time for the dog to rear up on his hind legs and put his paws on Caleb's chest.

Not looking freaked out in the least, he just rubbed the dog's sides. "Nice ball."

"Sorry, I failed horribly at teaching him manners," she said, hurrying forward. "Anchovy, get down."

The dog shot her a pained look but got down and went over to the couch, climbing up and curling into a ball on the blanket spread over his end.

"It's no biggie," Caleb said. "I love dogs. Wish I could have one but with my schedule, I'd be worried about even keeping a goldfish alive."

From what she'd read this week, she'd learned that hockey didn't have as many games a week as baseball, but the teams played around three games a week. It was a long-ass season going from preseason in September to possible Stanley Cup finals in late May or early June. It was just another example of why she'd been smart to make "no relationship" rule number one. The last thing she wanted was a repeat of the chaos of how she'd grown up, with her dad never having the same hours—or regular hours—and not being home very often when he was off work. Unreliability and a lack of stability were not in her life plan.

"Yeah, Mr. Friendly here has separation anxiety, so the fact that my office is my home works out really well for us." She sat down on the couch. "Did you pick out an episode?"

He glanced back at the TV, his jaw tightening, then pointed the remote at the screen and clicked play episode. "This one sounded interesting."

"Let's do it," she said, taking off her shoes and putting her feet up on the coffee table, her heels barely reaching.

He sat down beside her, leaving a few inches between them—right up until Anchovy ever so gracefully farted and then stretched out, his oversize paws pushing against Caleb and forcing him to scoot closer to her. His hip touched hers, and he extended his arm along the back of the couch behind her. Zara had never been more aware of her hip or the tops of her shoulders. Her chest tightened. She wouldn't relax back against him. She wouldn't. It wasn't against the rules, but it seemed like a bad idea.

Still, somehow, by the time the action on the screen had moved from the police investigating the crime to the district attorneys who prosecute the offenders, the back of her head was nestled in the hollow of his shoulder. His arm had moved from being across the back of the couch to wrapping around her waist. Neither of them said anything, but there was a tension tightening in her core, a thrill of anticipation brushing against her skin. Her every nerve was focused on him, the tease of his fingertips over her T-shirt; his deep, steady breaths in and out; and—finally—the soft, barely there snore that penetrated the haze of lust making her every thought center on sex.

Gently, she sat forward, pivoting to get a look at him. He was sacked out. Now *that* did wonders for a woman's ego.

Still, she couldn't help but look at him. It wasn't every day a hot guy like Caleb crashed out on her couch. She'd never realized his eyelashes were so long or that he had a faded scar near his left eye or that such a big, hard man could look so soft while he slept. It sucker punched her right in the feels. And while waking him up and sending him on his way home was the right decision, she just couldn't do it. Instead, she turned off the TV, grabbed the non-dog-hair-covered blanket in a basket by the couch, and covered him. The blanket, which spanned from her head to her toes, barely went from shoulders to knees on him.

Then, before she could give in to the urge to kiss him good night that she didn't understand, she got up and tiptoed to her bedroom.

$$\cdots$$

Caleb couldn't say what woke him up at first, just some instinctual knowledge that something wasn't right. His right shoulder was stiff from where he'd been lying on it—unusual, since his bed was worth almost as much as the rest of his bedroom furniture combined, a concession to the fact that a tweaked neck from sleeping weird could be the difference between a good game and a great one. Everything around him was dim, the first soft light of dawn barely coming in through the windows. He lay there listening, trying to climb through the sleepy haze making his brain slow to figure out why things felt off.

Then he heard it. A quiet shuffle. A light clink of glass.

Someone was in his house.

He didn't get any further than that before he jumped up, whacking his shin on something hard that shouldn't be near his bed, and sprinted, his eyes starting to acclimate to the low light, toward the noise. He cleared the space between his bed and the source of the noise like he was racing for the puck, connecting with its source. He wrapped his arms around the intruder and was about to slam them against the wall when a single noise cut through.

"Caleb."

Zara.

Everything in him stilled for a second as reality seeped in and he shook off the last of his sleepy confusion. The memories came as fast as heartbeats. He and Zara had made dinner. They'd come back to her place and watched *Law & Order*. He…must have crashed on her couch like the biggest asshole ever. And now he was holding her, clutched to his chest high enough that her feet were probably dangling in the air.

"Fuck." He sat her down so she was on her counter and took a step back, bringing up his hands palm forward in apology. "I'm so sorry. I didn't realize where I was. I just woke up and heard a noise."

"At least you're a better guard dog than Anchovy," she said, setting down the glass in her hand and shoving her long red hair out of her face. "He's still snoring."

Eyes more accustomed to the dim light of early dawn, he glanced back at her bedroom. Bookcases blocked most of it from being seen, but from this angle, he could see the corner of her bed, sheets rumpled, and a dark, unmoving lump that had to be the dog.

"Yeah, you might want to invest in an alarm system," he said with a laugh as he turned back to her.

As soon as he did, his amusement died away, replaced by a jolt of desire that went straight to his dick.

Like she'd been during their FaceTime conversation the other night, she was wearing a pair of tiny sleep shorts and a thin T-shirt that did nothing to hide the heavy sway of her tits or the way her nipples had formed hard, tempting little peaks. After that call, he'd grabbed his cock and had jerked off to the memory, stroking his dick until he came hard and fast.

Now, here she was, looking at him with desire dark in her eyes, nipples straining against the cotton of her shirt, her legs spread just enough that his could fit in the space between. Lust fired through him, tightening his muscles, hardening his dick, and making every nerve in his body focus only on Zara. All he wanted was to touch her, take her, make her come so hard on him that she wanted to do it again and again.

They shouldn't do this. It may not be against the rules, but that didn't make it a good idea.

Too bad it was getting harder and harder each time he was near Zara to remember.

He moved to take a step back, but she reached out, stopping him.

"Kiss me, Caleb," she said, her voice husky with need.

"What about the rules?" He hated himself for asking, but he was fighting to stick to what she wanted because all he wanted at the moment was her.

"They said no making love. It didn't mention kissing."

Maybe there were other men out there who would have continued to fight the attraction, to stay above it all. Well, they weren't him, because she had found the best loophole in the world.

His mouth was on hers in the next heartbeat and after

that, he was lost to her. It wasn't a nice kiss or a soft kiss; it had to be so much more because it was all they had. Desperate, hungry need ate away at his control as they lost themselves in the exploration of the hard, bruising kiss. Her tongue curling around his, daring him to give her more, demanding it. If it killed him, he was willing to give it all at this moment.

She moaned, her hands clutching his shoulders as she wrapped her legs around his waist. He didn't think, just reacted, stepping back and taking her with him, his hands cupping her ass as he carried her across the apartment and back to the couch, their mouths never leaving each other.

As soon as he sat down with her in his lap, straddling his hips, she rocked against him, seeking the same maddening friction he needed so damn badly. He tightened his grip on her hips, pulling her against him as she undulated, giving them both a taste of what they so desperately needed.

She arched her back, breaking the kiss and letting out a low mewl of pleasure as she moved against him. Even with the layers of clothes between them, he could feel her heat against his dick. Curling forward, she dipped her head down until their foreheads touched.

"We aren't kissing," she said.

He could fix that. Cupping the back of her head, he weaved his fingers through her red hair, pulling her mouth down to his, plundering its dangerous sweetness before trailing his lips down her neck, kissing and nipping his way along the low scooped collar of her T-shirt. She shivered in his arms when his lips brushed the upper swell of her tits, and he knew at that moment, the same way he knew the second he delivered a check, what the outcome would be. It wouldn't be today, and it may not even be by date five, but he was going to persuade her that there was more to this—more to them— than a PR stunt.

"Zara," he said, looking up at her as the sun turned the

sky pink and gave the apartment a soft glow. "I want to kiss you here." His thumb brushed over the hard tip of her still-covered nipple. "Can I kiss you there?"

He reached between them, inching the hem of her T-shirt up as he watched her face for any sign to stop, and when she pulled the bottom of her shirt out of his grasp and took it off, he offered up a prayer of thanks.

"Start here." She laid a fingertip at her freckle-covered collarbone. "Go here." She slid her finger across to the top of her tits. "Then here." Her finger glided down the side and underneath. "And finally, be sure to kiss here." She lifted up her breast, her thumb grazing against her nipple.

His dick strained against his jeans, and his balls tightened as a wave of need cross-checked him right into the boards, but he managed to get out a barely audible, "Yes, ma'am. I'm gonna give you that and more."

Then he went to work, because he could follow her coaching, but he could add a little off-the-tongue twists as well. He followed the path she'd laid out for him, and kissing his way over her skin, the freckles becoming lighter and spaced farther apart, he made his way to her pale-peach nipple, letting the overnight growth of his beard brush against the sensitive spot. He sucked the tip into his hot mouth, swirling his tongue around it and grazing his teeth over it, nipping with just enough pressure to make her moan. Her hands were in his hair, pulling him closer as she arched against him, her hands holding on to the back of the couch. Her hips rotated as she rubbed her core against him at an ever more desperate pace.

She needed relief—needed it bad—and there was nothing more he wanted at the moment than to taste her orgasm on his mouth. Raising his mouth from her, he skimmed his hands down her sides to her hips and lifted her so while she was still grasping the back of the couch, her legs were nearly straight.

He slid down so he was underneath the apex of her thighs.

He hooked his finger in the waistband of her shorts. "There's one more place I want to kiss."

"Yes, please." She lifted one leg as he brought her shorts down on that side and slipped it free.

As the shorts slid down the other leg, circling her ankle, he didn't care that her shorts weren't all the way off, not when they were both this close. He pulled her hips lower so her hot, wet core was against his mouth. Fuck, she was sweet, so good. He tasted her, licking and kissing and sucking her plump, wet folds.

"Caleb," she cried out when the tip of his tongue touched her clit.

When he circled his tongue around the sensitive nub while stroking his thumb in and out of her slick entrance, her thighs started to tremble. He pulled her down more, burying himself in her as he continued lapping and sucking her clit and fucking her with his thumb, circling her entrance and driving it inside over and over until her shaking thighs stilled half a second before they clamped closed on either side of his head and she came all over his mouth.

He slowly ran his palms over her ass and up and down her legs until her orgasm abated, then helped her lay down on the blanket she must have given him when he'd fallen asleep earlier. Dawn was full upon them now, the pink-orange rays bathing her in a golden pastel glow. God, she looked fucking delectable, sated and spent with her eyes half closed and the unmistakable red of beard burn on her inner thighs.

It was almost impossible to remember why dating Zara for real was a bad idea. In this moment, he couldn't shake the idea that there could be more than an agreement between them. That he wanted that. That it didn't seem like he had a choice in wanting her. That it was too late to try to fight it even if he wanted to.

"I think you broke me," she said, her lips curling into a

soft smile.

Before he could say anything dumb, like *me too*, his phone buzzed, vibrating on the coffee table. He glanced down at the notification reminding him that he had twenty minutes to get to the team practice facility for an early-morning team run. Coach Peppers loved bonding activities—especially if he could schedule one early enough that his players couldn't get up to anything stupid the night before.

"Duty calls?" she asked, sitting up and wrapping the blanket around herself like armor. The easy bliss was gone from her expression already.

He nodded. "Zara—"

"Don't say it," she interrupted, her gaze lowered so instead of looking him in the eye, her gaze was directed at his chin. "It was just kissing. Didn't mean a thing. I know."

She couldn't be more wrong, but now wasn't the moment to make his case, not with her chin up at that stubborn angle and her lips flattened into one thin line. He needed more time than the forty seconds he had before he needed to go or risk being too late to catch the subway to the facility—fines and lectures about being a disruptive force in the team would follow that, and he had to do everything he could to keep things on an even keel.

"We'll talk later," he said as he got up and walked backward toward the door.

"Sure, we still have an agreement, remember?" She gave him a wobbly smile. "Two more dates to go."

And that's when it hit him. She had her own reasons for going on the Bramble dates, and it wasn't to fall for a guy like him. Maybe what had just happened didn't mean anything to her, and he was just being a sucker thinking it might be—could be—more. Wiping away the last taste of her from his mouth, he just nodded and walked out of her apartment, his steps heavier than they had been when he'd walked in last night.

Chapter Ten

Zara still wasn't sure about the elephants. Of course, since Caleb had left right after she'd gone to town on his face and she had been avoiding his texts for the last two days, she'd been overthinking *everything*, so maybe this was more of that. Just a normal, everyday mental freak-out. That was all.

Perfectly normal.

Yep.

That was her and her mini elephants.

The miniatures scene was straight out of a fantasy, a parade of miniature rainbow-colored elephants marching up a waving ribbon of EEG readings. Each elephant followed the up-and-down path of the brain waves readings. The elephants and the ribbon got smaller and smaller the higher the EEG ribbon went until they disappeared into nothing. It was one of her earlier works when she did an entire series on idioms. She and Gemma were pulling the whole series and more out of her building's storage vaults so she could pick ten to display as part of the ultraexclusive cocktail party to celebrate the opening of ticket sales for the Friends of the

Library ball next month.

"An elephant never forgets?" Gemma asked as she set another scene on the kitchen island.

"Yeah, but I'm not sure if it's right for this show." Zara looked around, her gut doing a very uncomfortable version of the Cha-Cha Slide. "I'm not sure if any of these are right for the show. I just need to rethink this. Keep working on it. Maybe next year."

"What is this gibberish? These are awesome." Gemma took Zara by the shoulders and turned her so they were facing each other. "This is what you want. What you've been working toward—a chance to show the world what you can do, to share this joy."

"It's not good enough." Every miniatures artisan she followed on Insta showcased work that just blew her away. Each piece was an amazing fantasy. However, when she looked at her own pieces, all she saw was the work that went into it and never the joy she felt when she looked at other artists' work. "I can do better."

"So can we all." Gemma pulled her in for a quick hug and then walked over to the stove and poured boiling water from the whistling kettle into the two mugs on the counter. "That means your work will continue to evolve and continually be fresh."

Zara took out the tea bags from the cupboard and handed two to Gemma. "I want it to be perfect."

"If you wait for perfection, then you're never going to do it." After adding the tea to the mugs, she handed one to Zara. "That's not a dig, it's an acknowledgment of the fact that perfection is unachievable."

She didn't want to admit that. Life was too messy as it was. Part of the reason why she'd even begun working in miniatures was because the ability to control every last detail spoke to the need deep in her soul for order and stability.

Exposing that to someone else's eyes and asking for that judgment when every time she looked at a scene she saw something else to tweak or adjust made her palms sweaty.

"If I put it out there and it gets shot down, then I'll have to accept that all of this has just been a silly dream as dumb as my dad's get-rich-quick schemes." She took a sip of Earl Grey as she turned a skeptical gaze toward the ten scenes on the kitchen island. "Looking at this, all I can think is that I'm being an idiot for thinking that getting a face-to-face with Helene Carlyle at the ball would make any kind of impact— I'm just not ready."

"There's a big difference between showing your amazing art or talking to an influential collector and your dad's plan to start a cat-walking business."

Despite the emotion making the tip of her nose itch, Zara had to giggle. Her dad had gone so far as to buy professional walker leashes that would let him walk ten cats at once. The first time he'd tried it—with only five cats—had been an epic disaster. Her dad had taken the failing with a shrug and started work on his next scheme.

Zara shook her head. "That idea was almost as inane as this whole Bramble dating thing."

"Well, since you brought it up, have you seen Caleb's latest interview?" Gemma said with enough fizz-bang excitement in her voice to show just how much she'd been wanting to bring up this topic. "This one was just him and his mom, no Asha."

Zara's tea became incredibly interesting—okay, the smell wafting up from her mug was amazing, but the contents itself were not. It was just that looking down was a lot better than making eye contact with her bestie, who would be able to read her thoughts and therefore know what happened the other night. She could play this cool. She could. Really.

She didn't bother to look up from her mug because she knew that was a lie. "I haven't seen it."

"Oh, honey." Gemma dug her phone out of her purse, brought up the video, and hit play. "Take a look."

Zara tried to watch the right corner of the screen instead of Caleb's face. Then he started talking, and there was no way she could turn away. Her belly shimmied in that good-things-are-coming way as she took in the crooked line of his nose that she'd spent way too much time thinking about while thanking the universe that she hadn't broken it again when she'd come hard enough to make her ears ring.

Caleb and his mom sat next to each other, pivoted so they half faced each other, on the couch in the *Harbor City Wake Up* set.

"You actually cooked for your third date? I didn't think you'd go through with it," Britany said, her eyes wide with shock. "Did you burn the place down?"

"Very funny." He pulled a face at his mom. "But yeah, I was a little worried about that."

"I still remember that time when you were in high school and the fire department had to come because you got distracted by the hockey draft while making a grilled cheese," Britany said with a smile. "Of course, I did end up dating one of the firefighters for a while, so that almost made up for the smoke marks that went up to the ceiling."

"I'm never gonna live that down." He said it as if he was laughing with his mom, but there was a tension in his jaw that belied his tone.

"Doubtful." She did a good-natured one-shoulder shrug. "So what was it like cooking with Zara?"

Caleb's smile went from perfunctory to genuine, and it was enough to make Zara's heart beat faster.

"It was really fun," he said. "She has a way of making things that I would normally not be into really fun."

"So dinner and then what? A movie?"

"Sorta." The tips of Caleb's ears turned pink, and he

looked down at the coffee table in front of the couch that someone had decorated with oversize photography books about Harbor City. "We watched some TV."

His mom, obviously picking up on his telltale body language, leaned in. "And that's it?"

Zara stiffened.

Hello, Miss None of Your Business Even Though He's Your Son, you can just back off now.

Caleb must have been thinking the same thing because he didn't mince words. "I'm not having this conversation with you, Mom—especially not when it includes the entirety of Harbor City."

Britany Stuckey, though, didn't seem to be fazed. "Because you like her?"

It was just another invasive question from Caleb's mom, who didn't seem to understand personal boundaries very well, but it came out different than the others. Softer. Concerned. Hopeful.

Zara couldn't have looked away from Gemma's phone screen if Anchovy had started eating the just-finished, one-twelfth-size doll of Kamala Markandaya. She held her breath, not wanting to miss a syllable of his answer.

"Because it's the right thing to do and, yeah, because I like her," he said, the words coming out strong and sure. "She's really amazing. I just want to hang out with her as much as possible, even if that means learning to cook. Zara's special."

For a few seconds, Caleb and his mom just looked at each other, saying so much without uttering a word. Zara's skin was hot, and her lungs felt ready to burst, but still, she couldn't look away. If she had, she might have missed the quick one-two-three tap of Britany's finger on Caleb's forearm.

"And to think, I was the one who set up this play," Britany said with a wink.

Instead of rolling his eyes at his mom's outrageousness,

though, he just said, "Thanks, Mom."

The tip of Britany's nose turned red, and a bright splotch of color appeared at the base of her throat as she stared at her son for a moment, speechless. It was the first time Zara had ever seen Caleb's mom like that, but Zara could understand the feeling completely. Her own brain was in meltdown mode while her body was in heat-up mode, a totally inconvenient and unacceptable reaction to watching her not-dating partner talk to his mom about her on a video stream.

The video ended and the logo for *Harbor City Wake Up* appeared on the screen. Zara looked at Gemma, whose eyes were as big and round as saucers.

"Oh. My. God," Gemma said. "You slept with him."

Cheeks. Burning. Lava. Flames. "I did not."

But only because Caleb was the type to give orgasms and run, which was followed by a string of texts over the past few days that she'd ignored because she was a big, embarrassed chicken. What do you say to someone after you come all over his face like a woman who hasn't had a non-self-induced orgasm in literally forever? Was she supposed to text back "WYD?" Pour her heart out? Tell him her clit was usually broken when other people touched it? Demand he gets back to her apartment so she could tie him to the bed?

Gemma narrowed her eyes and crossed her arms, giving Zara a long, hard look. "You did something more with him than hold hands."

Zara folded like cardboard in the rain. "I might have ended up naked."

"You might have?" Gemma clapped. Literally. As if Zara had just won a spelling bee. "What about him?"

"Totally dressed." The work that zipper must have done, though...judging by the hard length of him that she'd dry humped.

God, her cheeks were burning even more just thinking

about it—in both a good and a bad way.

"And what happened while you were naked and he was fully clothed?" her bestie asked, because she, too, had never had a question she didn't need to air.

"He went to town downtown." Her core clenched just remembering the feel of his tongue against her.

"And...?"

Zara waited for a beat, screwing up her face, and prayed for courage because this next admission was going to cause shock waves. "I had an orgasm."

Gemma set down her mug on the counter with a loud *thunk*. Her jaw dropped, and she just stared at Zara, blinking occasionally as the truth of the matter sank in.

"Oh my God. Oh m-my God," she finally sputtered. "This is huge."

It wasn't like Zara went around telling everyone that she'd never had an orgasm with another person before. That kind of humiliation didn't need to be shared. Really, who wanted to know that her body was defective unless she was by herself grinding out a toe-curler? The only person she'd ever told had been her best friend. Together they'd pored over sexual health books, the internet, and Gemma had even tried to get her to go to a therapist. None of it had worked.

The fact was that the more time she spent during the deed thinking about how to have an orgasm or telling herself that she should have had one by now, the further away her climax felt. So she just let it go, figuring that she had a shy clit that only wanted to play when she was by herself.

"It's not that big of a deal," Zara protested, without really putting her heart into it. "It just means I probably should have had more sex with my other boyfriends while I was still half asleep so that my brain would stop spinning and I could actually experience the event instead of feeling like I was giving a barely listened-to guided tour in hopes of maybe getting a tip in the end."

"So that's what you're going with?" Gemma raised an eyebrow and tilted her chin down. "Hazy brain equals orgasms when you've never had one with other people before? Girl, forget your history of solo-only orgasms, if a dude is willing to get you over without even getting a handie, then you've found a keeper. That kind of giving is not found in a majority of the male population."

"We're not really dating," Zara said, not wanting to deal with the rest of that statement because really, what woman who was dating in today's world didn't deal with selfish lovers? "It's just a means to an end for both of us. Don't you have other friends you can pester about getting into relationships with people with whom they are not compatible?"

Gemma let out a loud cackle of a laugh that startled Anchovy from his midafternoon nap. "No one else who is dating Caleb Stuckey, first of his name, destroyer of vagina cobwebs, and bequeather of non-solo orgasms."

"You are so weird," Zara said with a laugh.

Her bestie shrugged and lifted her mug of tea in a toast. "And that's why you love me."

"True." She clinked her mug against Gemma's and snuck a peek at her own phone on the counter.

There were eight text message alerts she'd been pretending weren't there. She didn't need to hit the text icon to know who they were from, but she wished she knew what in the hell to say to him.

$\cdots$

"Stuckey," Coach Peppers yelled. "Get in my office."

Caleb heard Coach even though he had in his earbuds so he could listen to the video of Zara's dad interviewing her about the last date. He'd been waiting for a hint that

Anchovy had eaten her phone or that she'd been under a tight work deadline and that was why she hadn't texted him back beyond a couple of emojis—whatever the fuck they were supposed to mean. Of course, he didn't really care that she was blowing him off. Whatever he'd been dumb enough to think was maybe a possibility obviously wasn't. She'd set him straight on that by ignoring his messages.

He pocketed his earbuds and his phone, then pulled on his shirt and headed into the coach's office. Surprising no one, Coach wasn't alone. Zach Blackburn lounged against the window ledge, his tatted-up arms crossed and the eyebrow piercing he took out for games and practices back in place. The team captain looked every bit like a man about to take a chunk out of whoever pissed him off that day, which was pretty much Blackburn's usual expression.

Caleb stepped farther inside Coach's office. "You wanted me?"

"Sit down," Peppers said without looking up from his computer screen.

That didn't bode well. Usually, Coach just had little chats with his players in the locker room while he drank coffee spiked with enough sugar and milk to give only the barest hint of what it had been originally. Caleb went for an air of cocky confidence, but on the inside, he was that too-skinny kid with buck teeth in front of the classroom trying to read from the assigned chapter.

"Do you know why you're here in this facility and wearing that team logo?" Peppers jerked his chin toward the Ice Knights logo on Caleb's T-shirt.

"To play hockey," he said, not understanding where this was going but not liking it.

"Damn straight." Coach leaned forward, propping his elbows on his desk. "And what else?"

Beads of sweat popped out at the base of his skull, and

he tapped his fingers on his thigh, an old trick his mom had taught him to stay grounded when anxiety started to wind up in his belly. "To be a team player."

"Just a player or a leader?" Blackburn asked, his tone gruff and his expression inscrutable beyond his perma-glare.

He straightened in the guest chair. "A leader."

"Good, because that's what I see when I look at you, which is why your fuckup in the off-season hurt us so badly." Peppers exhaled a harsh breath in obvious frustration. "The new guys look up to you. The old guys want to play with you. The fans love you. More importantly, the boys thought they could depend on you to show the team in a good light and not to cause distraction or disruption."

"I know that." Caleb couldn't talk for other organizations, but with the Ice Knights, there was a sense of team that went beyond the logo on his jersey. Maybe it was because they'd fought their way out of the standings basement together, and none of them wanted to go back into the never-could bracket. "I'm willing to do whatever it takes."

"Like let your mom take over your Bramble app so the front office wouldn't trade you and Petrov?" Blackburn asked.

"Petrov's working his ass off." The center had put in so many hours to get back to the game that he'd practically worked an eighty-two-game season already. "He deserves to play for the team he's dreamed about being on since he was in juniors."

"Yeah, well, he's playing in tonight's game," Peppers said, then took a drink from the sugary concoction in his Harbor City Dental mug. "The front office has decided against trading him."

All the air whooshed out of his chest in relief. "Good."

"They're not trading you, either, but we're making a change to your jersey," Blackburn said as he tossed a piece of fabric into Caleb's lap.

He looked down at the blue A, picking it up with the

reverence that the letter denoting the alternate captain deserved.

Brain still processing what this meant, he looked up at Blackburn and Peppers. "But I fucked up."

"Are you gonna do that again?" Coach asked.

He shook his head. "No."

"Then take the A," Blackburn said.

"And don't worry about the Bramble thing," Peppers said. "I can talk to Lucy to get you out of it."

In a heartbeat, everything slammed back into action: his heart started beating again, his mental abilities caught up with the situation, and he almost jumped out of his chair—stopping himself just in time.

"No," Caleb said, the single word coming out like a curse. He cleared his throat and tried again. "I'll see it through."

"Might as well finish up the last two dates, eh?" Coach steepled his fingers and tapped them against his chin. "I like it. Shows you finish what you start. The front office will appreciate that."

That was nice but was not the reason Caleb was doing this—not that he was about to say it out loud. Still, the amused tilt of Blackburn's smirk meant Caleb wasn't entirely successful in keeping that information to himself. He glowered at his defensive partner, who just shrugged and flipped him off while Coach wasn't watching.

Yeah, Blackburn could suck it. Caleb had had to watch the other man fall like a boulder through thin ice for Fallon Hartigan last year—the last thing Caleb needed was for Mr. I Know Everything About Relationships Now to think that's what he wanted for himself. It wasn't.

This thing with Zara? It was just fun. No strings. No feelings. No commitment. Those were the rules. That's what they'd agreed to, and she was obviously sticking to it even if he had been starting to waver. He wouldn't be that dumb again.

Chapter Eleven

Shoulder still aching a bit from the hit he'd taken during last night's home game that had sent him crashing into the boards, Caleb eased his truck into the parallel parking spot on the busy Harbor City street near Zara's building and took his phone out of the glove box. He'd meant to drive across the Harbor Bay bridge home to Waterbury after this afternoon's practice. Instead, he'd driven in the exact opposite direction because he'd been driving with his dick—not literally but close enough. It was allowed, though, because this wasn't about a relationship. This was just for fun so everyone got off.

Engine off and phone in hand, he fired off a quick message.

Caleb: *You in?*

He didn't take his gaze off the screen. It remained stubbornly blank. He was an asshole—the kind who fucked around and ran off. Who could blame her for the past few days of emoji-only responses to his texts? She was sending a message, and he had to accept that. Then, three little text dots appeared on his screen and he whispered a "fuck yeah" in the empty cab of his truck.

Zara: *Yes, but I'm not fit for public.*

Caleb: *Bad day?*

Zara: *The worst cramps ever.*

His experience with that was all theoretical, but there were many benefits to growing up with sisters—one of which was knowing not to fuck with a woman dealing with period cramps.

Caleb: *Sorry.*

Zara: *It's okay. When I die, make sure someone comes and feeds Anchovy so he won't eat my corpse.*

Caleb: *Only cats would do that. Anchovy is a good boy. Speaking of which, I have something for him. Can I stop up real quick?*

Zara: *Thought you were in Toronto.*

If he looked in the rearview mirror about then, he had no doubt as to the goofy-ass grin he'd be wearing. His damn cheeks hurt. This was ridiculous. Thank God he was alone.

Caleb: *Not until tomorrow but you're following my games now?*

Zara: *Anchovy sat on the remote. I didn't have a choice.*

Caleb: *Uh-huh. Whatever you say.*

She only sent an eye roll emoji in response.

Caleb: *I actually found a parking spot only three*

blocks down from your place. Can I swing by?

Okay, the truth of it was that he'd driven around her neighborhood for a solid fifteen minutes hunting for a parking spot, but she didn't need to know that. He didn't want her to think he was a total creeper.

Zara: *All right, just know what you're in for.*

Caleb: *I grew up in an all-girl family. You can't scare me.*

Instead of making the left to go to her apartment building once he got out of his truck, he turned right so he could hit the corner store, where he grabbed a bottle of red with a pair of high heels on the label that reminded him of Zara and half a dozen different kinds of candy bars, hoping she'd like at least one of them. He was knocking on her front door five minutes after the old lady behind the counter handed him his change, gave an appraising look at his items as she bagged them, and wished him good luck.

Zara opened the door wearing yoga pants, a long-sleeve T-shirt, and fuzzy slippers that looked like Anchovy had munched on them a time or twelve. Her long red hair was pulled into a ponytail, and she was clutching a bag of chips.

"I brought you a present." He handed over the plastic bag.

She pulled out a Baby Ruth and the wine. Since he knew next to nothing about wine, he'd picked the label more than the bottle, but he must have done okay judging by the happy sigh she let out. Shit. He was in trouble. If Blackburn could see him now, the only thing the captain would say was *told you so.*

"Okay," Zara said, stepping back and giving him room to enter. "You're allowed in."

He made it all of three steps in before Anchovy loped over and helpfully lifted Caleb's hand with his head.

"You want a pet, huh?" Caleb delivered that and then reached in the bag Zara still held, pulling out a tennis ball with the Ice Knights logo on it. "Figured you might want a smaller one every once in a while, too."

Anchovy woofed his approval, took the ball from his palm, and then trotted off to the part of Zara's studio designated as a workspace. The dog lay down on a blanket under a table covered with miniature furniture and books.

The candy bar wrapper crinkled as Zara tore it open. "You've made a friend for life."

"Does that mean I can stay for a while?" That tight sense of anticipation made his nerves vibrate as she looked him up and down.

"Okay, but I'm invoking the rule that I don't have to pretend to be in a good mood."

He kept the victory grin off his face. "Works for me."

Two hours later and the fast-cars-and-loud-explosions movie was winding down while they sat next to each other on the couch. The bottle of wine was half empty, three crumpled-up candy bar wrappers sat in the middle of the coffee table, and Zara was tucked in against him. The team plane took off for Toronto at O-dark-hundred in the morning and he still had to pack, but he wasn't ready to go.

As the credits rolled faster than his brain could process the jumping letters, he let his eyes droop closed. This was what had happened last time. Just the no-pressure ease of sitting there together had lulled him into the kind of super-relaxed state that he usually only experienced after a hard-fought win. It was the kind of feeling that sank deep into his bones, melting away everything else until there was only the good of that moment. That's what it was like sitting on the couch with Zara. It made absolutely no sense, but there it was.

However, unlike last time, he wasn't going to crash out, not when they had to stop pretending that nothing had happened.

"Are we going to talk about what happened the other day?" he asked, the words out of his mouth before his brain had time to think better.

"You mean when you gave me my first non-solo orgasm ever." Zara's eyes rounded as she whirled around to face him, slapping her hand over her mouth in horror.

Caleb could practically smell the smoke from the sizzle of his brain exploding.

First.

Non-solo.

Orgasm.

What in the hell?

She dropped her hand to her lap and looked up at the ceiling, her eyes squeezed shut. "Ignore that. I did not say it. You did not hear anything. Fuck."

Yeah. That was not gonna happen. How in the world had she never— Ohhhhhhhh. Okay, this was a first for him since he'd lost his own V card.

"It's no big deal," he said, working to keep his tone neutral. "Being a virgin is cool."

Her responding groan of misery was loud enough to wake up Anchovy, who had been asleep on the floor using his new tennis ball as a doggie chin pillow.

"No," she said, fanning her face with her hands, but the movement didn't do anything to lessen the redness of her cheeks. "I'm not a virgin, and no, there is nothing wrong with being a virgin. I just don't happen to be one."

Caleb pivoted on the couch so that instead of sitting side by side, he was facing her. "And none of the people you've been with have helped you get there before?"

She shrugged. What a bunch of sad-sack losers. He wanted to go out and find every single one of them and smack them upside the head. How could they have done that to her—left her wanting—when there was nothing better than watching her come? It wasn't necessary for him to close his eyes to picture how she'd tossed her head back, arching her body in ecstasy above him. He wouldn't be forgetting it anytime soon. In fact, he couldn't wait to see it again.

He sat up straighter, pride puffing out his chest. "But I helped you come."

Egotistical ass? Him? Well, fuck yeah, he'd helped her get where all the rest of those assholes had failed to go.

"Yes." Opening her eyes, she shook her head and let out a sigh. "It's probably just because I was half awake."

Not his technique? Not even a little? He let out a grunt of protest.

"Sorry, what I mean is that we agreed that this"—she gestured between them—"is a temporary arrangement and not a relationship, so there's no pressure. Sex can just be sex. I don't have to think about how it will impact anything once we have our clothes on."

Pride pricked, he turned that over in his head for a minute. Sex for him had always been about wet friction and hard orgasms for all involved—but not for Zara, and that made him want to beat the crap out of all her old boyfriends again.

"What a bunch of selfish assholes," he muttered. "You wanna give me names and I'll go pay them a visit?"

• • •

It wasn't a sincere offer, but it made Zara smile. Her last boyfriend would shit a brick if he ever opened his front door and Caleb was standing there. That mental image alone was almost as good as the wine-and-chocolate cramp cure and the way he didn't freak out when she spilled the beans about her broken bean.

Thank you, wine on a chips-and-candy-bar stomach for that bit of wordplay.

"It's not *only* the guys' fault, although yeah, they were not all that into making sure I came or changing what they were doing to get me there." Why was she talking about this with him? She needed to stop. She was gonna stop. The words came out anyway. "I saw a therapist. She said I needed to live in the moment more."

He looked skeptical. "Did that help?"

"Not really." She scooted over on the couch, bringing her knees up to her chest and wrapping her arms around them. Telling herself to just relax got about the same results as when other people told her to. It wound her up more. "It's hard for me to turn off my brain. I've had to keep six steps ahead of things my whole life. I don't even mean to do it. It's just how I am."

It was how she'd grown up. She'd always had to be the responsible one, the one who made sure things got done. While her dad was out cheering up a neighbor, she was home calling in the grocery order or adding the second-notice-overdue bills to the magnetized chip clip on the fridge so he'd remember to pay them.

She always worried about something. It had become her neutral point—and that caused difficulties in ways she hadn't expected. Every time things got serious with a boyfriend and they had sex, she fell into that what-do-I-need-to-take-care-of stress spiral.

"I tried a glass of wine before sex to relax me. It just made me sleepy. I tried meditation and even tried thinking about the porn I enjoyed during my alone time, but that was a no go. I was too busy thinking about everything else from *was his tongue starting to develop a cramp from being down there so long* to *did I remember to put dog treats on the grocery list*. Ultimately, unless I gave myself a helping hand, it didn't happen. I'm broken."

Just like they weren't supposed to be sharing secrets, she was not supposed to be sharing tears, but her cheeks were wet anyway.

She wiped her cheek with the back of her hand and inhaled a sniffly breath, trying to focus her gaze on the TV instead of the man sitting next to her. It gave her some mental space to get everything put back into its correctly labeled emotional box. That worked out great right up until the screen went dark, showing off the reflection of the ten miniature scenes she'd picked out for the cocktail party celebrating tickets going on sale for the Friends of the Library ball. All the worries and the doubts about the one thing in her life that only she was in charge of and, therefore, could control slammed into her. Were they good enough? Was she just selling herself one of her dad's pipe dreams thinking they could be?

Fragile sense of equilibrium lost, Zara dropped her head to her knees and let out a pitiful moan. She'd warned Caleb that she was at peak crampy period misery, and he'd shown up anyway—no doubt a decision he was now regretting.

"You're not broken, and neither is your clit," he said, laying his big hand on the back of her neck and rolling the pad of his thumb over the knots there with just enough pressure to make her sigh.

"Why?" she asked. "Because you made me come? Do you subscribe to the magic tongue school of thought?"

He chuckled and continued to massage the tension out of her neck. "No, I think you might have had it right the first time. With us, it's different not because of my skills— although, for the record, I want it noted that I have them—but because I don't matter. I'm just temporary."

She lifted her head, the meaning of his words cutting through her own misery. Damn. She was a bitch. "I didn't mean it to sound so mean. I'm sorry."

He shrugged. "I'm tough. I can take it." His hand moved from the back of her neck to her ponytail, his fingers sliding through the length of it before he pulled away from touching her completely. "Still, we owe it to science to figure out if my hypothesis is correct."

The words had come out light, fun, almost teasing, but there was something real underneath the tone that called out to her. Still, it couldn't happen. What if that one time was just that—the one time? Then she would be back to having mediocre sex. Or it could happen again and then her ever-spinning brain wouldn't rest until she figured out why and what it meant.

"You gotta be kidding. That's the plot of a bad movie, and they always end up together." Her pulse picked up as she turned the idea over in her mind despite knowing it was probably a worse idea than the time her dad put their electric bill money on a sure-thing pony at the track. It was ridiculous. And foolhardy. And a disaster waiting to happen. And...oh God...she wanted to say yes anyway. "I'm not in this for orgasms. I want to go to the ball, but I'm not looking for Prince Charming in or out of bed. I most definitely am not looking for love or a relationship. Depending on other people is for suckers—I learned that the hard way."

Caleb tapped the bump on the curve of his crooked nose and raised an eyebrow. "Do I look like anyone's prince?"

That's where he was wrong. He might not have shown up at her door tonight on a white steed, but he'd come bearing chocolate and wine in her time of need. That counted for something—really, it counted for a lot.

"I'm serious," she said. "If I'm gonna consider this, I have to be able to depend on you sticking to the rules."

Because she wasn't so sure anymore that she could, and they both knew it would never work out between them. They were too different.

He held up one hand, three fingers extended toward the ceiling. His gaze slid down to the left as if he wasn't sure, but he grinned at her anyway even if it didn't look totally genuine. "I solemnly swear that I'm only trying to get into your pants and not your heart."

The tension inside her broke, and she laughed, hard and until she couldn't catch her breath. Anchovy wandered over from under her worktable and sat in front of them, squeezing his big body between the coffee table and the couch. As he switched his focus from her to Caleb and back again, she could practically hear the dog's thoughts that the humans had obviously lost it.

"We are six kinds of fucked-up," she said, once she finally got her lungs to function again.

"Probably," he said.

"I need a show of good faith that I can trust you to stick to it." Because she couldn't shake the prickly doubt that she might not be able to, and that scared her all the way down to her pink-painted toenails. "I told you my biggest secret tonight. You should reciprocate so we keep this an even playing field."

Caleb sat there for a while, scratching Anchovy under the chin until the dog nearly passed out from bliss. Finally, just when she thought he was going to call the whole thing off—and yeah, that may have been a little self-sabotage there on her part—he started talking.

"I can't read," he said, not looking at her.

She waited for the *just kidding*. It didn't come.

Three words, one syllable each, and they stopped the world from spinning. Images flashed in her mind. Caleb standing in front of her TV picking out a *Law & Order* episode, his jaw tight and gaze narrowed at the screen. Caleb sitting on the *Harbor City Wake Up* set and his mom asking him if he wanted her to read the release form. Caleb's teasing grin after they'd swapped from text to FaceTime, which they almost always did. Everything fell into place, and she had no idea how to react. Shock froze her.

"Okay, not technically, but it feels like it sometimes. I have dyslexia, but we didn't realize until middle school. I'd just figured the letters danced around the page for everyone," he said, continuing to pet Anchovy with slow, deliberate brushes of his palm over the dog's head. "I was good at covering, plus I'd had really great teachers who made learning fun even though it was hard. Then, in sixth grade, I got a teacher who was counting down to retirement, and his big thing was students reading out loud in front of the class."

Caleb paused, and she nearly reached out to him, but there was something in the hard line of his broad shoulders and the tight way he clenched his jaw that warned he didn't want her comfort, her pity. She understood. Some old hurts did that, burrowing deep under the skin until they were a part of a person's makeup, indistinguishable from what had been there before and what came after. And here she was making him pull back all the protective layers. Guilt and regret tugged her down low against the couch cushions.

"It's okay—you don't have to go on," she said.

He gritted his teeth, his gaze going up to the ceiling for a few beats before he let out a deep sigh as if he'd made up his mind.

"He'd call on me every day," Caleb said. "I'd get up to the front of the class and stumble through on a good day or freeze on a bad day. It pretty much sucked, and that feeling of everyone staring at me just waiting for me to fuck it up, it stuck with me. That's why I love being out on the ice. While I might literally be in front of thousands, it doesn't feel like it. During a game, it's just me, the puck, and my boys. The letters might dance when I look down at a page, but when it comes to reading a play, everything is solid. It all makes sense at first glance."

It took all of half a second for Zara to swap places with where Caleb had been earlier. She was more than ready to put on her shoes and go kick a stranger's ass. To torment anyone like that was awful, but to do it to a kid who was at that age when the only thing they wanted was to fit in instead of standing out? Definitely a punch-in-the-junk-worthy offense. And it was one that stuck with a person, had them going into defensive mode even when they may not know they're doing it.

"That explains your viral video." She sat forward, realization pulling her spine straight. "You're still trying to make sure no one sees you as that outsider standing in front of the class."

"Nah, that's just…" He let out a harsh breath and turned to her, his jaw slack. "Fuck. You're right."

What a pair they were. Totally blind to themselves and yet able to see the other so clearly. That was a disturbing thought. She did not need to go there with Caleb Stuckey. Five dates and done. That was the unbreakable rule, because there was no way they were compatible. She was a woman who craved stability, and he was a guy whose job demanded travel nearly ten months out of the year, plus he could be traded to another team at any moment. It was a bad mix in the long term. But in the short term? That no-emotionally-invested-sex rule? Well, that was on the table…or the couch…or the bed.

Caleb got up, the hem of his T-shirt raising above the waistband of his jeans when he stretched his arms, giving her a tantalizing glimpse of the top of his deep V-cut. She must have made a noise of appreciation because he let out a chuckle at the same time as Anchovy cocked his head to the side. Okay, could she embarrass herself any more tonight?

"I hate to analyze and run," he said. "But I still have to

pack for tomorrow's game in Toronto and Detroit after that."

Yes. Hockey. Lots of road trips. She sent up a prayer of thanks for the reminder of the most obvious reason for their incompatibility at a moment of weakness. She stood up and walked him to the door, pulling it open and standing to the side so he could leave.

But he didn't.

He got halfway through before stopping, his body so close to hers that his pheromones wrapped around her as solid as a touch as his eyes roamed her from head to toe. He didn't say anything. He didn't need to. She heard every heated want, every naughty vow, every dirty thought as if he were whispering in her ear, and it made her knees weak.

"Let me know when you're ready to see if we can make the magic happen again," he said.

She shivered. There was something in his rough tone that stripped her naked. "What makes you think I will?"

One side of his mouth curled upward in a sexy smirk that said everything he didn't need to, because they both knew the score. Then he turned and walked away while she stood in her open door, trying to catch her breath, already half on the verge of coming.

You are in so much trouble, girl.

Chapter Twelve

Per Coach Peppers's theory that early-morning activities equaled team cohesion, Caleb was in a suit getting half choked by a tie, walking across the tarmac to the team jet at six in the morning. As a solid member of team Sleep In, his eyes were barely open as he climbed the steps. Because he'd hardly slept at all thanks to a continual fantasy reel involving Zara Ambrose in all of her naked glory, he was a walking zombie. He sat down in the first empty window seat and yawned big enough that his jaw popped.

"Good morning, sunshine," Phillips said, plopping down next to him. "Out late with your date? Will there be another video soon?"

At the mere mention of the word "video," Christensen's and Petrov's heads popped up above the seats in the row in front of them like meerkats on one of those nature shows his mom liked to watch.

"Is she ready to dump your ass yet?" Christensen asked. "Because I would totally tap that. Forget a defenseman—she needs a forward with some skill and finesse."

"Nah, a center is more her speed," Petrov said. "I have the flexibility to go wherever she needs."

The two knuckleheads jabbered between themselves, each stating his case as that all-too-familiar unease had Caleb's every nerve flinching. There wasn't a spotlight and he wasn't standing in front of a class full of people—hell, he knew damn well they were just busting his chops—but still, the urge to play along to sink into the familiarity of the group was there. He could stay silent like he had in the Uber. Zara might never find out, but he would know, and he wasn't going down that road again. He let out a breath and took the metaphorical puck down the ice.

"You two are idiots," he said, giving them the glare they deserved. "Stop talking like a pair of privileged assholes— better yet, stop *thinking* like a pair of privileged assholes."

If they were offended, they didn't show it. Instead, they both stared at him, shit-eating, we-got-you grins on their faces.

"I think he likes her," Petrov said.

"Definitely." Christensen nodded. "Our little boy is falling in love."

Caleb flipped off the other men. "Is that what that was, just a way to rile me up?"

"Pretty much," Petrov said. "Thanks for falling for it."

Then he sat down, Christensen following suit.

Keeping his mouth shut, Caleb took a deep breath in through his nose, filling his lungs until they were just about to burst and letting it out slow and steady. The jangle of his nerves was more of a hum than a loud clanging, and the tightness in his lower back that always weaved its way up his spine didn't appear. Mild annoyance instead of gut-churning anxiety that made the back of his throat burn with bile.

"Don't let them get to you," Phillips said as he took his earbuds out of the case that looked like a floss container.

"They're just giving you a hard time because neither of them can keep a girl for longer than two dates."

"It's not that—it's that I should have been able to do that months ago in that stupid Uber, shut the rookies down." Which was the truth of it.

"No argument there." Phillips shook his head and pushed the button on the armrest to lower the back of his seat. "So was it a pocket-size redhead who helped you understand the stupidity of your ways?"

"Pretty much." Zara told it like it was, and that was one of the things he really liked about her.

"Sometimes we need someone else to get us to see things from another perspective, and then shit makes sense."

"Speaking from personal experience?"

"We're not talking about me," Phillips said, his tone easy but the pulsing vein in his temple giving away the fact that they *were* talking about him. "But take it from a fellow moron: text your girl before takeoff and hit her up again when we land. Communication is everything."

"She's not my girl." But the phrase sounded good in his head. "It's just an arrangement."

"You forget I've been at the fork in the road that either went to the good place or the bad place. Don't follow my footsteps. Text your girl." Then Phillips put his earbuds in, hit play on his phone, and closed his eyes.

Okay, taking advice from the guy who had such a messy personal life probably wasn't the best idea, but the man made sense. Caleb swiped his phone on and hit the text icon. He thumb-typed each word slowly, being careful to make sure each one was the one he wanted.

Caleb: *Thinking of you.*

And being a giant cheese-ass about it.
He hit the back button until all the words were gone.

Caleb: *Taking off for Buffalo.*

Hello, it's Itinerary Man here to text boring things.
Delete. Delete. Delete forever.

Caleb: *Have a kick-ass day.*

And now I'm a motivational bot.
He held his thumb down on the text and clicked select all and delete.

It shouldn't be this hard—with other women, it wasn't. He wasn't a player like Christensen or everybody-just-naturally-likes-me chill like Petrov, but he wasn't a clueless dork, either. Why couldn't he figure out what to say to Zara? Finally, after staring at the empty message box for a solid three minutes, he scrolled to the gif section. He picked one of a Great Dane who looked a little like Anchovy pulling a blanket down from on top of a crate as he walked inside of it and lay down, totally covered by the blanket. He hit send.

They were speeding down the runway when his phone pinged with a message from Zara. It was a picture of her and Anchovy sharing a pillow with the Ice Knights ball between them. There weren't any words, but he didn't need them. Just seeing her put that goofy-ass smile on his face.

• • •

For being so small, packing up her miniatures scenes for the Friends of the Library cocktail party was a giant pain in Zara's ass. Each had to be double-checked for flaws, surrounded by protective Bubble Wrap, and then placed inside boxes that were padded so nothing would move during delivery tomorrow. And she had to do all that while Anchovy kept trying to hand her his Ice Knights tennis ball—no doubt because he could feel the stress stringing her tight and figured a game of catch would loosen her right up.

Good thing being a woman often meant being a stellar multitasker, because she was able to toss the ball, box up the last of the scenes, and dance horribly without even a hint of coordination as Beyoncé sang. She'd just poured a glass of wine, raised a glass in celebration of the end of her period, and switched from Queen Bey to an episode of *Law & Order* (she really needed to find a new show, but there were so many episodes) when her phone buzzed with a FaceTime request from Caleb.

She tapped accept without thinking twice about her hair or her lack of makeup or that she was in her ratty sleep T-shirt again. "How's Detroit?"

"The food's good," he said as he moved around what looked like an upscale hotel room. "Petrov is originally from here, and he took us to this takeaway place called Chef Greg's Soul-N-the Wall, where he actually broke this crazy-strict nutritional regimen he's been on to get a Boogaloo Wonderland hoagie sandwich that was loaded with beef, sauce, cheese, and caramelized onions. The damn thing smelled so good, I had to get one, too. It did not disappoint."

She curled her legs underneath her and propped the phone up on the edge of the couch. "And now you're tucked back up in your room?"

"Yeah, the coach is a stickler for curfew and he sets an early one. What are you doing?"

"You know me." She flipped the camera so he could see the screen of her TV. "It's *Law and Order* time."

"You've got a serious problem," he said, settling back onto a bed, draping his arm overhead so it rested against his upholstered headboard.

The move gave her a very good view of his biceps, and the ornery glint in his dark eyes was all the proof she needed to confirm that he knew it. Hell. That wasn't fair. Like she hadn't spent enough time thinking about him since he'd walked out of her apartment the other night.

"What can I say?" she said, fighting not to fan herself right here and now. "I like what I like."

"What else do you like?"

Long walks on the beach, chatting with friends over tea, coming all over his face...the usual. Thank God her brain engaged to save her from herself before she could say that out loud. "Baby Ruths and red wine, as you found out the other night."

"And that T-shirt."

"What's wrong with this shirt?" She looked down, tugging her shirt lower and holding it out a bit to make sure it didn't have chip crumbs or anything on it. "It's comfy."

"Don't worry, I like it, too—especially how well loved it is."

She glanced down again, trying to figure out what he meant, and that's when she saw it. The dark shadows of her nipples were clearly visible under the threadbare cotton because of course they were. Things couldn't be simple and uncomplicated when it came to her. She had to have an auto headlight function when it came to Caleb Stuckey.

"When did you realize?"

He didn't even bother to look guilty. "That first night we watched TV together on FaceTime."

"And you didn't tell me?" She wasn't sure whether to be embarrassed, annoyed, or turned on. In truth, she was a little of all three—okay, a little of two and a lot of the last one. "Is that why you had to change clothes while I was watching?"

"Oh, you noticed that?" he asked as he stood up. The view on her phone was jostled a bit while he set his phone down on something and then stepped back and peeled off his shirt before dropping it to the floor. "And have you thought about it since?"

Warm desire flowed through her as her nipples, the ones she'd bet good money he was staring at right now, stiffened against her sleep shirt, the soft material not providing nearly enough of the rough friction she wanted right now. Caleb's phone was angled so she only got a view of him from the waist up, but there was no mistaking what he was doing. His hands dropped lower, out of the frame, and he pushed down his pants or jeans or shorts or whatever the hell he'd been wearing on his lower half.

Hot in here? Yes, yes it was. "What are you doing?"

"Getting ready for bed." He flipped off the overhead light, leaving only the bedside lamp.

The change in lighting did nothing to hide the lines of his body or the dark hint of the best kinds of trouble in his eyes. She should end the call. Say good night. Stop this while she still had the self-control to do it.

Who are you kidding?

"Why, does it bother you?" He picked up the phone and brought it close to his face so her view was now from the shoulder up. "Is that better?"

Oh, she was way past that. Her body was primed and aching for him. "You're tormenting me on purpose."

"I'd never do that." He walked back to his bed, sitting down so he was resting against the propped-up pillows. "I'm just trying to even the score, since I've seen you without a stitch on. It seemed the gentlemanly thing to do."

As if to prove his point, he kept the phone angled so all she got was him from the muscular shoulders up, which let her take in the dark scruff covering his jaw. She didn't even have to think hard to recall the feel of it against her inner thighs.

Her core clenched, and it took everything she had not to slide her fingers underneath the elastic waistband of her panties right then. "Are you naked, Caleb?"

"I'm not telling," he said, his voice rough and ready. "This is all the view you get tonight."

"I know you're just trying to get me worked up." Which she'd passed five minutes ago and was now at the door of press-me-against-any-horizontal-surface-and-fuck-me. "It's not working."

His gaze dropped from her face to her chest and back up again. "Really?"

"It's cold in here." She twisted the side of her sleep shirt around one finger, the move tightening the material across her breasts. If he wanted to play *let's tease*, she could do that.

His jaw tightened, and he moved his hand holding the phone, allowing her to watch as his hand slid over his pecs and down lower out of view. "So the flush in your cheeks is from the chill?"

Breath quickening, she ached for him. "Absolutely."

"Zara, you're damn good at just about everything I've seen you try, but you're a very bad liar. When I get back, we're going to have to have a long talk about that."

He moved the phone again, giving her just enough of an eyeful of his chest and abs to make her sigh out loud. Damn, he was good at this—and the cocky bastard knew it. Time to give him some of his own back.

"Good luck in the game tomorrow." She traced a finger across the scooped neckline of her sleep shirt, accidentally pushing it down lower, showing off her breasts from the top swells to almost her nipples. "I've gotta go and take care of something before bed."

"Gonna tell me your plans?" he asked, his hot gaze roaming her as good as a touch.

"You're not the only tease, Caleb." She dipped her finger lower, under the soft cotton of her shirt, letting her finger graze the stiff tip of her nipple as he watched—not to give him a show but because watching his reaction to the move was a huge turn-on. "Good night."

He let out a harsh groan. "Night, Zara."

She ended the call wired, on edge, and desperate for relief. Ever so grateful that she'd already taken Anchovy for his last walk of the evening and that the big dog was asleep on his cushiony bed instead of hers for once, she headed straight for her bed. She had her fingers between her legs when the first buzz sounded on her phone. Ignoring it, she circled her clit, slow and soft, making that tight high-wire feeling last as long as she could.

The second buzz, however, pulled her straight out and she grabbed her phone, more than a little annoyed. That changed as soon as she opened her text messages. The first was a pic of Caleb from the abs down, the thick outline of his hard dick against his boxer briefs breathtakingly visible. The second photo was a side view without any underwear. While his junk was hidden by the way his hips were shifted away from the camera, she had the perfect view of his high, muscular ass in profile.

Her brain stopped functioning, but her fingers didn't. Forget drawing it out. She rubbed faster, circling her clit and dipping down between her folds to slip a finger in her slick entrance before going back up to her clit, repeating the process while she looked at the photos until her orgasm hit. She was still trying to catch her breath when she took a picture of her own and hit send before she could second-guess it.

• • •

Caleb was already in the shower, his hand around his cock, when his phone dinged. He reached out past the shower curtain and grabbed it without losing a stroke. It was a photo of Zara's slightly spread legs from just above the knees down—nothing he wouldn't see at the beach except for one thing. Her black panties were around one ankle.

The water beating against his back could have been ice chips at that moment and he wouldn't have cared, even if he'd noticed. His girl was tormenting him in the best way possible. He set his phone down outside the shower before he dropped it and planted his hand against the tile wall.

Hand gripping tighter, moving faster, he closed his eyes and pictured sliding those panties off her. He'd toss them to the side, yank her down to the edge of the bed, and feast on that perfect pussy of hers. Her hands in his hair, her hips raising off the bed to help put his mouth exactly where she wanted it. Hearing her soft pants and the low, husky pleas to lick here and suck there. Then he'd reach down to squeeze his dick as she came all over his tongue.

The fantasy played in his head, so real he could almost taste her on his lips as he jacked his cock rough and fast until he came in a rush of sensation that left him breathless with his forehead pressed against the shower wall.

Zara Ambrose was taking over his brain, his fantasies, his plans. Hell, he'd already added taking her to Chef Greg's Soul-N-the Wall someday to his list of must-dos in the next off-season. If he kept going like this, he would end up like Phillips, in a messy situation with a woman who couldn't be his.

He only had her for two more dates. That's when rule number one would kick in—no relationships.

He was starting to fucking hate rule number one.

Chapter Thirteen

Caleb had three new stitches and a beauty of a shiner thanks to a high stick in the Detroit game when he walked into Fido's Café on Forty-Third Street and Westin Avenue for date number four.

Calling it a café was a local joke. It was a dog park surrounded by benches, and some entrepreneurial food truck vendors had set up on the street beside it. Every Saturday morning, the place was packed with dogs in the fenced-off play area making furry friends and their human counterparts milling around, trying to do the same.

He scanned the massive outdoor brunch crowd for a short redhead with a giant dog, spotting Anchovy first—or was it that the Great Dane spotted him? Either way, the beast came galloping across the green space outside of the fenced-in section, pulling Zara behind him. Bracing himself, Caleb prepped for the onslaught as an older woman next to him let out a squawk of alarm and a pair of young dads yanked their toddler out of the way. Anchovy was clueless to all of it. The dog didn't stop until his paws were on Caleb's chest and the dog's wet nose practically touched his.

"Hey there, fella." He scratched Anchovy on his special spot behind his ears. "Miss me?"

It was a rhetorical question when it came to the dog, but he really wanted an answer from Zara, because he sure as hell had missed her. The air around them was electrified as he watched her, wondering if she was wearing black panties again today. Were her nipples already straining against the material of her bra? Had she woken up wet, knowing they were in a countdown to getting to see each other again? Fuck, even thinking those questions had his dick getting thick against his thigh as he adjusted his stance before he embarrassed himself.

The dog must have realized there was an undercurrent, because Anchovy went back down on four legs, then sat down on the ground.

"Oh my God," Zara gasped, taking off her sunglasses and peering up at him. "Your face."

His hand went to the bandage covering his stitches. It looked worse than it was. "It's nothing."

Raising herself up on her tiptoes, she took a closer look. "It was that asshole who got away with that high stick, wasn't it?"

He was about to answer when the meaning behind her words sank in. "You watched my game?"

"It might have been on." She took a half step away and slid her sunglasses back on. "You know how Anchovy likes to sit on the remote."

"Don't try to cover it up," he said, his ego growing twelve sizes in three seconds. "You interrupted your *Law and Order* binge to watch my game."

"Fine. I was curious," she said. "Before I met you, I'd never watched a game before."

He almost fell over. "Never?"

"I'm more of a baseball person." She fanned her face with both hands. "There's nothing like those pants."

Caleb had spent his life in locker rooms; he knew when someone was busting his chops. "I'm going to take this as a challenge to win you over to the hockey side of things."

They spent the next half hour talking hockey while Anchovy played with a bunch of other dogs in the park. She'd just finished a question about the point of icing when a guy in a T-shirt emblazoned with the Doghouse Boot Camp logo on it blasted a whistle.

"Bramble daters! Bring your good boys and girls over here—it's time for Doghouse Boot Camp."

"I'll give the Bramble app one thing, the dates are definitely not your typical dinner and a movie," Zara said, getting up from their bench and holding out her hand. "You ready for date number four?"

He took her hand, entwining his fingers with her much smaller ones as if it was the most natural thing in the world. "I don't know about Anchovy, but I am."

• • •

Zara fought to hold in her laugh as Anchovy broke down Caleb one treat at a time.

Hands on his hips, ultraserious expression on his face, Caleb told the dog to sit. Anchovy just stared at him and wagged his tail.

Caleb nudged the stubborn dog's hind end. "Sit."

Her devious little beast didn't sit. Instead, he did that whole puppy-dog-eye thing, and the big tough hockey player folded like a half-cooked pancake and gave him the treat anyway.

"You can't do that," she said, doing her best to sound serious because she was right. "He'll never learn."

"It won't hurt anything," Caleb said as he fed the dog another biscuit.

Zara scoffed. "You saw how people scattered when he came sprinting over to you—he scared them half to death. He needs to learn some manners."

"He's got some, it's just that they're his own." Caleb reached out and patted the dog on the head.

Anchovy, traitor that he was, immediately sat down, gazing up adoringly at them both. What in the world was she going to do with them? They were both nothing but trouble. Of course, she only had Caleb for one more date. The fizzy little champagne bubbles popped one after another, leaving her deflated when she should have been elated.

She was nearly to her goal of completing five dates to help her dad get his SAG card (he was already filling out his paperwork) and to get her as Gemma's plus-one to the Friends of the Library charity ball. Plus, she had the added bonus of her vagina cobwebs being utterly and thoroughly cleaned out—which sounded gross when she thought it out loud in her head that way, but what the hell, it was true.

Caleb continued. "I just know that some people—and dogs—learn a little differently than others."

Her chest tightened as she pictured him alone in front of that classroom. If she had access to a time machine, she would love to go smack that teacher up side the head. "So what was your mom's reaction to that teacher who was such an ass?"

"She told me to buckle down, try my best." He squatted next to Anchovy, keeping all his attention on the dog, as if looking at her and saying the words was too much. "That's Coach Britany's answer to just about everything—figure out your goal and work harder. The thing was that I hadn't been slacking. It's a processing thing, not a lazy thing. I don't know that she understands that even today."

Emotion clogged her throat and her chest burned as she took the three steps over to him. For once, she towered over him, but she'd never felt more helpless. The lasting hurt of old wounds was something she knew all too well, and if she understood how to heal them, she would have done so by now. But she didn't. So she did the one thing she could to try to help—she ignored the little voice in her head warning her that she was on the edge of breaking the no-relationship rule and reached out to him. She combed her fingers through his thick hair, pulling his head close so he leaned it against her waist. They stood like that, her, Caleb, and Anchovy, an unbreakable triad if just for that minute, before breaking apart.

"Our parents make us who we are *and* they make us crazy," she said, wishing there was more she could do.

"Yeah," Caleb said, standing up and flashing a grin at her that almost reached his eyes. "We're completely well adjusted."

Okay, she could play along. "Which is why your mom picked out your date and my best friend blackmailed me into coming."

"Do you regret it?" he asked, dropping the act, his gaze searching her face.

They were on some sort of edge here; one move either way and they'd go straight over. He wasn't hers to fall for, though. They were total opposites in more than just mashed potatoes or dog training philosophies. They were opposites where it counted. He went by his gut and trusted his instincts. She couldn't help but admire that faith in the universe he seemed to have, but that wasn't her. It never would be. They couldn't work, and she needed to remember that. They both did.

"No. It's been fun," she said, putting enough cheer in her tone that it almost sounded genuine. "Now we have to get to teaching Anchovy the basics of rolling over."

She went straight to the handout the trainer had given them with step-by-step directions. Caleb, however, dropped into a plank position on the grass next to Anchovy. The dog, no doubt sensing fun was afoot, immediately did his best to copy the move. Then Caleb rolled over and the dog did the same.

"Sometimes you have to take a chance on something fun," he said. "It almost always works out."

And as they got back to getting Anchovy to work for his treat biscuits, she couldn't shake the idea that he might be right. How many times had she heard the same advice from Gemma or her dad? Maybe this time, taking a chance on something fun was just what her rigid, workaholic self needed—if only for the date and a half of time that was left with Caleb. As long as she kept remembering that, she'd be okay after it was all over.

· · ·

Caleb spent the next forty-five minutes with Zara trying to teach Anchovy some manners. It went about as well as could be expected for a dog who thought he was a human and didn't need any learning. The best part was watching him think around the trainer's tricks and doing just what needed to be done long enough to get a biscuit and a pet before going back to trying to start a mutiny among the other dogs to get back to the play park. By the time the session was up, even the trainer was laughing as Anchovy led the rest of the dogs in a game of chase.

"I definitely went wrong somewhere," she said, shaking her head.

"No way, that dog is golden." And so was this opportunity. This time he took Zara's hand as they walked back toward the bench near the play park, but instead of stopping there, he led her behind a tree next to it. Hands on either side of her hips, he bent down to kiss her, but she stopped him with the palm of her hand against his chest.

"Hold on." She stepped up onto a gnarled exposed root that gave her a few more inches off the ground. "Now you need to make up for making me wait so long to properly welcome you home."

She didn't have to tell him twice—especially not with that look on her face. Closing the distance between them, he dipped his head down and captured her mouth in a kiss that was the best he could do considering they were both dressed and in public. Her lips parted, and he slipped his tongue inside, tasting her, teasing her until she was pressed against him. It wasn't that the rest of the park disappeared, it was that it didn't matter anymore. He had Zara and she was making those sweet, needy sounds, and he could give her exactly what she wanted.

But not here.

He couldn't afford the bad headline of *Hockey Player Arrested For Public Indecency*, but more importantly, she didn't deserve to be at the center of all that. It took just about every last ounce of his self-control, but he pulled back from the edge. They were both sucking in deep breaths as they disentangled from each other.

"Welcome home," she said, her voice breathy.

Unable to stop himself from touching her, he brushed a strand of bright-red hair behind her ear. "Glad to be back."

Holding hands again, they walked back around the tree to the bench. Judging by the looks the other dog owners gave them, they hadn't been as discreet as he'd been hoping. Some people were amused, others openly curious, and a handful were staring hard, looking at him as if they knew him but just couldn't place how. All the attention made the back of his head itch and his lungs tighten.

All of a sudden, Zara's grip on his hand tightened and he looked down. Her face was serene, the sun highlighting the sixty billion freckles covering her face, but the tight lines of her mouth told him she'd noticed.

"So, what's the post-date video plan for this one?" she asked as they sat down on the bench with a perfect view of Anchovy playing with another dog. "Do you know?"

The question yanked him out of the panic zone, and he tapped his fingertip against his thigh three times, the old routine settling him.

"The instructions Bramble sent the team PR guru about this date was that we were supposed to do a casual video of ourselves, talking about the process and what we were hoping to get out of date five and beyond."

The last word hung in the air between them, a finish line he really didn't want to cross anymore.

"I guess it would be kinda mean to let them in on our rule number one of no actual relationship after all this," she said. "They really do have something cool here. I might try it again after the ball next week. Gemma is never going to let me hear the end of that, though, after she and a regrettable amount of tequila got me here in the first place."

If any part of him had been wondering—and to be truthful, all of him had—about what was beyond date five for them, that pretty much answered it. There would be no more adjusting the rules—and he fucking hated it.

Chapter Fourteen

Oh yeah, going on camera was exactly what Zara wanted right now. She couldn't wait to see if she could fake this smile long enough to get through a video where she had to listen to Caleb say all the things she wished were true.

"So how are we going to do this?" she asked, her spine stiff and her shoulders tight with tension.

"Why don't you start." He scooted down a bit on the bench, turning so he faced her as he held up his phone. "I'll ask the questions."

Deep breaths. *It's just for fun. It doesn't mean a thing, even if it's starting to feel like it.*

"Perfect." Her jaw was going to ache later from clamping it together like this. "I'm ready whenever you are."

"So what were your thoughts before that first date?"

Oh man, that seemed like a billion years ago and yesterday all at the same time. It had been hot, and she'd been annoyed, and there was that couple from out of town.

"That the whole thing would be a disaster." She chuckled remembering how she'd tried to speed-walk past the lollygaggers and had ended up eating the sidewalk. At the time, not funny. Now? Kinda funny. "I got tangled up in a pair of tourists on my way to the restaurant and I didn't want to be on the date in the first place."

He turned the phone around so the camera faced him, then pulled a funny face. "Sounds promising."

"Oh yeah, very." Especially considering she'd looked a total mess and had walked into the café and spotted him in all of his sexy pro-athlete glory. "Anyway, so I got there and you're, like, a billion miles tall and hot, and I figured this was going to be a giant waste of my time."

He lowered the phone enough that she could see the self-satisfied smirk on his face. "So you think I'm hot, huh?"

"That's what you're going to get stuck on?" She rolled her eyes. Men. "That part?" She swiped the phone away from him while he was trying to come up with an answer for that. "Okay, same question. What were your expectations for date one?"

"Someone taller," he teased.

Giggling, she flipped him off from behind the camera.

The smart-ass grin on his face faltered as he leaned forward into the camera, resting his elbows on his hard thighs. "And definitely not someone who was as funny as she was smart and gorgeous. With my mom picking my date, I was expecting someone who was type-A, a hockey fanatic, and probably could beat me in the forty-yard dash."

"Would that have been bad?"

"No." He looked right at her then, not at the phone's camera lens but at her. "But it wouldn't have been you."

Hello, heart, there is no reason to go into overdrive right now. Her heart didn't listen. Instead, it pounded a hectic beat against her ribs while she tried to figure out what to say to that.

No doubt taking advantage of the moment, he snagged his

phone back. "Then, we went on date two, where I found out you were just as competitive as the initial date I'd expected."

Okay, neutral ground. She could talk about that. "That obstacle course was fun."

"You know," he said, his focus going from the screen to her, his dark eyes serious. "That's when I knew you were going to always keep me on my toes, never knowing exactly what to expect."

It wasn't fair that he kept doing that, putting her at ease and then ramping things up again with words he didn't mean but she so wanted to hear. How had that happened? How had she gotten lost in a fantasy of fake dates? This was why she'd made the rules, kept mostly to her usual routine, and refused to consider the possibilities. The last thing she needed was another man in her life who acted like he could be Prince Charming only to leave time after time.

Needing desperately to regain a foothold, she reclaimed the phone, surprised her hand didn't shake when she did so.

"I wouldn't have guessed judging by how well you did on our cooking date that you didn't spend much time in the kitchen," she said.

Reaching out, he toyed with the string hanging from the rip in her jeans just above her knee, his thumb occasionally brushing the bare patch of her skin. "When it comes to getting to hang out with you, I'm pretty much willing to try anything."

"And you loved the food." The words came out in a rush as she tried not to melt under the most minimal of touches.

"Somehow I missed out on keeping any of the leftovers, though." He looked up at her, everything about him taking on an air of dangerous promise and sensual teasing. "I have no idea how that happened. Do you?"

The images came one after another. Being naked above him. The scratch of his beard against her thighs. Coming so hard she'd nearly collapsed on top of him.

"One of the great mysteries of life," she managed to squeak out before taking a deep breath and releasing it in an attempt to focus on the video at hand and not what she wanted his hands to do. "And now we just finished with date number four: trying to teach my dog some much-needed manners."

"Is the date over already?" He grinned, obviously aware of exactly what he'd done to her with that comment. "There should be more later. It's a gorgeous day. I know Anchovy would approve." He gave a whistle, and the dog came rushing over.

In the chaos of Anchovy getting onto the bench with them, finding a way to squeeze his big self in the small space between them, Caleb retook his phone. This time, though, instead of staying behind the lens, he stayed in the frame with her and Anchovy.

"Now this is a good-looking picture," Caleb said. "Thanks to you two."

As if he understood a single word, Anchovy let out a little doggie sigh of happiness and laid his fuzzy chin down on Caleb's shoulder. Was it possible to be jealous of her own dog? Because at that moment she was.

"So, that's it for us," Caleb said, addressing the people who'd be watching the video. "Four Bramble dates down with the amazing woman my mom picked out and with only one more to go before this parental-guidance experiment ends. Be sure to catch up with us after date number five."

He gave a little wave, but Zara just didn't have it in her to do the same. The realization hit her square in the heart that walking away from Caleb after one last date was going to hurt like a bitch.

The question was, could she take the pain—because even though it was all but guaranteed, she couldn't help but hope it just might work out.

. . .

An hour later, they'd brought Anchovy back to Zara's apartment along with a takeout bag's worth of fragrant Thai food from the place on the corner. Caleb followed her inside, using his elbow to shut the door behind him. Per usual, her space was clean and everything was in its place.

Almost a dozen miniature scenes were on her long worktable. He set the food down on her kitchen island and went over. They were as detailed and perfect as her work displayed at Hot Thang Review, but they were more fantasy than family, with tiny elephants and kittens climbing out of a bag. It was hard to look at them and not be in awe of how talented she was.

"You didn't have to buy dinner." Zara took out a couple of plates from the cupboard and silverware from a drawer. "The app was pretty clear about the date parameters, and you have officially completed them for date number four."

"True, but we were both hungry, and there's no harm in a good meal."

She raised an eyebrow in question as she added a generous amount of the stir-fried rice noodles to each plate.

"No one can resist pouring their stories out over good food. It's the key to good team bonding." He crossed over into the kitchen area. "Trust me, there's a reason why Peppers has us go out for team meals."

It was always fun to watch the rookies try not to geek out at being at a table with their heroes—especially since not that long ago, every veteran at the table had been a wide-eyed rookie. The longer the season went on, the more relaxed the meals got, until it was like eating with family.

"In that case," Zara said, handing him a plate, "you can

go first."

"Not yet. First we demolish all this amazing food."

And that's what they did. They sat on the windowsill leading out to her tiny balcony that was really more of a glorified fire escape and ate pad Thai, sitting so close together that their knees touched as they held their plates on their laps. As it was warm for late September, they basked in the sun, ate, and laughed at Anchovy's attempts to garner enough pity to get him a bowl of noodles.

He laid his fork down on his plate and let out a satisfied sigh. "I'm gonna have to move to your neighborhood just so I can be closer to that takeout."

Zara chuckled as she wound the last of her noodles around her fork. "I'm sure your team nutritionist would approve."

"The bigger problem would be our trainer, Smitty. He's a hard-ass." And whatever plan he came up with always worked. All he had to do was take a look at Petrov's faster-than-expected comeback to understand that.

"But you still love playing hockey."

It wasn't a question. It didn't need to be. "For as long as I can do it."

"And after?" She took his plate, stacked it on top of hers, and set them both down on the little table near the open window they'd crawled out of. "Or is that verboten to talk about?"

"Some guys are superstitious about it, but I'm not. It'll happen; I'd rather prepare for it. There are benefits to being Britany Stuckey's son, and that's one of them."

"You want to go into coaching?" she asked, making the logical deduction.

"Hell no." Even the idea of it made his entire chest seize up. "My plan, which I've had since high school, is to go into sports management. Being raised by a woman—who I love—

but who is a giant pain in the ass always driving each of us kids to be more, do more, get better grades, try for harder classes, leave it all out on the ice, doesn't really give you room to take things as they come—especially not if half your class thought the only thing getting you from one grade level to the next was your hockey skill."

She got that snarly look to her again, one that, if he was facing off against her on the ice, would have him thinking twice before he dropped the gloves. "What a bunch of jerks."

"We were kids." He shrugged, more interested in the patch of skin above her knee that was visible thanks to the very convenient hole in her jeans than in talking about the bad old days. "We were dumb."

"You're a helluva lot nicer about it than I would be."

He took a long pull from his beer, trying to figure out how to put it into words that didn't make him sound like a total whiner. "That's only because the worst part wasn't the other kids, it was coming home with that report card, knowing I was going to disappoint the woman who sacrificed so much to get food on our tables and keep the rent paid and had the drive to become the only female boys' hockey coach in the state and one of the few in the nation."

"You're right." Zara's shoulders slumped, and she seemed to sink into herself. "I have no idea what that's like, not with my dad."

"You haven't told me the story. Honestly, he comes off as a pretty nice guy." In the few times he'd met her dad, Jasper had seemed like a guy who loved his daughter, wanted the best for her, and had a pretty good sense of humor.

"He does—and he is," she said, a bone-deep weariness seeping into her thousand-mile gaze. "Everyone who meets him loves him, and for good reason. You need a shirt? He'll take the one off his back to give to you. Need a little bit of cash to make it through until payday? He'll cover you without a second thought. The problem was that growing up, he did that without regard to whether we had enough in the bank for rent or utilities or groceries. It was kind of like being out on the ocean in a dinghy, never knowing when a giant wave was going to crash down on you and take you under."

What did he say to that? How did he make up for a dad who seemed to prioritize his own daughter below the rest of the neighborhood? The reality was that no matter how much he wanted to, he couldn't. All he could do was pull her close, picking her up enough to slide her onto his lap so she could rest her head against his chest.

"So I'm warning you now that I'm a fuckup," he said, letting the words come out before he could think better of it. "The viral video that started this whole thing? I almost got one of my teammates traded because of it."

She looked up at him, the sweet understanding on her face making his chest tight. "I'm not following."

"The front office figured the video was proof that we weren't a cohesive team. Trading someone made sense to them, and Petrov wasn't supposed to make it back to the lineup for another few months. Any team that got him would be excited enough to sacrifice a few draft picks because once he got healthy, he'd be an animal on the ice." Guilt twisted his gut. "The thing is, there wasn't another team in the league that Petrov wanted to play for like he wanted to play for the Ice Knights."

"Then you ended up on Bramble to fix it, probably without ever telling him." She straightened, twisting in his lap so her face was only inches from his, her look fierce. "That's not being a fuckup; that's accepting responsibility and making amends. That's a helluva lot better of a reason than why I ended up on the app and my whole clear the cobwebs line." She groaned and closed her eyes, her cheeks turning pink. "I'm gonna kill Gemma one of these days for letting me hit send on that. There is such a thing as the girl code. Then she taunts me with that stupid bet."

"What bet?"

Her pink cheeks turned a deep red. "The one where I bet her I would not have sex with you. But the thing is…" She braced her hands on his shoulders and did a spin move on his lap so she was straddling him. "I think I need to take your advice from earlier."

His hands automatically went to her hips, pulling her hard against him. "What's that?"

She leaned forward, teasing him with her nearness. "To try something just for fun."

A million things went through his mind, but thank God his body took over, and he threaded his fingers through her hair, cupping the back of her head, and brought her in for a kiss because for once she was going to let go and live in the now.

Chapter Fifteen

Zara knew she was probably making a mistake, but kissing Caleb, feeling him against her, rocking her core against him, all of it felt too good for her to change her mind now even if she'd wanted to—and she very much did not. This was what she'd been thinking about since he'd shown up at the park for their date today. She'd taken one look at him in his perfect-fitting jeans and T-shirt that stretched snugly over his muscular chest and her breath had caught. Then, they'd had dinner and her heart had shuffled and skipped. And when he'd opened up to her, trusted her? That was it. She was a goner. There was no turning back. She might only have him until the end of their next date, but she was going to fall into the moment and for once in her life let go of what was next.

Hands in his hair and her mouth on his in a kiss that had her reaching for more already, she moved against him, hating the layers of clothing between them. It had been bad enough the other night when only he'd been dressed. Having both of them like this was unbearable.

Planting her hands on his chest, she pushed herself back,

not stopping until her feet were on the floor. "We have to go inside or Mrs. Cooper across the way will call the cops. I'm surprised she hasn't already."

The woman was infamous on the block for calling Harbor City's finest at even the hint of a disturbance. Two naked people going at it on a balcony would definitely end up in a call from Mrs. Cooper.

Instead of letting her go, Caleb slipped his hands under the hem of her shirt. "If we were at my house in Waterbury, there's not a neighbor who could see us."

She grabbed his wrist, halting his progress before she lost all sense. "Well, unless you want to wait until we're across the harbor to get me naked again, then I suggest we go inside right now."

"Naked again" seemed to be the magic words.

His eyes darkened with desire. "Excellent plan."

Caleb went in first, and when she climbed over the window, extending her leg as far as she could so she almost touched the floor in her living room, he scooped her up and carried her across the room. Anchovy, thinking it was a game, started hop-walking around them, letting out a playful bark as they made their way to her bedroom. Once inside the area behind the room divider bookshelves, Caleb turned a circle.

"No door?" he asked.

"It's a studio," she said, kissing her way up the side of his neck. "There are no doors."

Caleb looked over at Anchovy. "What are we going to do about him?"

"Put me down for a second."

Caleb looked like he was about to argue, but smart man that he was, he thought better of trying to get his two cents in. The second she was standing, she waved Anchovy to the other side of the bookshelves, then pulled a baby gate from behind her dresser and set it up so it was leaning against the shelves in front of the opening that served as her bedroom door.

Caleb took one look at the gate leaning against the shelves, then glanced over at Anchovy, who could easily step over it or knock it down.

"He won't do it," she said. "He's scared of the gate."

As if to prove her point, the dog lowered his ears, dropped his tail in dejection, and let out a sad whine before turning around and heading over to his bed. Turning, she walked back to Caleb, wanting to touch him everywhere at once, as if giving herself permission to be with him had unleashed a floodgate of want.

However, he kept looking toward the gate. "Are you sure that'll work?"

"Afraid Anchovy will come get you in a delicate moment?" It wouldn't be the first time that had happened. There was a reason, after all, that she'd developed the gate trick.

Any thought of anyone else scattered when Caleb picked her up and carried her over to the bed, laying her down on it. "Zara, honey, there's *nothing* delicate about me."

She lay down on the bed, turning on her side to face him and propping up her head on her hand. "Why don't you show me? You've been teasing long enough."

He reached behind his head, pulling his T-shirt off in one fluid motion. Running his hands down his chest, over his washboard abs, and down to the button of his jeans, he never looked away from her.

"Should I keep going?"

The idea of him stopping now was like being told the world's entire chocolate supply had vanished. "Yes please."

"So polite for someone who wants to see me naked so badly." He flipped off his shoes and unbuttoned his jeans.

The work his poor zipper was doing at that moment bordered on heroic—or at least it would if she hadn't wanted it to fail. She sat up, no longer able to even pretend at nonchalance when her entire body was practically vibrating with lust. She wet her lips with her tongue and watched as he tugged that zipper down. Slowly. She couldn't look away, couldn't blink; the thought of missing even a second had her wound up tight, her hands clutching at her bedspread so she wouldn't touch herself—at least not yet.

And just when she thought she was going to make it, he dropped his hand away from his now-open zipper and walked toward her, his strides solid and bold. He stopped just out of reach.

She looked up at him, all solid muscle and cocksure attitude. "You are not nice."

"Never said I was." He didn't even crack a smile. The man was as close to the edge of his self-control as she was. "If you want to keep going, you have to take them off."

"Why?"

"Because this isn't a one-person show." He cupped her chin, the pad of his thumb grazing her bottom lip, dipping inside her mouth, and retreating. "Not for me. Not for you." He leaned down, delivering a brief, hard kiss before straightening back up. "We're in this together."

Heart pounding loud enough that she was surprised he couldn't hear it, she reached out, hooked her fingers in the waistband of his jeans and boxer briefs, and pulled them down. Damn, he was glorious. There was nothing miniaturized about him. Hard and smooth, his cock was like the rest of him, almost too much and just the right amount at the same time.

She wrapped her hand around his width, stroking up and down his length, testing the pace and her grip. When she sped up just a bit, she was rewarded with a hiss of pleasure from him and a few drops of pre-cum on his tip. Using her thumb, she smoothed it around, then dipped her head and took him in her mouth.

"Zara, holy shit, that feels amazing."

She reached down, lower, cupping his balls as she took him in deep and shallow over and over again, loving the feel of him, until he stepped back.

"I'd like to take my time with you tonight, but I can't promise that this first time."

She swallowed. Hard. "First?"

"If you think we're stopping with one, then you have the wrong guy, because I'm going to fuck you until you are wrung out, satisfied, and too dick drunk to ask for one more orgasm."

"I've heard promises before." She was going for unimpressed, but it came out breathy and hungry even to her own ears.

"Well, I deliver," he said, his voice low and the best kind of dangerous. "Now get those clothes off."

• • •

Caleb was going to die from lack of oxygen going to his brain, right here in the next thirty seconds. He was okay with that as long as he got to touch her first.

That was as close as he could come to processing the feeling of watching Zara strip. That night when he'd fallen asleep on her couch? That had been a rush of lust so strong it had swept both of them along. Tonight couldn't be like that. It needed to be deliberate. He wasn't joking when he'd said this was about them. He'd meant every word.

Her chin high, her eyes daring him, she raised the hem of her T-shirt, pulling it over her head. All the air he didn't realize he still had in his lungs came out in a whoosh. Reaching behind her, she unsnapped her bra, letting it fall away and giving him a view of her full tits, dotted with freckles, tipped with stiff nipples he couldn't wait to touch. Next came her jeans. She stood up and made fast work of those, kicking them off so they went sailing across the room, landing with a soft *thump* near her closet. Still watching him, a coy smile playing at her lips because she knew exactly what she was doing to him, she slid her thumbs under the waistband of her black panties and started to lower them.

"Wait," he said, blood pounding in his ears.

She cocked her head to the side but paused.

"I've been thinking about this since you sent that picture."

Smoothing her hands over the black lace, she let her touch linger against her hips. "You liked that one?"

He moved behind her, pressing close so that his cock was against the small of her back. "You know the answer to that."

Reaching around, he cupped her tits, taking her nipples between his fingers and rolling them, tugging them. As he continued his explorations, moving from her tits, to the small of her waist, to the flare of her hips, he listened for the changes in her response, circling back to repeat the things that had her mewling with pleasure and arching into his touch. Listening to her, feeling her respond, sent a rush through him that turned his dick to iron. It was good, so fucking good, but it wasn't enough.

Without letting go, he nudged her toward the extended edge of her platform bed that stuck out a few inches past her mattress. "Step up."

Her cheeks were flush and her eyes hazy when she shot him a questioning look over her shoulder, but she did it. The move brought her up half a foot, bringing their bodies more in line. He wrapped an arm around her waist, tugging her back until she was firm against him, his dick nestled against the firm curve of her ass.

Dipping his head so his lips were against the sensitive spot behind her ear, he kissed her. "I've got you."

Then he slid his fingers under the lace of her panties. Her breath hitched when he parted her tight curls and didn't start again until he brushed over the hard tip of her clit.

"You're so wet for me." He kept his voice low, each word coming out ragged because he was a man on the verge of losing it. But he wouldn't—couldn't—yet. "Is this what you like, me touching you like this?"

"So good." She laid her head back against him and widened her stance.

He glided his fingers lower, exploring her soft folds and noting when she tensed, when she went slack, and when she let out a strained "fuck yes." Tuning in to her was like the best part of being out on the ice before a game—it was all possibility and anticipation. Sinking a finger inside her slick entrance, he curled it forward, pressing and rubbing against the bundle of nerves there while he used his thumb to circle and press against her clit.

"Caleb." Her hands reached back, grabbing his thighs. "Don't stop."

"I won't," he promised.

Her breath came in quicker bursts as her body grew tense against him. She was there, close, her hips thrusting forward to meet his fingers. But on the next breath, things changed. It wasn't a lot: it was a subtle relaxing in her shoulders, a deepening of her breath. Determined not to let this moment go without satisfying her, he adjusted his arm—still keeping her safe from falling but now he could cup her tits, which was exactly what he did.

• • •

Zara ached; her entire body was primed, but it felt like there was an entire ocean of space between her and her orgasm and with every breath she was inching further and further back.

And just when she was about to give up, accept the other night as a fluke, Caleb moved just enough to cup her breast, tugging her nipple taut as he kissed his way down the back of her neck.

It was like he was everywhere at once, hitting multiple pleasure points and drowning out the constant hum of you're-not-gonna-get-there that was always just under the surface. Sensations rocketed through her, and she dug her fingers into the unyielding muscles of his thighs and rocked against the hard length of him pressing against her ass.

The tight ball of pure electricity in her belly started small, growing with each brush of his thumb on her clit, each in-and-out plunge of his fingers inside her, each nip of his teeth against that spot where her shoulder met her neck, and each pleasurable roll of her nipple between his fingers. It was nearly too much for her body to take at one time, but she gave in to it, let it wash over her. She couldn't plan her next move, couldn't wonder about the sounds she was making, couldn't think about the grocery list—the way he was touching her overwhelmed all of that. Vibrations of pure pleasure racked her body as she rode his fingers higher and higher until the tide rushed back and her orgasm exploded inside her in a sizzling burst of energy that made her cry out.

"That was the hottest thing I've ever seen in my life," he said, his breath coming almost as hard as her own.

Her pulse pounded in her ears, and part of her just wanted to collapse onto the bed, but tonight was far from over. "Thank you."

"For what?"

She didn't answer. How in the hell was she supposed to put into words what it was like to come back from resignation that her lot in life was to be non-solo-orgasm free? Once was a fluke. Twice had promise. If it happened again, that was a pattern, and she was fucking here for that—but not alone.

Turning on the edge of the platform to face Caleb, she cupped his face in her hands, kissing him, demanding—needing—more. Breaking the kiss, she glided her hands over his body, loving the way his flat nipples puckered at her touch, the hiss of a groan when she wrapped her hand around his cock again.

"Please tell me you have a condom."

"You're not the only planner," he said with a grin. "I brought several."

Without another word, he stepped back, grabbed his jeans from the floor, took out a three-pack from his pocket, and tossed them on the bed. "Lose the panties."

Maybe it was an orgasm aftershock, maybe it was just the way he'd said that, but her body reacted with a tightening in her belly and a warm flood of desire through her.

He stalked toward her, muscles undulating and intensity coming off him in waves. "I've spent almost every moment when I wasn't on skates thinking about this. I know exactly what I want to do next."

"Do tell." She had no idea how she'd managed to string two words together when he was looking at her like that, but she did it.

He stopped, a wicked grin not doing a damn thing to lessen the sexual ferocity surrounding him. "Showing you is better." He wrapped one hand around his cock. "Take off your panties and lay down on your back."

There was something in the demanding way he said it with that almost growl that sent a shiver of pleasure up her spine. She got rid of her panties and lay back, legs spread, pussy aching to be touched again already. He didn't move, didn't rush to put on the condom and fuck her senseless. Instead, he stayed where he was, watching as if he had to memorize every bit of her.

"Are you just going to look?" she asked, the first shades

of uncertainty raising the doubts and worries in her mind.

He moved his hand in a slow stroke up and down his length. "Show me how you touch yourself."

She hesitated, but only for the briefest of seconds before something in the way he looked at her settled her mind, and she reached for her clit and rubbed slow circles around it before slipping down and sinking two fingers inside. He let out a harsh breath, his face hard as he watched, his hand still moving at that slow pace up and down his cock. Then, just when she thought he was only going to watch her play with herself, he closed the distance between them, dropping to his knees between her splayed legs.

"Don't stop," he said, his voice low and reverent. "I want to lick you while you do that. Is that okay?"

She nodded, and the second his tongue touched her while she was rubbing her clit, her toes curled. Then he started to kiss and lick her in a solid, slow rhythm, and she knew he was jacking his cock while eating her, and her thighs started to vibrate.

"Fuck, you taste so good," he said, his words teasing her sensitive flesh.

He reached up with his free hand, spreading her wide, opening her up to him as she strained closer and closer to the edge again. Her fingers flying on her clit, his tongue going at a more leisurely pace while the movement of him rocking against her while he stroked himself pushed her right over into the abyss, and she came, her hips rocketing off the bed as her entire body went rigid with pleasure.

• • •

Her taste still on his lips, Caleb stood up, looking down at Zara as she came back to herself. The flushed tint of her skin almost camouflaged the riot of freckles covering her body.

They were everywhere, from her collarbone to her kneecaps, and he couldn't wait to kiss each one as he explored her body, but not yet. Right now his cock ached from need and his balls were already drawn up tight.

Zara watched him through hooded eyes, a satisfied smile playing on her lips, as he tore open one of the condoms and rolled it on.

"Stay right where you are." He came down between her legs, lining himself up with her core.

"So bossy," she said, but there wasn't any censure in her blissed-out tone. "I thought that was my role."

"If I'm gonna make it until I get inside you, it's gotta be mine." He slid in her, just the head, and closed his eyes. Even this was good enough to make him suck in a breath through his clenched teeth. "You have me ready to tip over."

She lifted her hips, changing the angle and taking him deeper. "Then don't wait."

Fuck. How in the hell had he gotten this lucky? It was almost too much to process, which made it a damn good thing he didn't need his brain right now. This thing between them, this pull, he didn't understand, it was all heart and instinct and knowing this was right. Thrusting forward, he went as deep as he could before pulling back and doing it all again and again. Sweat beaded at the base of his neck as he fought to hold out, to make this last. That wasn't going to happen, though—it was too good, and he was too close already before he'd even gotten fully inside her. His balls tingled as he buried himself to the hilt one more time and came so hard his vision blacked out.

When he could see again, it was to see her smiling underneath him, and something shifted in his chest. He hadn't realized it until this moment, but he'd been waiting for Zara Ambrose. No-relationship rule or not, he couldn't lose her now.

Chapter Sixteen

A few days later, Caleb pulled to a stop outside of a house in Waterbury that looked like one of those that Zara usually drove by and wondered how long it took to vacuum the entire place. It was two stories with a three-car garage and a circular driveway protected by a gate that needed a code. She inhaled a deep breath and let it out slowly.

Why had she agreed to go to an Ice Knights team barbecue at Cole Phillips's house? It wasn't like they were in a relationship. She didn't *need* to meet his friends, but it had seemed like a good idea when he'd shown up at her place this morning with a spur-of-the-moment invitation.

Now? Her stomach flopped around inside her like a fish out of water. Everyone at the barbecue would tower over her, even though she'd put on her I-am-a-badass super-high heels today. The athletes and their model girlfriends would take one look at her with her bright-red hair, gargantuan number of freckles, and clearance-rack clothes before dismissing her.

She was gonna have a panic attack right here in Caleb's truck as he parked next to a sports car glossed to a high sheen.

"This isn't a date, right?" she asked for the billionth time since he made her come again this morning and she was so high on happy hormones that she agreed to come. "So if your friends hate me, it doesn't matter."

"No, it's not an official date; it's a hangout. The Bramble people don't need to know a thing about it," Caleb said. "And if my friends hate you, we're just gonna throw them in the pool."

"There's a pool?" *Dumb question, girl. It's a McMansion behind a security gate. Of course there is a pool.*

He squeezed her hand with his much bigger one. "They're good guys; they're gonna love you."

Nerves still making her stomach burble, she arranged her face into what she hoped was a not-a-complete-weirdo smile and got out of the truck. Caleb knocked on the front door but didn't wait for an answer before walking inside. They headed through the house with its rich mahogany hardwood floors and modern furniture that looked like it came out of a spread in *Interior Design* magazine and toward the kitchen, where all the noise seemed to be coming from.

"Is your place like this?" Because compared to her studio apartment, this was Texas, and she wasn't sure how to deal with that difference.

Of course, you don't have to worry about it, since you're not dating him for real. She mentally smacked herself for that unnecessary bit of reality. The voice in her head could be a real asshole sometimes.

"It's not as clean. Phillips is a neat freak," Caleb said, stopping in the hall before they turned into the kitchen. "You'll have to come over this week. Maybe after the next home game?"

She looked up at the high ceilings and around at the hallway wide enough for one of those kid-driven cars. "I'd be afraid of getting lost in all this space."

"Just for you, I'll block off the west wing and east tower," he said, pulling her closer.

"You're such a smart-ass." She punctuated the declaration by lifting herself up onto her tiptoes and kissing him before he could make another rejoinder.

It worked. He dropped one hand to her hips, pulling her close and deepening the kiss. She was just wrapping her arms around his neck when someone cleared his throat behind them.

Because of course—*of course*—she'd meet someone after he walked in on her making out with her not-date the first time she was invited inside. *Way to make a great first impression.* She turned around, but Caleb didn't didn't remove his reassuring touch.

"About time you showed up, Stuckey," the guy said. "Tell me you brought the brats."

Caleb lifted the bag in his hand that wasn't still planted firmly on her hip. "Ta-da."

"Thank God." He snagged the bag. "I get one of these cheat days a month, and I'm making it count."

"Zara Ambrose, meet Cole Phillips, who, despite his obsession with dusting and insistence that everyone use a coaster, is actually a pretty chill dude," Caleb said. "Phillips, this is Zara. She is a massively talented miniatures artisan and you don't stand a chance with her because she has a Great Dane."

Cole grimaced. "Oh God, the only thing worse than dogs is kids. Sorry, I'm sure your dog is the special one that doesn't shed or lick things."

"Oh no, Anchovy does all of that, plus he steals and farts." She cringed as soon as the words were out of her mouth.

Cole, who looked like he worked as a model during the off-season, just stared blankly at her for a second. Yes, there she was, continuing to make the world's worst first impression.

Then, when she was ready to chop through the hardwood floor to make her own hole to crawl into, Cole started laughing, and she let out the breath she hadn't realized she was holding.

"You are always welcome. Your dog, not so much," Cole said. "Come on out by the pool. The grill is ready to go, and Petrov and Christensen are playing some kind of ping-pong death match."

They followed Cole out onto the patio. While she'd been expecting a crush of people, there was only about a dozen. Most were Ice Knights players, including Zach Blackburn and Fallon Hartigan, who she, like most of Harbor City, had watched fall in love. She had been firmly #TeamZuck, and meeting them now was a little awkward. Okay, a lot awkward. She may have called Fallon Lady Luck, which really was better than referring to Zach by his former nickname as the most hated man in Harbor City...but still embarrassing.

Two strikes, Ambrose.

"Don't even stress about it," Fallon said when Zach and Caleb wandered off to go get cheeseburgers and beers for them all. "Meeting everyone can be weird. I met everyone at a paintball game and was so excited, I told Stuckey his own stats."

"Thanks," she said, relieved at the other woman's kindness. "That's really nice of you."

"Just don't let it get out." Fallon gave her an ornery grin, nodding toward the two guys who'd been playing ping-pong and who were now making their way over. "I have a reputation as a ballbuster to uphold."

"I'll never tell," Zara said with a laugh as the men stopped at their table and sat down with them.

"Oh, come on, you can tell me everything." One of the men stuck his hand out. "Alex Christensen. You must be Zara, the woman who has our boy all twisted up six ways from Sunday."

God, how did she explain the straightforward plan she and Caleb had come up with that had twisted into a complicated mess all of a sudden? "It's not like that."

"The Bramble dates are a PR setup? Yeah, I figured that," the other man said, lifting his chin in greeting. "Ian Petrov."

"Oh, you're Petrov," she said, excited to have a face to put with the name. "Caleb was telling me all about how they were going to trade you if he didn't do the dating thing. I'm so glad everything worked out."

The words were out of her mouth in a burst of nervous rambling, and as soon as they were, she knew she'd fucked up.

Ian leaned forward, his eyes narrowing and his shoulders tensing. "Trade me?"

Strike three, you're out, Ambrose. You have officially messed up everything within the first ten minutes of being here. Way to go.

She gulped. "I guess I forgot you didn't know that part?"

"No," Ian said in a harsh voice. "Stuckey seems to have forgotten all about telling me that very vital piece of information about my career."

Of course, Caleb walked back to their table with two plates of cheeseburgers at that moment. Zara wanted to warn him, but she didn't get a chance.

"So it seems I have you to thank for my job." But Ian didn't sound thankful—not in the least little bit—as he stood up and faced off with Caleb. "Here I'd thought I was back in the lineup because of all that hard work I'd put in at the gym and the PT regimen that left me praying for death some days. I gave up motherfucking *cookies* because I didn't want to leave anything to chance."

Fallon leaned over and whispered, "He loves cookies, like could-be-Santa-Claus loves them."

Caleb didn't seem put out by the other man's aggressive

attitude. He just sighed and rolled his eyes.

"And this is why I didn't say anything to you." Caleb laid the paper plates ladened with enough food for five on the table. "You and that big-ass chip on your shoulder because of your last name. You got your spot back all by yourself, not because of me and not because your dad's in the Hall of Fame. You put in the work; I just made sure you had the time to make it happen."

The two men were practically nose to nose, chests puffed up, both of them refusing to back down. Zara opened her mouth to say something—anything—in way of an apology for causing trouble, but Fallon reached out and covered her hand, giving her a discreet nah-don't-do-it shake of her head and mouthing the word "men" while rolling her eyes.

"I made it happen on my own," Ian said. "They aren't trading me."

"Yeah, I know. They told me last week before they gave me the A." Smiling, Caleb slapped his hand down on the other man's shoulder. "The front office wants to have your damn babies now—especially after that game against Detroit. They're looking at you like the glue this team was missing last season."

The vein in Ian's temple pulsed, and his jaw was clamped shut so tightly, she worried a dentist would need to get called in to fix his teeth, but after a few tense seconds, he relaxed. "Next time, don't think you can fly in and fix things without telling people first. You are always pulling that shit."

"You are," Phillips said, sitting down at the table as if it hadn't just been World War III. "Even with that stupid video, you took the heat on your own. You're not alone out there, you know. We can help you, too."

"Jesus," Zach grumbled, popping open two beers and handing one to Fallon. "Are you gonna sit here and talk about your feelings the whole afternoon? Because you are ruining my appetite."

"Always the charmer," Fallon said, shaking her head.

He winked at his girlfriend. "Only for you."

All the tension in the air around them disappeared as Zach and Fallon started eating their cheeseburgers as if Ian and Caleb hadn't just almost come to blows. Everyone else seemed to treat the moment that way, too, walking off to grab a beer or a burger. Finally, Caleb sat down and picked up a burger from one of the overloaded plates, then pushed the plate to her.

"Sorry about that," she said, wondering how in the world she was going to make it up to him. "I forgot that he didn't know."

"I should have told him, let him in from the beginning." Caleb shrugged and took a bite. "I guess I'm more like my mom than I realized. She's always pulling this crap where she thinks she knows what's best for someone and just does it without even asking first."

"Kinda like suggesting the Bramble stunt to Lucy?" Fallon asked.

Zara's chin almost hit the table. Caleb must have been just as shocked because for once, he didn't have a response. He just stared at Fallon, his eyes wide.

"Why are you so shocked?" Zach asked. "You said yourself that your mom is known for her behind-the-scenes planning and play-making."

"I can't believe it," Zara said, thinking back on her interactions with Britany to see if there had been any hint, any clue that she'd missed.

Caleb threw back his head and laughed. "I can. As she always says, you don't get to be at the top of your game by playing it soft." He turned to Zara, heat in his eyes. "You gotta fight to make it happen."

Her breath caught, and a million words swirled around

in her head, all of them a bad idea when it came to keeping her heart in one piece. The truth of it was that it was already too late. Maybe not in reality, but her heart had broken rule number one, and she had no idea what to do about it.

Before she could accidentally voice any of that, though, Ian, Cole, and Alex grabbed Caleb's chair, carried it over to the deep end, and dumped him—burger and all—into the water. They may have been pranking Caleb, but she couldn't help but think they'd just saved her from saying something she was bound to regret.

It was, after all, rule number one: five dates and done.

• • •

On the day sandwiched between the team barbecue and their final preseason road trip out west, Caleb had one thing on his mind—seeing Zara. They'd been able to FaceTime a few minutes here and there, but nothing like before. She'd been working all hours to finish up her miniatures scene for the Friends of the Library silent auction during the organization's ball in a few days. Meanwhile, he'd been spending more time in the sin bin than Coach Peppers liked after a few players got chippy with him and brought Zara into the on-ice discussion.

But today? Today he was taking the steps up to her apartment two at a time to get to her door just a few seconds sooner. He made it to her floor, and his phone vibrated. Since he had a meeting scheduled in a little bit with Lucy, he couldn't ignore it.

The notification, though, wasn't from her. It was from the Bramble app. The app's icon now had a big red circle with the number four inside it, notifying him of how many days it had been since his first reminder to schedule date number five. He'd been ignoring the notifications, a practice he had no plans to change.

Unfortunately, he wasn't sure how much longer he'd be able to, because the Bramble people were calling Lucy and Lucy was calling him and the whole world wanted this PR stunt wrapped up by the first game of the regular season— except for him. And that's why he was outside of Zara's apartment, knocking on the door instead of using the app to officially schedule their final date.

"Hey there," she said, using her entire body to keep an excitedly wiggling Anchovy from bursting out into the hall.

She looked delectable. Her hair was up in a big poof on top of her head, and she had on a pair of yoga pants and an Ice Knights sweatshirt that he'd never seen her in before. If it was his number, he wasn't going to remember his promise to himself to play it cool. There was just— She turned around to shush Anchovy, and he saw the number. It was his.

Something came over him and he swept her up, pulling the door closed behind her to block Anchovy inside, and gave in to the overwhelming need to kiss her until she forgot everything else but him. He cupped her ass as she wrapped her legs around his waist and he was lost in the feel of her. Damn. He was so screwed, but as long as he was kissing her, he didn't give two shits. Unfortunately, though, he'd acted before his brain had caught up, and they were definitely on the wrong side of her front door for him to get to do all the things he wanted to.

He broke the kiss but didn't let her down.

"I was in the neighborhood for a meeting and thought you might have some time to go grab coffee," he said at the same time as the dog let out a sad wail on the other side of the door. "We could take Anchovy."

She didn't hesitate. "Let me grab his leash."

He didn't want to let her go but did anyway, staying out in the hall because he didn't trust himself not to strip her down the second they were alone. So he watched as she hurried around the apartment, slipping on her shoes and then putting her tools away. The dollhouse she'd been working on for weeks with all the authors reading one another's books looked finished, and it was amazing. He wanted to take a closer look but again, he'd get her naked and have her coming on his lips instead of making his can't-miss appointment with Lucy.

Zara grabbed her keys while Anchovy went to a basket by the door and pulled out a leash. He snapped it onto the dog's collar, and the three of them walked down the stairs. If anyone had asked if he'd taken Zara's hand or if she'd grabbed his, he couldn't have answered. All he knew was that by the time they walked out into the afternoon sunshine, their feet crunching on the first fallen leaves of the season, they were holding hands.

They went to a walk-through coffee joint a few blocks down from her place and a few blocks up from the Carlyle Building. He told her about the extra-hot hot sauce they'd gotten a rookie to drink in Atlanta, and she told him about the rush order she'd gotten for thirty-six miniature antelopes. They were laughing trying to come up with the most ridiculous miniature scene they could think up that would require that many antelopes when they turned the corner to the Carlyle Building and nearly ran right into Lucy.

"Oh, just look at this good boy! You're a good boy, aren't you?" Lucy asked, turning into a nearly unrecognizable softie in the presence of Anchovy, squatting down and giving the dog the kind of attention he clearly thought he deserved. "I don't know what you did this time, Stuckey, but if you always bring this boy over to my office, I will find a way to fix it."

"I didn't do anything," he said. "We had an appointment."

Lucy turned her attention from him to Zara, giving her an assessing once-over. "Are you going to introduce me to the woman who saved your ass?"

Caleb rolled his eyes. "Zara, meet Lucy Kavanagh, the most sought-after crisis management public relations person in Harbor City. Lucy, meet Zara, who not only saved my ass but happens to own Anchovy."

"Nice to meet you. Have you worked in this building long?" Zara asked. "It's my favorite one in the city."

"A few years," Lucy said, looking at the skyscraper that seemed to reach up and touch the sky. "The Carlyles are big Ice Knights fans, and when the office came open, I was able to sweet-talk my way into a lease.

"But I'm guessing you two aren't here to talk buildings," Lucy said. "We have Bramble business. Zara, are you coming up, too?"

"No, Caleb just rescued me from my workaholic ways long enough to grab a walk and some coffee," Zara said with a laugh. "And this is probably presumptuous, but have you ever met Helen Carlyle?"

Lucy shook her head and gave Anchovy a scratch under the chin. "Usually people want to know about her sons, Hudson and Sawyer, but no, I haven't met her."

"Too bad. I was hoping for some insight." Zara looked up at him, an embarrassed flush making her cheeks pink. "She'll be at the charity ball I'm going to next week and she's a huge miniatures collector. I was hoping to be able to make a connection so I wouldn't make a bunch of conversational fumbles like I did at the barbecue."

He squeezed her hand and ran his thumb across her knuckles to reassure her, but there was no missing the worry in the tightness around her mouth. With the ball coming up, he knew her stress level had to be at a peak. She wasn't one who ever seemed to want to let herself dream—and he couldn't blame her after she'd told him about all of her dad's schemes.

"Sorry I couldn't be of help." Lucy gave Anchovy one

last pat on his head and stood.

"No worries," Zara said. "Well, I know you two have a lot to talk about and I have a piece to finish." She turned to Caleb. "Talk to you later?"

Their schedules had been at odds lately, and he was hitting the road tonight for a four-day west coast trip, but he'd always have time for her. Lifting her hand, he kissed the trio of freckles on the inside of her wrist. "Without a doubt."

. . .

"So what happened after that?" Gemma asked the next morning as she ate a bite of double-caffeinated, triple-chocolate doughnut with rainbow sprinkles. "He just went up into the building? He didn't carry you away on his horse into the sunset? He didn't even kiss you properly, only on your wrist like a rakish Regency duke?"

Zara almost choked on her sea salt and caramel doughnut with coconut flakes. "Oh my God, warn a person before you say something so ridiculous! He's not my boyfriend. It's just a mutually beneficial partnership with one date left to go."

She looked around at the other customers at the Donut Emporium on Sixty-Eighth Street who were all noshing on Harbor City's best carb and sugar concoctions. No one paid them any mind.

It was a Saturday-morning tradition to meet Gemma and do some carb loading for the definitely-not-doing-a-marathon activities ahead of them. It was also the best time to catch up on everything they'd been missing. Between Gemma doing all her wedding planning and Zara working her ass off to finish her latest piece before the ball—not to mention going out on as many dates and non-dates with Caleb as possible— it had been hard to get together with her best friend. So this morning she'd pushed aside the unusual disappointment at waking up in a bed by herself—unless she counted Anchovy snoring beside her, which she did not—and had leashed the Great Dane. They'd walked the four blocks to one of the best outdoor eating spots in her neighborhood, where all dogs were welcome as long as they stayed on the outside of a short iron fence that surrounded the tables.

"Okay, fine." Gemma took a sip of her hot tea, the steam floating up into the air of the first crisp fall morning of the season. "He can carry you off into the sunset on the Ice Knights' Zamboni."

"Not everyone gets a happily ever after." Unease settled into Zara's belly, turning the coconut flakes and sugary goodness into something acidic and foul, which pretty much made her the worst friend ever, considering she was sitting across from her best friend who was only a few months away from wedded bliss. "I mean, you do, obviously, because you and Hank are perfect for each other."

"You don't think there's anyone perfect for you?" Gemma asked.

"I have to be realistic." Zara reached over and gave Anchovy a few pets on the top of his head, his smooth fur settling her nerves. "I'm happy with a couple of orgasms and a good time." Her fingers trembled, so she wrapped them firmly around her paper cup, letting its heat seep into her. "Isn't that what the whole point of this Bramble date thing was? To clear out the cobwebs, not find forever." She took in a deep breath, willing that stupid clock that always seemed to be ticking away in her subconscious to shut the hell up. She was getting exactly what she wanted and she was *thrilled*. Her throat burned, but she was determined to get the last bit out. "Well, I'm happy to report that they're gone."

Gemma raised an eyebrow. "So why do you sound like you're about to cry?"

"I don't cry. It's allergies." She wrinkled her tingly nose, blinking extra-hard to clear out the pollen that must have come out of nowhere. "And I'll have you know that I don't expect some knight in shining armor or Prince Charming to come rescue me from my life. I like my job. I have a goal I'm working toward." She shoved a bite of doughnut into her mouth with more effort than necessary, part of it crumbling in her fingers. "Things were going well before Caleb Stuckey and they'll go well after date five."

"Which is why you've made sure to schedule that last date," Gemma said, nodding as if Zara's explanation made perfect sense while her eyes all but screamed that her pants were on fire.

Date five? She had six notifications from Bramble to schedule it. She'd ignored every single one like it was a dirty plate someone else had put in the sink instead of the dishwasher—resentfully and often.

"We've been busy." No, that didn't sound lame at all.

Gemma scoffed, dropping any pretense at believing any of the bullshit was real. "Why can't you just admit that you really like him? That you finally found someone who you feel safe with? Who you aren't going to have to worry will spring life-changing surprises on you in an effort to change the world in one fell swoop? Are you afraid it'll just make all of this too real?"

"It's not that." *It's totally that, you big liar.* "I mean, look at my history. It's been one undependable guy after another in my life, from my dad and his crazy schemes to every boyfriend I've had." Fear and panic and worry and a million other emotions went to battle inside her, leaving her bleeding and aching and wondering if she could survive this. "Is it really smart for me to fall for a guy who travels ten months out of the year? One who only dated me because his mom picked me out of a digital lineup? One who lives by the philosophy of going with his gut instead of solid, hardcore planning? What about any of that sounds like it could be forever?"

"You gotta let yourself believe." Gemma reached across the table and laid her hands on top of Zara's, giving her a gentle squeeze. "Have a little faith that something good can happen."

But would it? The idea of answering *yes* was nearly overwhelming, leaving her lungs tight with anticipation and an elusive hope that began to feel a little more real with each day she spent with Caleb.

Chapter Seventeen

It was day two of Caleb being on the road, and Zara was dragging. Nothing felt right. She kept forgetting what she opened the fridge to get or that her female authors dollhouse was already packed up and waiting to be displayed at the Friends of the Library charity ball, so she couldn't even make little last-minute adjustments. When it came to her art, nothing was ever finished, she just ran out of time.

And now her life seemed to be nothing but time. She should be out at a museum or taking Anchovy to Fido's Café or meeting Gemma for drinks. Instead, she was wandering around her tiny studio apartment wondering what Caleb was up to and sneaking glances at her phone to make sure she hadn't missed his call. She hadn't. The damn thing had been obnoxiously silent. She'd shot off a few gif texts—feeling as awkward as a fourteen-year-old messaging her first crush— but hadn't gotten anything back. Not even a K or an emoji.

"Not that it matters. It's not a relationship," she told Anchovy as he watched her pace from one end of her apartment to the other. "He's just busy. Working. Having team dinners with the other players. Sleeping."

There. It all made perfect sense.

Unfortunately, that lizard part of her brain that held on to every fear and unquenchable worry she'd ever had in her life was reminding her with each passing minute of all the times she paced waiting for her dad. When she was ten waiting to see if his sure-thing pony had come in first like his buddy had sworn he would. When she was fourteen and he'd gone off to sweet-talk their landlord into floating them another week on the rent. When she was seventeen and he'd been so sure that taking out a loan for an oxygen bar was the winning idea he'd always been waiting on. The other day, when she'd waited for two hours for him to stop by to help her pack her author dollhouse for the ball and he'd never shown, leaving a voicemail later telling her he'd ran into a friend from the neighborhood. In each of those instances, she'd come last, been his lowest priority. Oh, her dad had never meant to make her feel that way, but it didn't change anything.

Now here she was again, wearing a hole in her apartment's carpeting while the person she loved left her hanging without any communication.

She jolted to a stop, all the oxygen in the room gone.

Loved.

Fuck. Fuck. Fuckity fuck. She'd skipped over breaking rule number one and had landed smack-dab in the middle of falling in love.

The white-noise static filling the space between her ears where her brain had been previously was so loud, she almost missed the *chirp-chirp* sound of her incoming text notification.

Caleb: *New phone. Left mine in the truck before we left. Just got replacement and downloaded contacts from the cloud.*

All the pent-up ugly in her whooshed out in one deep exhale.

Zara: *That's crazy.*

Caleb: *Miss you.*

She *wasn't* goofy smiling. She wasn't *goofy smiling.* She was totally goofy smiling.

Zara: *Miss you too.*

Caleb: *Gotta go, plane's about to take off for Vancouver. Can't wait to see you when I get back.*

All the bounce returned to her step, and she did a shimmy dance move across her apartment. She was in love and in trouble and so far out of her comfort zone, she didn't know what to do, but for tonight, at least, she'd go with it, let herself go with her gut. Feeling like she did right now, it didn't seem like anything could go wrong.

• • •

Caleb couldn't explain it, but the ice smelled different when the clock had ticked down to almost regular season. He moved faster on the ice, checked harder when it counted, and got the puck like it was meant for him. At least that's how it usually went. During today's game, though, he was sucking wind.

He sat on the bench in front of his locker with his forearms resting on his knees and the towel draped around his neck. Something was off, making it hard to concentrate, but he couldn't figure out what. He hadn't changed his skate laces. The tape on his stick was the same as he always used. He'd even put on his socks left and then right, just like always.

"Is it the tape?" Phillips asked, because if there was one

thing that united all hockey players besides their love of the game, it was their belief in the power of superstition and routine.

"Nah," Caleb said. "I put it on myself."

"How about Zara?" Petrov asked, no doubt still grudge-holding about the no-trade thing. "Has she finally kicked you to the curb?"

He glared at the center, who was dripping everywhere because the asshole never bothered to use a towel, preferring to air-dry. "She's not available for other dates."

"Has she agreed to that? If not…" Petrov shrugged. "By my count of the videos, you guys only have one more date."

Caleb wasn't going to take the bait—he wouldn't give him the satisfaction. He fell into it anyway, all but snarling at the other man and all but hearing a countdown clock on his time with Zara. "That's not how it's gonna go."

"What are you going to do to make that happen?" Blackburn asked as he sat on the bench opposite and tied his street shoes.

"I have no fucking clue."

And wasn't that the case. The rules had made perfect sense in the beginning. Neither of them wanted to be there. Now, he didn't want to stop being with her. Everything was better when Zara was there.

Christensen, fresh from the shower, stopped in front of his locker next to Caleb's. "You need help winning a woman? I have the answers."

Everyone in the locker room laughed. On the ice and off it, the forward was known for playing fast and loose. Taking advice about women from Christensen was just asking for trouble.

Petrov chucked an empty water bottle at their line mate. "When was the last time you were with someone for more than three dates?"

"Survey says never," Christensen said, not sounding like he cared. "But that doesn't change that I am a man who has serious game. The ladies love me."

"Oh yeah," Phillips said. "Right up until they've spent more than forty-eight hours with you."

Christensen flipped them off, but before he could launch into another defense of his studliness, Blackburn stepped into the fray, crossing the locker room to stand in front of Stuckey.

He looked at all the players and gave a disgusted huff. "Seeing as how I'm captain and I'm the only one of you chuckleheads in anything like a relationship—no offense, Phillips, but whatever it is that you have with Marti is too messy to be called a relationship—I believe I'm the only one here who can comment on what Stuckey should be doing to fix his Zara problem."

Denying that he was in deep was useless. These guys knew him too well for that. Between the months of September and June, they spent more time with one another than their own families. That was the hockey life. He'd chosen it. He wouldn't change it for the world. Now he just wanted to add Zara to it.

"So what do I do?" he asked, almost desperate enough to take advice from Christensen.

Blackburn crossed his arms and gave him a hard look. "What's the goal?"

He didn't even have to think about it. "I want to be with her."

"For a night or for longer?"

"The second." Without a doubt.

Blackburn rubbed his chin for at least a ten count, then just when Caleb was convinced the other man was going full vow-of-silence monk on him, he shrugged and said, "Then find a way to make that happen."

Fucking A. He could have come up with that shit advice

all by himself. "That's what I'm asking you to tell me how to do."

"I don't want to date her; I don't fucking know what specific thing will apply to her," Blackburn said. "You gotta figure it out."

Caleb considered strangling himself or Blackburn with the towel but just balled it up and threw it at the captain instead. "You are horrible at giving advice."

"But I'm really good at telling people to get their head out of their ass, which is exactly what you need to do." Blackburn dropped the towel in a laundry bin and picked up one of the new mini pucks the marketing department would be handing out when they got back home to all the fans on opening night, tossing it to him. "Figure it out, Stuckey."

Then he walked away, leaving Caleb staring at the tiny puck that wasn't even half as detailed or clever as it would have been if Zara had made it. She would have painted the team logo on it and given it some scuff marks as if it had been used in a game. She would—

How in the hell did he convince Zara that being with him, going beyond—way beyond—five dates was worth it, that taking a chance on love was worth it? Lucky for him, he knew just the Miss Fix It to consult.

• • •

Caleb walked out of the Carlyle Building the next day with part one of his game plan completed.

He'd gotten a promise from Lucy for tickets to the Friends of the Library charity ball in a few days. Once he was there, he'd be back up in case Zara needed help getting an introduction to Helene Carlyle. His secret weapon there? The fact that both Carlyle sons were huge Ice Knights fans. He'd get Phillips and a couple of the other guys to come with him to help smooth the way for Zara with some Carlyle meet and greets, but only if she needed it. Knowing her, she wouldn't, but he wanted to be there for her just like that safety net had been at their obstacle course date.

Hooking a left and heading toward Zara's apartment, he slow rolled when he spotted a limo at the corner with a well-dressed older woman standing nearby.

The guy in a chauffeur's hat put a suitcase into the trunk. "Is this everything you need for the airport, Ms. Carlyle?"

"Yes, Linus," the woman said. "Thank you so much. It was good to come back, but I'm ready to get home to Italy."

He caught the last bit in full as he was passing by and jolted to a stop. Airport? Italy? Now?

Shit.

Zara would be devastated. She'd been waiting for the ball just to be able to meet with Ms. Carlyle. He was moving again before he even thought about it, powered forward by instinct and the undeniable urge to help Zara.

"Ms. Carlyle?" He stopped a few feet away, making sure to stay out of her personal space as the words rushed out. "I'm sorry to interrupt, but I overheard you're leaving and my girlfriend— Well, she's not my girlfriend, not yet, but she's a miniatures artist and she's been working her ass off—pardon the language—to put together the perfect piece to show you. Are you really going to miss the ball?"

"I'm afraid I am," Ms. Carlyle said. "What's your friend's name?"

"Zara Ambrose."

She looked up toward the sky as if she was going through her mental contacts list. "I'm afraid I haven't heard of her."

"Here, hold on." He grabbed his phone and pulled up some pictures of the dollhouse that he'd taken last time he'd been at Zara's apartment. "These aren't the greatest photos, but you can see she does amazing work."

She took his phone, giving him an assessing look as if she was trying to place him. "What was your name?"

"Caleb Stuckey."

"The Ice Knights defenseman?"

Okay, his wasn't a household name for most people, let alone someone known for her bank account and art collection rather than for being a rabid hockey fan.

He nodded. "Yes, ma'am."

She let out a soft chuckle. "Don't be so shocked. A mother always takes an interest in whatever fascinates her children." She glanced down at the phone, enlarged the photo, and made several little *hmmm* sounds. "I truly am sorry to miss seeing her work." She handed him back his phone. "It is impressive."

As she made her move to get into her limo, the determined desperation that came in the final minute of a game when his team was down by a goal slammed into him.

"Her studio is only a few blocks away," he said, trying like hell not to sound like someone her driver should be giving serious side eye and possible a hard elbow to. "You could get a look for yourself in person before your flight, if you have time."

One steel-gray eyebrow went up. "And you say this Zara isn't your girlfriend?"

"It's a long story." But starting to feel shorter by the minute.

"Well, I hope you can squeeze it into a short car ride." Ms. Carlyle slid inside the back seat. "Are you coming, Mr. Stuckey?"

A soft buzz of warning vibrated against the back of his skull, but there was only one answer he could give. Zara deserved to have her chance.

"Yes, ma'am," he said and got into the back of the limo.

• • •

Zara was on her hands and knees in the bathroom, scrubbing the base of the toilet with a rag made from an old T-shirt soaked in a mix of cleaning product and water that still smelled strong enough that Anchovy was keeping his distance. The dog may not be thrilled with this turn of events, but deep cleaning was her go-to fix for when nothing in her life made sense. Her room in high school had always been beyond clean.

Shocker.

The rest of her apartment was a wreck, but she was going to clean the bathroom until her life started to make sense again. She'd spent her entire life depending only on herself. The idea of being able to depend on someone else had her cleaning her toilets like she worshipped at the altar of Pine-Sol and Magic Erasers.

She had just wrung out the rag when Anchovy let out an excited woof half a second before the knock on her front door. Peeling off her protective gloves, she stood up and went to the door. After scooching Anchovy over so she could get in front of the peephole, she raised herself on her tiptoes to see who it was. Her heart sped up the moment she spotted Caleb. Just the sight of him on the other side of her door settled all of the whirling mess of anxiety that had knocked her off-balance.

He was here. Just like he said he would be.

The realization that she could always depend on him for that nearly knocked her off her feet—well, that and the fact that Anchovy's tale was thwacking her.

Excitement bubbling up inside her, she flung open the door and all but jumped into his arms. "Caleb."

He wrapped his strong arms around her, deftly dodging Anchovy's attempts to join in on the fun, and kissed her. The brush of his lips electrified her all the way down to her toes, but it was over too quickly. He set her down and took her by the shoulders, turning her to face the woman he was with. Zara had never met her before, but she didn't need an introduction.

Helene Carlyle was standing in the hallway outside her apartment.

Zara's brain had to still be functioning because her lungs were working and she hadn't keeled over from a heart attack, but she couldn't manage to get any words out of her mouth.

"It's so good to meet you, Zara. Caleb has said so many interesting things about you this morning," Helene said, looking every bit like the Harbor City grand dame who spent half her year in Italy with her second husband. "May I come in?"

Still mute, Zara nodded and led the way inside her apartment. The bleach smell of cleaning that had been comforting only a moment ago hit her nose like a stinging slap. There were dishes in the sink. The box of cereal she'd had for breakfast was still on the counter. Her bed, visible from where they were just inside the front door, was unmade, and Anchovy sat on it with a bedraggled toy that at one time had been an oversize neon ball. He thumped his tail hard against the bed but thankfully had gone into visitors mode and would stay on the bed until given permission to come say hello thanks to the gate set up in front of the bedroom door.

"Sorry for the mess," she said, immediately comparing every inch of her messy apartment to the immaculate Helene and finding herself more than wanting.

This was not the impression she wanted to make. The only thing keeping her from drowning in a puddle of embarrassment was the fact that she'd get a second chance at the Friends of the Library charity ball.

"Well, I was leaving the Carlyle Building when your young man stopped me, and I just had to come look at your work right away," she said, glancing around the apartment, her gaze stopping on Zara's near-barren worktable. She walked over to it, Caleb going with her. "I was intrigued."

My work?

A horrible realization began to dawn. This was her shot at impressing the country's most influential miniatures collector, and she had nothing to show her. Her gut twisted and her palms turned clammy. What had Caleb done bringing Helene Carlyle here?

Okay, there's a way to save this. Everything isn't lost. Not yet.

She pasted on her best everything-hasn't-just-turned-to-shit smile. "I'm so sorry, but everything is with the Friends of the Library to be auctioned at their charity ball."

"That's too bad," Helene said, the initial interest lighting her eyes dimming as she turned away from the workbench. "I'm flying back to Italy tonight and won't be able to attend the event as planned."

"What about the antelopes?" Caleb asked as he handed two of the animals over to Helene, sending a look of apology to Zara.

The other woman gave the pieces a cursory once-over but handed them back to him with only a quiet, "How lovely." Zara took a shaky step back, her pulse thundering in her ears as she watched the dream she'd nurtured in secret and then taken the first baby steps toward fall apart before her eyes. She knew what *how lovely* meant. It was half a step above *bless her heart* when it came to dismissal disguised by pretty words.

She turned to Helene, desperation clawing at her as she tried to stay calm and recover the moment. "I'd been really hoping to meet you at the ball and get a chance to show you my work that will be featured there."

She flinched at the sound of her own voice. It reminded her so much of every time her dad had promised that this time, this plan, would be different. And he'd been wrong just like she was.

However, the carefully neutral look on the other woman's face told her just how late it was for that. There would be no recovery. This was it. The best option now was just to accept it.

Fighting to keep her shoulders from slumping in defeat, she lifted her chin and faced Helene. "I'm so sorry for wasting your time today."

"It's never a waste to meet someone with a vision." The other woman traced a finger over one of the planning sketches on Zara's workbench before picking up a small stack of others and quickly flipping through them. "Perhaps I'll see your work at next year's ball."

Translation: *Don't close your Etsy shop.*

"I hope so," Zara said, managing to keep her voice even.

The word hope left a bad taste in her mouth, and as Helene offered a quick goodbye, saying that her driver was waiting out front for her, Zara had a hard time concentrating on the other woman's words.

As soon as the door closed behind Helene, Zara sank down onto the couch, her legs too shaky to hold her anymore. "Why did you do that?"

For a big man, Caleb looked so small to her. He seemed to have shrunk into himself. Walking toward her, he opened his arms as if to gather her up.

She stopped him with a look. "What in the hell was that, Caleb?"

"Me helping," he said, squatting down so they were eye level as she sat on the couch.

"Wow. I'd hate to see what you *not* helping is like." The words spilled out of her, harsher than needed, but she couldn't seem to stop herself. Hurt and frustration churned through her, twisting her insides into thorn-covered knots. "Do you know what just happened? You showed leftovers and commercial dreck to one of the country's foremost miniatures collectors." A hot rush of humiliation blasted through her. "My best work probably isn't ready for Helene Carlyle, let alone a collection of antelopes bound for Peoria."

"I know it's not the outcome you want," he said, taking one of her hands in his. "But she did mention next year."

How could he still be so damn hopeful? How had she missed that he was just another dreamer like her dad, convinced that something not just better was around the corner but something amazing? What in the hell had she been thinking? It wasn't his job that had made her hold back or the strangeness of the circumstances that had brought them together—it was the fact that deep down she'd known all along that Caleb Stuckey was another foolish dreamer.

"She was being polite." Zara pulled her hand away. "She didn't actually mean it, which you'd understand if you could ever read a room."

"What the fuck?" He jerked back and stood up in one fluid motion. "I try to do something nice for you—to help you—and you throw reading in my face?"

Hating that she'd said that, hating that she hurt, hating that she'd been wrong about a possible future with Caleb, she reached out for him, but he evaded her touch. "That's not what I meant."

"If only I was smart enough to follow along, huh?" he asked, his voice quiet with a ribbon of pure, cold fury wound around each word. "Well let me tell you what I am smart enough to understand. You're scared and you react by pulling into yourself. You can't depend on anyone else? More like you can't stand to let yourself even try to. And do you want to know why you're really acting like this? It's not because of Helene. It's because you finally let down your guard with me, and it scares the shit out of you."

He was wrong. He couldn't be more wrong. While his

anger might be cold, hers was burning hot, stoking a fire in her that turned the last of her self-control to ash. She stood up on the couch, giving herself enough height to look him straight in the eye.

"Fuck you, Caleb," she said, her voice trembling with emotion that made her entire body jittery. "You don't know what you're talking about. You think you can just waltz in here and tell me what to do just like your mom or your coach does to you? Is there anyone in your life who doesn't tell you what to do, or is there a decision you can make for yourself that doesn't fuck something up?"

The air crackled around them with a low, mean energy that made the hairs on her arms stand up. Adrenaline poured through her as she stared at him, her breaths coming in fast bursts as if she'd just run at full speed down a mountain. From that angle, she had the perfect view to see the change in Caleb's expression as he shut down in front of her, leaving only a mocking sneer in place of genuine emotion.

"That's a low fucking blow, Zara."

"I'm short; that's where my punches land." She hopped off the couch and stalked over to the front door, yanking it open. "If you can't take it, why don't you just leave?"

He strode to the door, his long legs eating up the space between them until he was right next to her, looking down. "Don't worry. I'm already gone."

She slammed the door shut behind him and made it three small steps away before she crumpled to the floor, her chest heaving with tears coming so hard and so fast that she couldn't even make a noise.

Chapter Eighteen

Caleb was at home in the penalty box. Tonight, he'd spent a good chunk of the last home preseason game against Philadelphia in there, snarling about that high-sticking asshole on the other team who'd drawn penalty after penalty. And after the game, he was still salty enough that his teammates gave him plenty of space in the locker room—everyone but Blackburn, Phillips, Christensen, and Petrov.

The nosy foursome crowded in front of him while he was tying his shoes. He ignored them. For once, his mouth wasn't moving faster than his brain, because he wasn't talking at all and didn't have any plans to change that.

"What in the fuck was wrong with you?" Petrov asked, breaking the silence.

"It's the last preseason game," Caleb said, not bothering to look up from what he was doing. "It doesn't matter."

"Bullshit," Blackburn all but growled. "It always matters when you have that A on your jersey."

So much frustration was boiling just under the surface that it took everything he had not to step to his captain. So instead, he straightened up, giving the other man his full attention and letting just how much he did not give at that moment show on his face. "Then take it back."

Blackburn's jaw tightened, and the vein in his temple bulged. He didn't move, not even an inch, but Caleb knew if he could push just a little bit more, he'd get a reaction. That was what he wanted. He wanted to brawl. What he'd left out on the ice tonight wasn't enough to cancel out all the angry dark swirling around inside him.

He stood up, but instead of getting in Blackburn's face, Christensen put his pretty-boy mug in between Caleb and the captain.

"What's wrong, Zara decide she'd rather date me?" Christensen asked. "I heard you telling Coach that a fifth Bramble date wasn't going to happen. I'm thinking I'll give her a week and then go tap that a—"

That was as far as Christensen got before Caleb snapped. He vaulted forward, taking the other man down to the carpet right on top of the Ice Knights logo. They rolled, battling for superiority, but Christensen wasn't a fighter, had no idea how to brawl, and Caleb not only had the skills, he had enough pissed-off in reserve to take on the entire first line. The forward didn't stand a chance. Caleb had the other man down on his back and his fist pulled back ready to let loose when an unmistakable voice cut through the angry red haze.

"Caleb Stuckey, treat that logo with some respect and get the hell off it," his mom said.

Britany walked in like she owned the joint—then again, that was pretty much how his mom entered any room. No doubts. No panic. No fear of failure. She didn't fuck up over and over and over again until she ended up sprawled out on the floor of the locker room trying to take one of her friends' head off.

Caleb got up, hands still curled into fists, and looked

around at the men who made up his line. Usually they watched over one another on and off the ice. Last season when the world found out about what Blackburn's parents had done to him, it was their line who got him furniture and refused to let him lone-wolf out anymore. And now every one of those men was looking at him the way they'd all looked at Blackburn: not with anger or pity but with sympathy.

"You're all a bunch of assholes," Christensen said, brushing himself off as he stood up. "Why did I have to be the one to push him until he snapped?"

"Because out of all of us, you're the one who needs to be popped in the head most often," Phillips said.

All the fury whooshed right out of Caleb. "What are you talking about?"

"Psychology," Blackburn said, looking too satisfied by a mile. "You were so busy thinking about whatever it was that fucked up things with Zara that resulted in no date number five that you couldn't concentrate on how to move forward and fix it."

Stunned at how well he'd been punked, Caleb just stared slack-jawed at Blackburn. It took about three seconds for the reality of what he said—and how right he was—to sink in.

"Zach, you just might make a good coach someday," Caleb's mom said before giving the rest of the guys in the room the look that sent her players scurrying for cover. "Now, do you boys mind giving me some time with my son?"

She didn't have to ask twice—everyone scattered. Caleb sat back down on the bench in front of his locker, letting his head rest against the wood frame. Now that he didn't have the anger to fuel him, weariness seeped in, dragging him down.

His mom sat beside him. "So why don't you tell me what happened."

Letting his shoulders droop, he exhaled, and then he gave her the entire story, from the rules he and Zara had agreed to on the first date to the fun they had on the other dates to the barbecue with the team to the fight.

"She said some things. I said some things. Then it got ugly and she told me to leave." His whole body ached, every single muscle and bone, as if he'd been picked up by a tornado and thrown against Mount Rushmore. "Like an idiot, I stormed out and never looked back."

How could he have done that? He should have stayed. Pleaded his case. Instead, he'd just quit on her.

"Do you know why I picked out Zara from all of the bios I saw on Bramble?" his mom asked.

He shook his head. "No."

"Because she was honest about what she wanted," she said. "Sure, it was a little more straightforward about things I really don't need to know about, but she presented herself as she was without apology. That's something to be appreciated and respected. Just because you love someone doesn't mean you get to take away their agency. It's a hard lesson to learn, believe it or not."

She tapped her finger three times on his leg. It was their code since he'd gotten to that age where having his mom tell him she loved him in public just seemed like one more thing to get embarrassed about. Instead, it was three taps for "I love you." He tapped her on the knee right back.

"Do you love Zara?"

"Yeah," he said, not even needing to think about it. "I do."

"Does she love you?"

There was that gut punch again. "I don't know."

"So you apologize and you make amends. Then you hope for the best." She tapped him three times again. "Life is like hockey—you put in the preparation, you put in the work, and you pray like hell that the calls will go your way."

"And when they don't?"

"You play harder." She grinned at him. "Do you

remember that awful middle school teacher you had?"

Yeah, he wasn't likely to forget that prick ever. "The one who didn't care about teaching because he was about to retire? Yeah, he was awful."

His mom raised an eyebrow in disbelief. "He wasn't about to retire. He was forced to when I found out what was going on and how he was treating you at school because of your dyslexia."

"How?" Then he remembered who he was talking to. His mom was a master tactician. "You found a way."

"Always. And I would have sooner if I would have known. I wish you'd have felt you could come to me. There's nothing, *nothing*, in the world that I wouldn't do for you. I'm so sorry I didn't realize sooner."

"I should have said something," he said, shaking his head at the nervous little boy afraid of sticking out in any way. He wasn't that kid anymore, but how much had he really changed?

"Well, prove that's a lesson learned by not letting it happen again," his mom said, the tone in her voice proclaiming she was back in coach mode. "You can't keep how you're feeling bottled up again. You have to let Zara know how you feel."

He sat up, the wheels already turning in his head. It was the beginning of the third period. He still had time. He could fix this.

• • •

Zara knew she was in trouble when her dad showed up at her door with Gemma.

Okay, so she'd spent most of the past forty-eight hours since her fight with Caleb in front of her TV binge-watching *The Great British Bake Off* while eating chocolate frosting right out of the can. She hadn't returned calls. She'd ignored social media. She'd deleted her Bramble app because the little dings of her notifications reminding her to go on date number five made her hiccup-cry. Even with all of that, she'd managed to pretend just well enough to fool her pride that she'd been right and everything would work out.

However, the moment she opened her door and found her dad and Gemma, she burst into tears. Both of them freaked out while Anchovy tried to give her a ball. It was the Ice Knights ball Caleb had given him. She just cried harder. After confiscating her frosting-eating spoon, Gemma left with Anchovy, leaving Zara alone with her dad. He looked about as thrilled with that as she was.

Pacing the length of her couch and then back again, he kept his hands gripped behind his back. Every few steps, he'd look over at her and give her what he probably meant as an encouraging smile that actually came across as more of a nervous baring of teeth.

"Dad, it's okay," she said, sinking farther down into the couch, wishing it could swallow her up. "You don't have to pretend."

He stopped mid-step and pivoted to look straight at her. "Pretend what?"

She didn't want to say, but the words burned in her throat. It was time to let them out—past time, really.

"That you want to be here," she said. "When I was growing up, you were always off making plans or helping other people in the neighborhood. If I'm not used to it by now, I never will be."

All of the color drained out of Jasper's face. "What are you talking about, Button?"

She tried to answer, but the words just wouldn't come. All she could do was stare at him and feel all the same hurt she had when she was poring over the bills while he was buying rounds to cheer up the neighborhood after the community center burned down. She'd never doubted his sincerity to help people; she'd just always known that her place in the rankings for people who needed some of Jasper Ambrose's kindness was near the bottom.

His chin trembled just once before he firmed it. "We both know I wasn't the greatest dad when you were growing up. I'm still not." He came over and sat beside her on the couch. "When your mom left, it hit me hard. It killed my hope, and that had been the one thing that had filled me since we brought you home from the hospital. Once we had you, I was sure that everything was going to work out."

How many times had she heard that as a kid? *Don't worry about the light bill; it will work itself out. Don't worry about the landlord; the rent will work itself out.*

"But it didn't," she said. "Not with Mom or your business plans or anything."

He let out a long sigh and then gave her a sad little shadow of a smile. "You know what I learned from all that failure? That you can't force it." He reached for her hand, curling both of his around her one. "You can't force things to go your way just because you want them so badly that it shakes your whole world, and you can't force it away when it breaks something inside you that you thought could never be broken. That's what I learned from your mother." A bone-deep hurt filled his eyes, and it was raw enough to steal Zara's breath. "Your mom, well, I always said she was troubled. The truth was that, after you were born, she developed a drinking problem, and I thought if I loved her enough, I could help her beat it. I hadn't realized yet that you can't change people. They have to want to change themselves." He paused, turning away from her for a minute so she couldn't see his face as he lifted a hand up and wiped something away before turning back to her. "And once she was gone, I saw how it affected you. God, you were the happiest girl when you were little. No fantasy was too big, no dream too unlikely. But after she left, all of that changed." He squeezed her hand as a tear spilled over onto his cheek. "All those schemes and crazy ideas, they were all an effort to bring that spark back to you. I thought that if you could feel that sense of hope just one more time, that it would stick. That what had been broken would be repaired. In reality, I just ended up doing more damage, didn't I, Button? I'm so sorry."

It was a shift in paradigm and perception that she couldn't wrap her head around, but what she could do was give her dad a hug. It wasn't much. It probably wasn't enough, but she did it anyway.

"I'm so sorry," she said, tightening her grip as he hugged her back. "I never realized."

"Yeah, well, I didn't exactly do a great job of communicating," he said as he sat back, already sounding more like himself. "I just tried to *do* instead of talking."

Ouch. That hit close to home. "That kinda sounds familiar."

"You want to tell me about it?"

All of it came in one huge run-on sentence punctuated by sniffles and the occasional blowing of her nose. She'd just gotten to the part where Helene Carlyle showed up outside her apartment when Gemma came back with Anchovy. Her bestie sat cross-legged on the floor while petting the dog's belly for the rest of the story, adding in the appropriate gasps and *tsk-tsk* noises when necessary.

"Don't take this the wrong way," Gemma said, cringing back just a bit. "But, oh, honey, you just might have overreacted a bit. He did the wrong thing, but he really was trying to help."

Coming from anyone else, that little bit of truth telling would have rankled. However, she'd been friends with Gemma for so long that there really wasn't anything they couldn't say to each other—especially when it was an oh-honey moment.

"I know, but I don't know what to do about it." Regret burned a hole in her belly as she contemplated her options, which basically came down to null and nada. "He's never going to talk to me again, and who can blame him? I was a total bitch."

"Don't you think you owe him the opportunity to make that decision for himself?" her dad asked. "Dig deep into that Ambrose heritage and go big with hope."

"I do still have tickets to the ball tonight," Gemma said, a wide grin erasing the worry from her face. "And you know the Ice Knights are one of the major sponsors, so I bet he'll be there."

It was a ridiculous idea, almost as out of the bounds of reality as falling for the man who answered an ad on an online dating app calling for someone to clean out her vagina cobwebs. Oh my God, when this worked out, she was going to have to do whatever it took to make sure that ad was deleted from the app's servers. *When it works out.* Oh yeah, she, the woman who never dreamed, was going to make that happen. She just couldn't do it on her own.

She turned to her soon-to-be knights in shining armor. "Which one of you is going to be my fairy godmother, because I'm going to need help turning this fantasy into a reality."

"I do believe that's my calling," her dad said, rubbing his hands together in anticipation. "Let me work my magic, and then you can go win back your Prince Charming."

All she needed was a trusty steed. Anchovy let out a happy woof.

It turned out that doing almost everyone in the neighborhood a favor every now and then meant Jasper was able to send a call out for help that was answered almost immediately.

Jasper tapped into his line of contacts, and within a

couple of hours, she was sitting on a stool in her kitchen while Andrea from The Hair Bar did alchemy-level magic turning the rat's nest on Zara's head into some kind of dreamy updo that involved braids, waves, and enough bobby pins to pick a million locks—if Zara had that skill.

"Close your eyes and stretch your eyebrows up to the ceiling," Jayse from the fifth floor told her before applying winged eyeliner to her. "There, finished."

Zara opened her eyes. Her little apartment was filled with people. Mrs. Spatz had come over with three of her granddaughter's old prom dresses to pick from. Amelia from the Donut Emporium had brought over a dozen of her most popular, sprinkle-covered sugar and carb bombs. Devon had his limo out on the street, waiting to take her to the ball.

Anchovy was in heaven. She was amazed, flabbergasted, and thankful.

"Dad, I can't believe you made this happen with just a few calls," she said, giving him a hug. "I never would have dreamed it was possible."

"Now you know better." He twirled her around just like he had when she was a kid and they'd dance in the kitchen after the dishes were done. "It doesn't always work out, but when it does, it's so very worth it."

Tears were threatening to ruin Jayse's hard work when Gemma burst out of Zara's bedroom.

"I found the perfect pair," she said, holding up a pair of knock-off heels covered in glass crystals that made them sparkle in the light. "Hurry up and put them on. You're already late."

Zara did as she was told, gave everyone thank-you hugs, and hustled out her door. She had no idea what she was going to say or how Caleb would respond, but she had a whole ride across town to figure it out. Fingers crossed, she hurried down the stairs and outside.

Chapter Nineteen

Not even a thirty-minute ride was long enough to figure out what would come next. She had no plan and no ideas, but every ounce of hope was clutched tight to her chest.

Zara got out of the car, too jacked-up to wait for Devon to make his way around to her door, and walked as fast as she could into the hotel. Everyone was in designer ball gowns and tuxedos, drinking champagne and ignoring the waiters with trays of canapés. Even in the heels that were pinching her toes with every step, she couldn't get a good enough look at the crowd to find Caleb. She had to find higher ground.

She made it up to the mezzanine overlooking the ballroom. It would give her the perfect view. Rushing to the decorative stone railing, she peeked over the edge.

"Oh, my dear, are you hiding out or on an assassin mission?" Helene Carlyle asked as she sat in a chair set in a nearby alcove. She put her phone with its case decorated with famous paintings by Hughston in her purse. "Either way, I support it; these things are always dreadfully boring."

Zara jumped up in the air and whirled around before

catching her breath as she stared at the older woman in shock. She wasn't supposed to be here. Helene Carlyle was supposed to be on her way to Italy.

"Neither," Zara said as she turned away to scan the crowd again without any luck. "Just trying to find my prince."

Helene chuckled. "I like how high you set your goals... almost as much as I like your work."

That got Zara's full attention, and she spun around, the glass crystals on her shoes scratching her toes. "I thought you weren't coming to the ball."

"I got all the way to the family jet, sat down, buckled the seat belt, and realized I couldn't go," Helene said. "If your actual pieces were as good as those sketches I saw, my nemesis Patricia would snap them up at the auction and lord it over me for the next decade. The woman is a horrid little nit. So I told the pilot we needed to delay the flight. It was worth it. No one is going to beat me at the silent auction. I sweet-talked..." She paused and took a sip of her wine. "Okay, fine, I scared the bejesus out of some of those hockey players to keep watch on the bidding sheets for me and to make a bid in my name if I wasn't the top price."

Before Zara had written her Bramble bio, she would have zeroed in on what Helene was saying about her work and what it meant for her career and block everything else out as she freaked out. That squealing fit of oh-my-God-yes would come, but not now, not when Helene had said the magic word.

"You said hockey players?" she asked, her heart thundering in her chest. "Was one of them Caleb Stuckey?"

"I like that young man of yours, reminds me of my first husband—all drive and ambition with biceps that made my breath catch." Helene looked over the railing and pointed toward a table near the band. "I stationed him there. If you pull him away from that bidding station, get a replacement. There is no way I'm going to let Patricia take home a dollhouse full of my favorite writers."

A giddy jolt of adrenaline shot through her, and she gave Helene a grateful hug before heading back to the stairs leading to the ballroom. Weaving through the crowd like a lifelong Harbor City resident who knew from birth how to get around slow-walking tourists, she got to the dance floor when she felt the first snap of the thin crystal-covered strap across her toes giving way. Another three steps and it tore free, sending her stumbling forward right into the hard chest of the man she loved.

Caleb saved her from nose planting and swept her up into his arms. Looking at him, feeling his arms around her, everything settled into place inside her. This was it. This was right. She hadn't been hoping for a Prince Charming to come into her life, but by some kind of luck, he'd done it anyway.

"We gotta stop meeting like this," he said as he set her back down on her feet.

They stood there, so close but not touching, and the rest of the world faded away until it was just them standing on the edge of a dance floor.

"My shoe broke," she said. "Which really is just the topper of a total hell day—really a hell month—that all started because I filled out a form on a dating app after a couple of shots of tequila."

His smile flattened. Her gut dropped.

"I understand," he said, turning and walking away.

Oh yes, Zara, please open your mouth and ruin the moment.

"That didn't come out right," she said as she did the up-down clomping walk over to him because she only had on one shoe. "It's hell because I keep fucking it up, not because it happened."

Caleb stopped and turned, crossing his arms over his chest. Damn. Some people shouldn't be allowed to wear tuxes. The combination of Caleb plus tuxedo was lethal. Her stomach twisted as she realized she might never see him like this again if she couldn't find the right words to fix things.

"You were right." She reached deep for the courage to keep going as she stood in front of him, one foot in a shoe and the other raised up on her toes. "I was scared. I've always been scared, so I retreated back into work, creating little worlds where I got to control *everything*. It was all going wonderfully until I met you, because you made me want more than my little worlds." She took in a raggedy breath because everything rode on this next thing. "I'm hoping you'll give me—give us—another chance. We still have one more Bramble date to go, so what do you say?"

The people swarmed around them on their way to the dance floor, oblivious to the drama playing out right in front of their noses. Meanwhile, Zara was seconds away from a heart attack as she waited for Caleb's answer. Everything hung on this moment, *everything*.

After an eternity of looking at her, his gaze moving from the hem of her baby-blue gown to her face, he shook his head. "No."

All the air in her lungs evaporated, leaving her chest empty and aching. Tears pricked at the backs of her eyes as she clenched her teeth together to keep from crying. She wouldn't do that here. She'd wait until she got into the Uber for that, just like someone who hadn't been decimated by a two-letter word.

"Oh, okay…" she said, floundering for words. "I'll just…" She bit the inside of her cheek. "Yeah, I'll go."

She stumbled back a few steps—heel, flat foot, heel, flat foot—needing to get out of there before she broke down.

"Zara," he said, a smile tugging at the corners of his mouth. "When was the last time you checked your Bramble app?"

The question was such a non sequitur that it stopped her backward motion. "I was sad and mad and all of the things, so I got rid of it."

"Download it." He closed the space between them; what had taken her five bumbling steps took him two. "Right now."

Hesitating, Zara tried to make sense of the request. They were past the Bramble app, weren't they? He'd said no. He didn't want to go on a fifth date. This thing between them, it was done.

"Zara." Caleb reached out and took her broken shoe from her grasp. "Trust me."

And despite what had just happened and the upheaval making her jittery, she did. So she took her phone out of her purse and tried not to freak out when she saw the red battery alert and the low signal bars. She swiped open the App Store and tapped download again on the Bramble app, not knowing what would happen next but sending up a prayer that it wouldn't break her.

• • •

Caleb was not a patient man, but even if he had been, this whole thing was taking too long. His palms were getting itchy watching her mess with her phone, but he wasn't going to use his phone and show her what he'd done, not after what had happened with Helene Carlyle. This wasn't his play to make. She had to be in charge.

Zara held up her hand, one finger raised. "Almost there."

Thank God. He started to let out the breath he was holding.

"Yes." She did an off-balance shimmy dance while the people around them pretending to be oblivious to what was going on pretended not to watch. "Now I just have to log in."

He wanted a time machine just so he could go back and smack himself in the head before he came up with such a dumb-ass plan.

"Shit," she mumbled. "Wrong password." She looked up at him, her expression tight. "Let me try again. I'm sure I just typed it incorrectly." Her fingers shook as she tried it again. When she got denied again, she handed her phone over to him, panic and worry coming off her in waves. "It's Anchovy. You try it."

"Your password is your dog's name?" He shook his head. One of his sisters was a cyber security consultant. She'd have a field day if she knew.

"I know it's dumb, but it's not like my Bramble account is tied to anything important." Zara smacked her hand over her mouth. "Oh my God, that's not what I meant."

He froze for a second, translating what she'd said into what she'd meant. Yeah, it was a good thing his brain was wired so he was used to having to translate garbage signals. The next few decades were going to be pretty interesting.

"I know." He typed in her password, brought up the video on the app's home screen, and handed her phone back to her. "Press play. I had to make this to explain why I couldn't complete the five dates I was obligated to go on and why I never would. It'll only be on your home screen unless you okay it going wide. I mean every word of this, but I didn't want to pressure you in any way by doing a huge public grand gesture. This is your call."

Even though she'd already given him her answer, having to sit back so she could see him ask the question was nerve-racking. The same jittery sizzles that snapped in the air around him before a game had him on alert to every flicker of emotion that crossed Zara's face. And when she hit play, he sent up a quick prayer that what she was about to watch wouldn't ruin everything.

"Hi, everyone, Caleb Stuckey here, and I'm going to tell you why I'm quitting this app and why some of you should not use Bramble—especially not if you're a professional hockey player just trying to get the world to stop seeing you as a complete bag of dicks," video him said. "Let me tell you my story so you understand why."

She let out a little gasp and plopped down in a nearby chair, her face twisting up, but she kept watching. He crossed his fingers that that was a good sign.

"First off, my mom—yes, my mom—picked out my date because Bramble has this whole parental-guidance angle to it." He ignored that asshole in his head telling him his voice sounded weird when he heard it played back and concentrated on watching Zara. "That was bad because who wants their mom picking their hookups? No one. I didn't have a choice, though, so I went along with it. My date was this pocket-size redhead who didn't want to be there any more than I did."

The first hint of a smile tugged at the corners of her mouth, and some of the tension in his body began to ebb.

"We came to a meeting of the minds and developed some rules to get through the whole process with as little pain as possible," video him said. "One of the rules was no going past date five because this was an arrangement, not a relationship."

A deep pink bloomed on her cheeks at the mention of the rules. Then she looked down at her fancy gown, which she looked amazing in, but she looked damn good in everything, including the jeans and T-shirts she normally wore. He tugged at the collar of his tux. Damn. They were not very good at following their own rules.

Video him wasn't done, though. "Everything seemed like it was going well, but something awful happened. I've dealt with overeager dates, angry fans, and a mom who thinks she knows everything, but I've never met anyone like Zara Ambrose. She's tough, talented, smart, funny, and her dog is a force of nature. All good, right? Well, I fell in love with her, hard, and I didn't even realize it at first. Who knew that finding the one person you were meant for kind of felt like the stomach flu and like you needed to smack your head against a wall repeatedly? For the uninitiated out there, I don't recommend falling in love unless you're made of stern stuff. You will end up in the penalty box—in my case literally and repeatedly—but it's worth it."

She looked up at him then, her full bottom lip starting to tremble, and she reached for him. He didn't have to be told twice. Taking her hand in his, he sat down next to her, not realizing until then that half of his teammates were gathered around the table where he and Zara were sitting. Each of the guys was watching the phone screen. Caleb sat for a second, waiting to be hit with that awful gut twist of panic from being the center of attention when he was off the ice.

It never came. It never seemed to when he was with Zara.

"All I wanted to do was fix my fuckup, get back on the ice, and keep my team together," video him said. "Then I fell in love and realized that I wanted so much more. Zara, we agreed to five dates, and then we were done. I'm here promising that I will never *ever* go on that fifth date with you, because I don't want what we have to end, and I hope you don't, either. I love you, Zara Ambrose. Now please tell me that you'll be my girlfriend so we'll never have to go out on another Bramble date again?"

The video ended, and he sat there, silent, holding his breath and waiting to see what she'd say. He didn't have to wait long.

"I love you, too, Caleb Stuckey, and I'd be more than happy to never ever go on another Bramble date with you in my entire life. There's no reason to, I already found the person I didn't know I'd been looking for."

There may have been cheering at that point, but he didn't hear it. The only person who mattered in that moment was Zara, and as he pulled her into his arms for a kiss, he realized that that was how it should be. Together, they fit. They worked. That was love.

Epilogue

Three Years Later...

The *Harbor City Wake Up* set had changed since the last time Zara and Caleb visited, but there were several people Zara remembered, including Asha Kapoor. The host walked over, her hand planted firmly on her lower back to support the weight of her pregnant belly.

"Oh, look at you," Zara said, giving the other woman a hug. "You're glowing! Pregnancy really agrees with you."

"Not at two in the morning when this one likes to do his acrobatics," Asha said with a chuckle. "He keeps early-morning-TV hours."

"Enjoy even the little bit of sleep you're getting now. Sometimes it seems like Lizzy has yet to sleep through the night," Zara said. "She's a total vampire baby and Anchovy only encourages her. I swear that dog sleeps under her crib just so he can be the first one to respond when she wakes up."

"Speaking of your little angel, here she comes, ready to do her interview with Mommy and Daddy," Asha said before turning to her producer for some last-minute show notes.

Zara turned around, and her heart sped up just like it always did when she spotted her family. Even after a baby and two years of marriage, she still was hit with wonder every time she saw them. Growing up, she never dreamed she'd get so lucky. Good thing she found just the man to prove her wrong.

Caleb had done his best to try to get Lizzy's bright-red cowlick to not stick straight up, but despite the amount of water he must have put on her head, it stubbornly stood sky-high. As soon as Lizzy saw Zara, she let out a squeal and did the drunk toddler stumble walk all the way over, only falling three times before getting to the couch and lifting up her arms in an unspoken demand to be picked up.

"Come here, cutie pie." She picked up her daughter and snuggled her in her arms.

"I see how it is," Caleb said, sitting down next to her on the couch and giving her a quick kiss that kicked up her pulse rate. "I get splashed in the bathroom, and Mommy gets the cuddling."

Lizzy let loose with a little baby giggle and reached for Caleb's playoff beard.

"Are Cole and Ian still coming over tonight with their little broods?" she asked. The dads club they'd formed began when each of the players had given newborn jerseys with their own numbers on them instead of the baby's daddy's number. The three of them never seemed to get tired of busting one another's chops.

"You can't have your own all-star mighty mites hockey team unless you start early," Caleb said as he made funny faces at Lizzy. "Cole's boy might be three, but he's already skating like his dad."

"Somehow I think that might be a bit of an exaggeration."

"Okay, he skates like me," he said, grinning at her.

"A defenseman who can't wait to get home every night to his gorgeous and extremely talented wife and adorable daughter—at least when you two aren't traveling with me so you can attend another gallery show opening now that your dad has found his true calling as your promo man setting up shows for you."

Yeah, that wasn't heart arrhythmia; she missed a beat every time he said something like that to her, which was pretty much all the time. "Don't forget we have a couple plans tomorrow."

His face got serious. "But it's not a date."

"Of course not—that would be breaking the rules." She leaned close and brushed a kiss across his lips. "Five dates and it's all over, remember?"

"I think I can manage to not date you for at least six more decades," he said.

"That sounds like the best plan ever." And it was. It really, really was.

The show's producer finished chatting with Asha and hustled off the set.

"You two ready for this?" Asha asked, playing a quick game of peekaboo with Lizzy.

Caleb took Zara's hand, the touch sending a sizzle of anticipation through her, and they both nodded. Then the cameraman started the countdown, and after five, the red light above the lens clicked on.

"So," Asha said, beginning the interview, "it's been a little over three years since you two sat on this set after your first Bramble date. I have to say, it looks like it went well."

Zara didn't even have to think about it. "Better than I'd ever dared to hope."

Turn the page to start reading book two, *Awk-weird*!

Chapter One

Tess Gardner was just about all peopled out, but leaving wasn't an option.

Standing in the shadow of one of the potted palms along the edges of the Hayes Resort dining room, she sipped her wine and counted down the minutes until she could go up to her room, slip between the ridiculously high thread count sheets at the luxury hotel, and fall back into the book she was reading. They'd barely finished with dessert, and there would be more toasts and lots of dancing celebrating her best friend Lucy's wedding tomorrow.

It wasn't that Tess wasn't thrilled for Lucy and her soon-to-be husband, Frankie—she was. However, over the course of the past year, Tess had become a seventh wheel in their friend group. Everyone but her had paired up. Now she was standing off to the side at a fancy lodge resort outside Harbor City watching Lucy dance with Frankie, Fallon laugh with Zach, and Gina kiss Ford. It was amazing and awesome and awful all at the same time.

Her three best friends were moving on without her. Oh,

no one would actually say that out loud. In fact, her girls probably didn't even realize it was happening, but growing up like Tess had, being shuffled from relative to relative like an unwanted familial obligation, had given her a sixth sense about not belonging. Sure, there was still their weekly girls' night at Paint and Sip, but how much longer would that continue? Not long. So even as she knew she'd stand up as one of Lucy's bridesmaids tomorrow and be genuinely happy for her friends, she'd be resigning herself to the reality of the situation as well.

Everyone left. That's just how life worked.

Maybe she should get a cat or a dwarf pig or a goat or something to help fill the inevitable friend void. She could name it Kahn and then reenact the great Captain Kirk bellow of "Kahn!" whenever it was time to call it in for dinner. Or she could always go with Darth or Rey. A puppy named Boba Fetch would be pretty funny.

"Gouda and Edam are cities in what country?" one of the guys gathered around a nearby table asked.

A group of the Ice Knights hockey players who Lucy worked with as a PR goddess had been sitting there for the past ten minutes playing some trivia app. So far, they'd been doing okay, but it still hurt to hear so many wrong answers get hurled out. This question was a prime example. They were going through every popular city in Italy and France as the app's timer *beep-beep*ed its way down to the limit.

"The Netherlands," she said quietly to herself as she watched Frankie spin Lucy around on the dance floor.

One of the players, the one with the curly hair who Lucy had introduced as Ian Petrov, called out "The Netherlands" as the answer and then asked the next question to pop up on the app. "What is another name for the star fruit?"

There was a moment of silence followed by grumbles along the lines of, *What the hell is a star fruit* and *Where are the sports questions?*

"Carambola." Tess sipped her wine as the information about the fruit scrolled through her head, one word after another, just like it had her entire life.

The yellow-green fruit originated in Sri Lanka and grew on a small tree that produced bell-shaped blooms that eventually became star fruit. She could go on with more facts and stats. Sometimes, she couldn't stop her brain. It had always been like this. Factoid after factoid getting downloaded onto a massive mental server that never seemed to fill up and always seemed to come out at the worst times.

Like now.

The Thor look-alike Ice Knights player, whom she hadn't met, must have caught her saying that last answer because he wasn't laughing at his friends like he'd been doing for the past ten minutes. Instead, he was watching her, assessing her with a calculating gaze as cool as the ice blue of his eyes. Then he winked at her.

Pulse kicked into high gear, she whipped her head around so her gaze was back on the dance floor, if not her attention.

Shit. Shit. Shit.

The first rule of being the odd woman out was to not be so fucking obvious about it that strangers noticed. And yet, here she was lurking near a group of people she didn't know, answering all the trivia questions in a game they were playing without her like a supreme dork. And she'd gotten caught.

She pulled her phone out of her bag and glanced down at it, hoping it looked like she'd just gotten a text from someone. Was it late enough that she could escape? How much more attention would she draw to herself if she sprinted away like her body was screaming at her to do?

More than an injured gazelle limping through the lion enclosure at the Harbor City Zoo.

Take deep breaths. Scroll through old texts from Gina,

Lucy, and Fallon. Smile as if you aren't in a fight-or-flight panic moment right now. In a minute, you can calmly walk away without flagging yourself as being completely and utterly awkweird.

"Perfecto, torpedo, and parejo are all shapes of what?" asked Ian, reading off the question from the app.

Before Tess could answer—in her head this time because humiliation was not her kink—Not Thor answered.

"Cigars," he said.

She didn't mean to look over at him. It just sort of happened. And because this was her life, which was filled with one uncomfortable situation after another, he was staring right at her. Unlike Tess, he didn't seem to have a single qualm about getting caught watching. The other men at the table groaned, and someone told him to fuck off. He shrugged away the curse and flipped the bird at his buddies, but his gaze never left hers.

Looking away now would be good, Tess. Go on. Turn your head. Turn it.

But she didn't. She couldn't. Maybe there was something in her wine pinning her to the spot.

Ian asked, "What was the first name of the real Chef Boyardee?"

Not Thor raised an eyebrow, challenging her to answer.

"Hector," she said, meaning to do so only in a soft whisper, but the combination of the song ending, the wine, and the man who watched her as if she were the most fascinating person in the room made her voice louder than she intended.

"Holy shit, that's right," Ian said. "How did you know that?"

How many times in her life had she been asked that? Too many to count, and unlike any of the trivia questions he'd been asking, she didn't have an answer. It was the way her brain had always worked.

"Let's make this interesting," Not Thor said. "Miss Chef Boyardee and me against all six of you, best out of three sets."

Wait, what? How had she gotten involved in this? She glanced around the room for backup. However, her girls were all preoccupied with the men they'd fallen for, and everyone at the other tables who she kind of knew—including the entire Hartigan family—was either dancing or sitting at one of the many tables around the parquet floor laughing and taking pictures. It was just her.

"What's on the line?" one of the other guys asked.

Not Thor lifted up his glass of what looked like scotch on the rocks. "Losers cover the bar tab for the weekend."

Another player Lucy had introduced her to, Alex Christensen, let out a low whistle. "Considering this is one of our few weeks off until the season ends, that bar tab will be substantial."

"Worried, Christensen?"

Alex snorted. "Just trying not to make that famously locked-up-tight wallet of yours cry."

"You won't because we aren't gonna lose." Not Thor glanced over at her, everything about him screaming ultra-confident sex god, from his blond hair that brushed his shoulders to the dimple in his chin to his not-of-this-world muscular forearms visible below his rolled-up sleeves. "Right?"

She was not the woman guys like Not Thor talked to. She was the one in the corner in a fandom T-shirt with bookish earrings. Okay, tonight she had on a dress, and her obnoxiously curly hair was pulled back instead of corkscrewing around her face and getting caught in her glasses, but still, she was not even close to being *that* woman.

"Everyone loses," she said, the words slipping out before she could stop them. Nerves and old habits made the possibility of stopping a random factoid from spilling out next to impossible. "Stephen King's *Carrie* was rejected thirty times before it was accepted."

"But we're gonna be number thirty-one." He stood up and pulled an empty chair out for her. "Come join the fun."

Peopling was never fun. It was fraught with danger and embarrassment and that sickly damp-palmed feeling that she was about to make a mistake, or more likely a million of them. Walking away was her best choice, but she didn't, and she had no idea what to think about that.

• • •

"Oh my God, Thor, how did you know that minimum wage was twenty-five cents an hour in 1938 but *not* that Lisbon is the capital of Portugal?"

Cole Phillips let the Thor comment go. When Tess had sat down at their table, there had been introductions all around, but she'd stuck with her nickname for him. Cole had given up on correcting her when she'd gotten ten questions in a row right. He knew better than to fuck with someone's process. As long as they won and he didn't end up footing what was going to be an epic bar tab, Tess could call him Scrumdiddlyumptious while spanking his ass if she wanted.

Still, his ego couldn't take that comment lying down—especially not after he'd watched his ex sneak out an hour ago with the Wall Street type she'd been dating for the past month. Sure, his pride was dinged up about it, but it didn't bother him as much as he'd figured it would when he'd heard she was coming. Maybe change wasn't Satan on a pair of roller skates after all.

"Not everyone is such a trivia nerd that they're gonna know that Cincinnati was known at Pordo...Porso...Portopolis in the nineteenth century," he said, stumbling over the word.

"Porkopolis," she said with a giggle that was a little breezier than it had been a glass of wine ago. "Oink. Oink."

Damn, she was cute with her big blue eyes that her glasses didn't do a thing to hide. Even the curls that had slipped free from her pulled-back hair and the pale-blue dress cut like she was a pinup girl couldn't take away from the fact that Tess was the human equivalent of a cinnamon roll—sugar and spice and everything nice. If he was the kind of guy who did cute, he might be tempted.

But he didn't do cute.

Really, he only did one type of woman, and her name was Marti Peppers and she hated his guts. They'd been on-again, off-again since he'd joined the league six years ago. They'd been off for the past six months, and this time it wasn't going back on again. She'd been explicitly clear on that. He'd given her his heart, and she'd given him, well, not a pen but about a dozen paintballs to the back and a single-finger salute.

Christensen turned to the other Ice Knights players who'd come upstate for the weekend for Lucy's wedding. "How are these two drunk assholes beating us?"

Tess let out a squawk of protest. "We're not drunk; we're happy."

He nodded in agreement. "What she said."

Okay, there were too many jagged pieces where his heart had been for him to be happy, but he definitely wasn't drunk. Slightly off-kilter? Yes. Blasted? No.

"Last question for the six," Ian said, using the fake announcer voice he used in the locker room to make everyone laugh. "If you chuckleheads miss, then team twosome gets a chance to steal. If they miss it, you win. Either way, I'm going to drink my weight in beer and you fools are covering the bill. Ready?"

The others nodded.

"In what country was Arthur Conan Doyle born?" Ian

asked.

Svoboda cocked his head to the side. "Who?"

"The guy who wrote *Sherlock Holmes*," Christensen answered.

One of the rookies, Thibault, took a drink from his beer and said, "I thought that was a TV show."

"It was a book first," Christensen said, giving the rookie a don't-be-a-dumb-ass glare. "It's gotta be England. Holmes was the greatest English detective."

"Wrong!" Ian exclaimed.

Everyone on the other side of the table groaned. Christensen sank down in his chair while the rookie tried—and failed—to keep a serves-you-right smirk off his face. Ian turned to Cole and Tess.

"He was…" Tess paused. "Can I confer with my partner for a second?"

Ian nodded.

She waved him closer, and he leaned half out of his chair so he'd be close enough for this little chat about who in the hell knew what because it wasn't like either of them didn't know Doyle was born in Scotland. She pivoted in her chair so her back was mostly turned away from the guys on the other side of the table to give them a modicum of privacy. The move gave him a perfect view of the top swells of her tits—or it would have if he'd looked. He did not. At least not for long.

"The league minimum is around three-quarters of a million dollars," she said, her voice low. "You make at least that, right?"

"More." A lot more, but he didn't need to put that out there.

"Oh," she said, surprise lifting her tone. "Are you a really good player?"

Maybe he was a little more than off-kilter because he couldn't wrap his brain around the fact that she didn't know the answer to that. He did have a billboard up in the middle of Harbor City's touristy hot spot, he had a contract with Under Armour, he was in the sports news pretty much all the time. "You know the league minimum but not if I'm any good at hockey?"

"People aren't really my thing." She played with the tail of the bow holding the straps of her dress in place. "And the other guys, some of them are rookies, so they make a lot less?"

If he hadn't been so distracted by the way she toyed with the bow, wondering if it was going to hold, he would have caught on to her plan sooner. "You're not thinking…»

She nodded. "I am."

His wallet cried out in metaphorical protest, but how was he supposed to say no to that face? "You are a horrible influence."

"Nothing could be further from the truth." She smiled, showing off a dimple that could probably cause cavities. "I'm completely harmless."

He didn't believe that, not even for a second.

"You're sure?" she asked, turning serious.

When he nodded, she smiled, and it gave him the same buzz he'd gotten when they'd made the playoffs.

Turning back so she faced the table, Tess said in a loud, clear voice, "While I disagree, my partner insists he's right. Sir Arthur Conan Doyle was from Australia."

"Wrong," Ian said, smacking his palm down on the table for emphasis. "He was born in Scotland."

Cole couldn't believe it. She'd gotten him to pay the bar tab *and* thrown him under the bus. Australian? That wasn't even in the right hemisphere of the correct answer, and she knew it. There was definitely some tart to her sweetness.

While the other players erupted in high fives and smack talk, Cole wrapped his fingers around the arm of her chair and tugged it close. "That was not very nice."

"True," she said, not seeming the least bit sorry. "But look how happy you've made them."

Of course they were thrilled. The lucky bastards were going to be drinking on him all weekend—and he wasn't going to hear the end of it pretty much ever. In fact, Christensen had that look that always preceded enough shit-talking to fertilize every cornfield in Nebraska.

"But now *you* have to figure out a way to get me out of here without it looking like a retreat so I don't have to deal with all of that." He waved a hand at the celebratory dance moves Christensen and Svoboda were trying to pull off. "That would be cruel and unusual punishment on top of that bar bill."

She looked guilty for about three seconds, then said as she stood, "Well, we may have lost, but at least we don't have to dance or anything like that."

His fellow Ice Knights players clamped on to what she'd made sound like a throwaway line that most definitely wasn't.

"Dance! Dance! Dance!" they chanted in unison.

Not laughing wasn't an option, so he gave in to what had lately been a foreign reaction. "What have you done?"

Given the fact that he'd had to almost yell to be heard over his idiot teammates, he wasn't surprised when instead of hollering back, she raised herself up on her tiptoes and leaned in close.

"Giving you an escape," she said, her lips nearly touching his ear. "Come on, once around the dance floor and we can go out through the conservatory doors."

He glanced over at the door on the other side of the mostly packed dance floor. It would take some weaving and skill to get through the crowd without looking like they were running, but he was a guy used to moving the puck through a line of professional athletes paid highly to get it away by stick or by check, so this would be easy.

Grinning down at her, he grabbed her hand. "Good plan."

And it was, right up until they moved onto the dance floor and he had her in his arms. His steps were half a beat too slow, but more due to his own inability to dance than the scotch. His hand spanned the small of her back, resting against the smooth silk of her skin exposed by the backless dress, and her head fit against the pocket of his shoulder, because of course it had changed to a slow song as soon as they stepped on the parquet.

He noticed everything about her as they swayed to the beat: the hitch of her breath when he brushed his thumb against her skin, the way she moved closer as they made their way across the floor, and the tease of her curly hair against his neck. All of it combined into a heady mix of anticipation and desire that had him searching for the door before he did something stupid like give in to the urge to kiss her in the middle of the dance floor.

Then she looked up at him, her full lips slightly parted and desire on full display in her eyes. Suddenly, doing something stupid seemed like a very good idea.

"On the count of three, we make a break for the door," he said, forcing the words to almost sound normal.

And what came after that? Hell if he couldn't wait to find out.

Chapter Two

Tess's pillow was tickling her nose as it moved up and down in a smooth, steady rhythm as if it was taking deep, steady breaths—her heart paused and her lungs stopped functioning as she jackknifed into a sitting position, her eyes squeezed closed because looking meant seeing and that meant…she peeked.

Oh my God. It hasn't been a steaming-hot dream.

She'd had sex with Cole Phillips.

Cole.

Fucking.

Phillips.

Not Thor himself.

Multiple times.

In the conservatory.

In the foyer of his massive hotel room.

Finally, in the ginormous bed that was only being half used because they had been curled up together until about ten seconds ago.

Oh my fucking God.

She had obviously lost her mind. Oh sure, she could blame the three glasses of wine or the wedding atmosphere for helping to lower her guard, but one of Lucy's clients? A professional athlete? A guy she'd just met? For a woman who had three friends and figured that was more than enough, she didn't make new friends let alone lovers in an evening.

Next to her, Cole started to move, his hand patting the bed for her. "It's too early to get up, Mar—" He jolted up.

Now both of them were sitting in bed, staring at each other with horror-filled eyes and breathing as hard as if they'd just gotten done outrunning a pack of zombies.

Good thing she was the type of woman who accepted that fate had it in for her. If not, she would have been painfully disabused of that notion as soon as the metaphorical light bulb went on over her head that the first guy she'd had sex with in nearly forever had woken up thinking she was his ex-girlfriend. That would have been some real ouch right there.

"Tess," she said, gathering the sheet close to her chest and scooting one butt cheek at a time over to the edge of the bed. "My name's Tess."

"Of course it is." Cole shoved his fingers through his hair, and it magically fell untangled to his shoulders like he was in some kind of shampoo commercial. "I just wasn't all the way awake."

That wasn't fair—his perfect morning hair, not what he said. A giant whatever on almost calling her Marti, because it wasn't like she had any delusions about who she was and who he was and what the hell had just happened. Nope. She was all about unvarnished truth regarding her interactions with all but a handful of people. It's why she loved trivia. Facts were simple, straightforward, and easily defined. People were very much not that. Ever. Which she knew more than anyone and why the bold truth that she'd fallen prey to the wedding curse felt even worse. Judging by the way Not Thor's gaze was darting all over the hotel room, landing on every piece of furniture twice but not her a single time, he didn't get it.

"Don't freak out," she said as she lowered one foot to the floor and stood up, taking the sheet with her. "We got weddinged."

Of course he looked at her now, while she was trying to hold up the sheet with one hand and put on her panties she'd swiped off the carpet with the other. One-handed pantie put-on-ing was not easy for the non-coordinated like herself. Looking up at the ceiling and away from the man in the bed seemed to help, though, so that's what she did, using a standing-on-one-foot hop move followed by a quick yank up to get her undies in place.

"Weddinged? What does that mean?" Cole asked.

"We got caught up in the whatever of the happy occasion." She glanced down at him. That was a mistake. He was totally naked, but the sheet around his waist stopped her from getting the whole view in the morning light. "Then this happened."

"Weddinged." He added a little *huh* sound to the end of it, as if he was putting the new vocab word in a mental filing cabinet for use later.

"Exactly." She clutched the sheet to her chest as if he hadn't already seen, touched, and licked every bit of her, which she was not at all thinking about as she walked sideways to the chair where her dress had landed in the rush to get naked last night. "But hopefully it's still early enough that I can get back to my room without being seen."

He grabbed his phone off the bedside table. "It's ten."

"What?" An electric zap of panic shocked her right down to her toes. *Shit. No.*

Abandoning the sheet, she sprinted the rest of the way to the chair, grabbed her dress, and tugged it over her head as she hurried to the door. "I was supposed to be in Lucy's suite getting my hair done thirty minutes ago." She grabbed her purse, stuffed her bra inside it, and picked up her shoes from the floor by the door where she'd left them last night. "I gotta go."

"I'll see you later at the wedding."

Later? She had to face him again after this? *Oh, fuck me running.*

And since she had no idea what to say to that, she did what she always did and fell back on her friends the random factoids, whether she wanted to or not.

"Romans used to give newlyweds a special loaf of bread, and some grooms would break it over the bride's head, which is why we have wedding cakes now," she said.

Shut up, weird brain.

Cole chuckled. "I really hope Frankie doesn't try that with Lucy. I don't see it going over well."

She didn't disagree, but she didn't trust herself not to give a whole lecture on the history of that phrase, so she opted for brevity. "Bye."

And she all but ran from the room, down the nearby stairs and to her floor. Setting a speed record, she showered, got dressed, grabbed her bridesmaid's dress, and hustled with still damp curls to Lucy's suite. Her girls were all there. Lucy was getting her makeup done. Gina sat on a stool while a hairstylist pulled her hair into a complicated updo that seemed to be held together by hope and hairspray, but there were probably a million hairpins in there. Fallon sat in the corner, dress already on, hair pulled into a simple French braid as she watched hockey highlights on her phone.

"Look who finally arrived," Lucy said with a smile as she gave Tess an assessing once-over.

Tess jerked to a stop, biting the inside of her cheek to keep from spilling secrets or factoids. She did not want them to know what just went down. Cole would forget about her before the vows were said, and she was totally okay with that. She knew how to deal with being forgotten about. What she didn't know how to handle was her three best friends all looking at her like she was a king cake with a surprise hidden inside.

These women knew her. There was no way she'd hold up under an interrogation. Her best option might be to beg the makeup artist to do something drastic with her look so she'd have to stay perfectly still and couldn't move or talk or make eye contact. Was that possible outside of getting a *Mission Impossible*–type mask? Probably not. She was definitely screwed.

Gina let out a relieved sigh. "We were about to send the search party."

"That would be me," Fallon said, raising her hand.

"Sorry," Tess said, sitting down in the on-deck chair for the makeup artist. "I forgot to set an alarm."

"So it had nothing to do with sneaking off with Cole Phillips last night?" Lucy asked.

"We went into the conservatory for some quiet," Tess said, clasping her hands tight in her lap. "The DJ was loud."

"Poor Cole," Gina said between blasts of hairspray from the stylist. "That guy is in a rough way. Thanks for hanging out with him."

"How do you mean *rough*?" Not that she cared, but she *was* naturally curious. That was all.

Gina shook her head, much to her stylist's annoyance. "He's been dating and not dating Coach Peppers's daughter, Marti, for about a million years, and she finally called it off a while back. According to the online gossip, he's totally brokenhearted."

"Yeah," Lucy said before blotting her bright-red lipstick. "But will this one take?"

"That's the million-dollar question." Gina got down from

the chair as the stylist checked her over from every direction. "But she seems serious about it, even if he may not be ready to walk away. Oh, I hope it works out."

And that was Gina in a nutshell. No matter how she used to deny it before she met Ford, Gina was a total romantic at heart, and it was no surprise she'd become a wedding planner. She was all about the happily ever afters.

Tess? Not even close.

"Honestly, Tess, you're the best for keeping him from moping," Lucy said. "If anyone sees him doing it at the reception, especially when Marti is nearby, please send up flares. The guy needs all the friends he can get because he is a mess right now."

"He sure is playing like one," Fallon, the resident Ice Knights superfan, said. "He's distracted, and it shows on the ice."

"Not everyone gets a Lady Luck," Tess muttered.

Fallon rolled her eyes. "Don't even. Zach turning his game around had nothing to do with me."

"Well, either way, we Ice Knights fans salute you," Gina said.

Tess's brain was spinning. Things had just gone from her normal level of awkweird to something approaching epic levels of oh-my-God-run-away awkweird. She'd done something totally out of character for her and banged a guy she'd just met six ways from Sunday. Then—to make it even more uncomfortable—*he* was hung up on another chick, and they were all going to be at the wedding together.

There was no way this was going to be anything other than a disaster.

• • •

Cole was in hell, and they were playing the "Electric Slide."

There wasn't enough alcohol in the world for this—which was good because he was still footing the tab for the team. Sure, there was an open bar, but everyone but the rookies thought it was funnier to go to the hotel bar and not the wedding reception bar for their drinks. Assholes. Sure, they weren't wrong, it was funnier, but they were still assholes. There was no way it could get worse.

"So." Petrov drew the single-syllable word out into at least four. "You disappeared with the curly-haired chick last night."

Obviously, Cole's previous declarative statement was now rendered false.

Sliding his attention away from the dance floor and over to the man sitting next to him, he saw the center had ditched his bow tie, and he had a glass of top-shelf single malt in his hand and a shit-eating grin on his face. This was going to be worse.

Cole shrugged. "It was a dance."

"Then a disappearance."

Followed by some damn good sex and—oh yeah—the totally awesome move of waking up and calling the woman he was in bed with by his ex's name. That had been a shit move even if remembering his own name when he first woke up was a challenge. He'd spent the past six months waiting for Marti to agree to give it another go—which she always did—and turning away every single opportunity to get it on with anyone else. Then he'd gotten weddinged. Something the quick-thinking center next to him wasn't going to let him forget, so he might as well dig in and get chippy about it.

"You have a point to make, Petrov?" Cole asked.

"Just an observation and a hell-yeah for finally moving on." Petrov clinked his glass against Cole's. "I haven't seen you with anyone in months, despite the efforts of some of our more creative fans."

"I don't need to move on from anything." Eventually things would realign and go back to the way they had always been. Solid. Sure. Unchanging. Just the way he liked it. This was just a temporary glitch, not forever.

"You trying to tell me that nothing happened last night? Bullshit. I saw how you looked at her."

"Nothing important happened." Inwardly he cringed at what an asshole he sounded like, but he kept that internal, covered under fourteen layers of ice. However, if he gave Petrov even a hint that it had been more, he'd never hear the end of it. "It was a nice time."

Three nice times. He'd gone around and searched his room until he'd found the two torn-open condom packets on the dresser top and the one stuffed into the pocket of his suit pants from the time in the conservatory, just to double-check his memory that they'd been three nice, protected times.

The other forward on his line, Alex Christensen, had packed his wallet with condoms for, as he put it, "the premium opportunities a wedding offered." Cole had figured it for the hazing it was. Using them had never crossed his mind until Tess talked him into doing the one thing he never did voluntarily—lose. What in the world was going on?

"First Christensen lines my wallet with condoms, and now you're whispering in my ear about Tess," he mumbled to himself before looking up at the god-awful fresco on the ceiling of the reception room that had been painted with a Greek god theme, never mind that they had Icarus flying away from the sun instead of toward it.

"Maybe we all think it's time you tried a new path," Petrov said, completely missing that Cole's question had been rhetorical. "Ever think that maybe, even though Marti is one of the coolest chicks we know, you should just walk away after this breakup? It's been six months." He gestured toward the dance floor. "She seems to have moved on. Follow her lead.

You've been ignoring the other women throwing themselves at you for months, but last night you fall in with Tess? Sounds to me like you're ready to move on."

Cole looked over toward the dance floor. He didn't have to search to find her. Marti was dancing with that Wall Street guy, who looked like he couldn't make up his mind between ogling her tits or stealing from a widows and orphans charity fund. Where had she found this prick? She was better than him.

"If I could have everyone's attention," the DJ said over the music, loud enough to clear the questions from Cole's head. "It's time for the garter and bouquet toss."

A chair was brought out to the dance floor and a laughing Lucy was led out to it by the redheaded giant, Frankie, she'd married. As she sat down, Frankie whispered something in her ear that had the toughest, no-nonsense shark of a public relations crisis management guru blushing, and then he reached under her dress and pulled her lace garter down her leg.

"If we can get all the single men to line up at the far end of the dance floor and the single ladies at the opposite end here by me," the DJ said.

Cole had absolutely no intention of moving from his seat, but Christensen and Petrov each hooked an arm under his, hauled him up out of his seat, and force-marched him to where all the single dudes were milling about.

"I'm not catching that thing," Cole said, stuffing his hands deep in his pockets.

Christensen just grinned that never-lost-a-tooth miracle smile of his. "Don't worry, the plan is for us to catch it for you."

"You two are assholes," he said with a sigh.

Petrov lifted one shoulder in a lazy shrug. "Something you already knew to be true."

"One," the DJ said, starting the countdown.

Frankie twirled the garter around one finger and eyeballed the crowd of single guys. Cole took a step back deeper into the crowd, only to be shoved none too gently back to the front by a pair of his line mates who really needed to get a hobby or a girlfriend or both.

"Two."

Frankie pulled back on the garter like it was a slingshot and aimed at a part of the crowd farthest away from Cole. He looked over his shoulders at Christensen and Petrov, shooting them a smirk. The only way to keep him at the front was if they both stayed there blocking his path, but that left the entire rest of the crowd unguarded if they were going to snatch that garter out of midair for him as they'd planned. It was the curse of the double-team.

"Three."

At the last second, Frankie pivoted and shot the garter straight at Cole. It flew through the air like a puck zinging toward the goal. He didn't mean to reach up and grab the flying lace, but muscle memory was a helluva thing. The garter was in his hand before he realized he was reaching for it.

Motherfucker.

He shoved the damn thing into his pocket as fast as he could and ignored the self-satisfied laughter coming from the two chuckleheads behind him. Maybe no one noticed.

"And we have our bachelor winner," the DJ said. "Now, all the single ladies lined up on my side of the dance floor, get ready because here comes the bouquet!"

Lucy turned her back to the gaggle of women, did a couple of I'm-about-to-toss-it-but-didn't moves, and then—finally—let the bouquet go. It arced across the opening before smacking Tess hard in the face and then falling to the floor as everyone in the room let out a collective gasp.

"I'm all right," Tess said as she picked red rose petals out of her hair. "'Tis only a flesh wound."

Old school Monty Python? He grinned despite his annoyance at the whole garter thing.

"Let's give a hand to our lucky guests who will get the dancing started," the DJ said, his shaking voice obviously an attempt to cover his laughter.

The fuck? A dance? No. This whole carrying-around-Lucy's-garter thing was weird enough without adding in a very public slow dance with the woman he'd gotten weddinged with last night.

He didn't move. Neither did Tess. Instead they both stood there on opposite sides of the dance floor, her looking just as horrified as he felt.

"Mr. Garter Belt and Ms. Bouquet to the Face." The DJ laughed at his own joke. "You're up."

"But I didn't catch it," Tess said, her voice going up at the last word.

No one seemed to be listening to her valid argument, though. Instead, her people were doing pretty much the same thing as his—shoving him out onto the dance floor as a slow song started playing. Last night, he'd curled an arm around her waist and pulled her close without a second thought. Not so much today. Without the high of the trivia game and the social lubrication of a few drinks, everything seemed to move slower with a higher level of awkward.

"I'm not gonna turn into a stalker," she said as she settled her left hand on his shoulder. "You don't have to worry."

Way to go, dumb-ass, you made her feel like shit. You should bottle that talent. "Who said I was worried?"

She looked up at him as they moved around the dance floor, filling up with other couples. "So you do that a lot and don't have weird stalker problems?"

"Do what?" How had he not noticed last night that she

had one blue eye and one green? It was subtle, only a few shades different, and she was wearing glasses, adding in a protective layer between her and the world, but still he should have noticed. "You have heterochromia iridum."

"It's not uncommon," she said, narrowing her eyes at him. "More than two hundred thousand cases are diagnosed each year, but don't change the subject. I know you're still hung up on your ex. I have no delusions that last night was anything more than just us getting weddinged."

Her no-nonsense declaration hit with the sharp crack of a stick to the cheek. For reasons unknown, it burned, stung, and just might have drawn blood. Not that it mattered. It didn't. It wasn't like Tess was interested in him anyway.

He spun them around a little faster than the beat, needing to move. "Good to know."

After that, they both kept their mouths shut, which was for the best. Last night had been a fluke occurrence. His tomorrows were already planned right down to the alphabetized books on the shelves in his den, the breakfast he'd been having every day since he was ten, and the woman he was going to end up with—Marti. The first girl he'd ever kissed and the one who had always been there for him no matter what. They'd find their way back to each other. They always did.

"Did you know the garter toss originated in England and France because guests would try to tear off a piece of the bride's dress for good luck?" Tess asked, her grip on his shoulder a bit tenser than it had been before. "Grooms started flinging part of the bride's wedding outfit to calm the crowd and stop the wife from having a nervous breakdown at the idea of having her outfit ripped to shreds while she was wearing it."

"I didn't." He mentally shook off the unease that crept in whenever he thought about a possible change in his routine and dug for a wedding factoid of his own. Competitive? Him? Fuck yeah. "Did you know bouquets were originally garlic, herbs, and spices carried by the bride to ward off evil spirits?"

Tess cracked a smile for the first time since she'd gotten a face full of rosebuds. "I'll add that one to my list."

The tension seeped out of his shoulders, and even though he didn't mean to, he drew her in closer and they swayed to the last bars of the song. Moving on to something up-tempo, the DJ called to the crowd to put on their dancing shoes. Yeah, Cole definitely didn't own any of those and, judging by the way Tess just stood there and looked around at everyone else, she didn't, either. Finally, her gaze landed back on him.

"Good luck with her, your ex," Tess said, taking a step back out of his arms. "I hope it all works out."

Before he could say anything in response, Tess hustled away from him, disappearing into the crowd. Looking down, he spotted a couple of rose petals clinging, against the odds, to his tux lapel. He wasn't likely to see Tess ever again, but he still slipped the petals into his pocket as he walked off the dance floor, wondering what factoid she would be able to tell him about roses, the origin of the tuxedo, and the stats for the most popular wedding songs. He'd have to figure out for himself, though, because she was right. They had gotten weddinged. Really, what were the chances of ever running into Tess again? Zilch. Zero. Nada. And that was a good thing. Really.

So why was he staring at the spot where she'd disappeared instead of over at Marti and her idiot date like he usually would have been? Fuck if he knew. He was a hockey player, not Freud.

Chapter Three

One month later...

If there was anything Tess could count on in life, it was her period coming every twenty-eight days like a perfectly engineered clock made of cramps and Almond Joy cravings. Today was day twenty-nine, according to her tracking app, and she was sitting on the edge of the tub in her tiny bathroom not breathing and watching four home pregnancy tests lined up on the counter next to the sink while Kahn weaved around and in between her calves.

Were four tests overkill for what would no doubt be a negative result? Probably. They'd used condoms. Three of them. It had only been one night. More than likely it was just the stress of her asshole landlord threatening to raise the rent on her flower shop and her apartment above it. Forever in Bloom was finally turning a healthy profit, and she had plans to use that extra cash to hire an accountant so she wouldn't be doing the books herself.

Kahn mewled and took a bite out of Tess's leg with his

pointy little teeth.

"Ow!" She massaged the spot right above her ankle to rub the sting out. "What was that for?"

The kitten, a puffball of black and white fur, just flicked his tail and stared up at Tess as if she'd somehow disappointed him by even having to ask the question. It had only been a week and they were still getting to know each other, but damn, Kahn's teeth were no joke, and from the kneecaps down she was starting to look like a pincushion.

Her phone buzzed as it vibrated against the counter, and she sat up straight, bite forgotten and nervous swirling in her belly remembered. If she'd been all in for the test result to come back one way or another, this experience might be different. Calmer? More hopeful? Instead, she was just a jumble of mixed-up emotions ranging from please-let-it-be-yes to oh-my-fucking-God-no and everything in between.

Family was something she'd never really had until she met her girls Lucy, Fallon, and Gina. Her mom saw her mostly as an inconvenience to be dropped off at various relatives' houses whenever possible for as long as possible. Those aunts and uncles never let her forget that she was an obligation and it was only because of their Christian duty that they welcomed her into their homes—even if that welcome was more of a tired tolerance. But a baby? That would be creating her own family. She could make sure to do it right because she'd seen firsthand how it could be done wrong.

Doubt circled upward, twisting and distorting all of that hopefulness because what if she really wasn't meant to have a family? How many times did she have to learn that lesson? Even if she kept the baby—if there *was* a baby—did she really think she'd be enough as a single mom? Or would she just repeat every mistake that had been visited onto her?

Kahn took a swipe at her shin and narrowed his little eyes at her as if to say, *Just look already.*

"I thought the whole cats-rule-the-humans thing was an exaggeration," Tess said more to herself than the kitten and stood up so she could lean over and look at the pregnancy test result screens on each of the four sticks.

Plus.

She stared, blinking and uncomprehending.

Plus.

Her pulse skyrocketed.

Plus.

A lump—of excitement? anxiety? wonder?—formed in her throat.

Plus.

Before she kept forgetting to breathe, and now, it felt like she couldn't stop inhaling and exhaling air, but she was doing it so quickly that none of it was actually getting to her lungs. She pressed her fist to her belly, holding it firmly in place, and then jerked it away.

Baby.

There.

Okay, not really. And it wasn't a baby yet, but a fetus so small an ultrasound tech would probably be able to circle something on a screen but to Tess it would be indecipherable. That didn't change the fact that this was happening. She was pregnant.

She plopped back down on the edge of the tub, her knees too weak to keep her upright, and focused on her breathing enough to actually slow the panicked hyperventilating thing she had going on and inhale a long, smooth breath through her nose and out her mouth. She repeated that five more times before she gave in to the constant whir of her brain and tried to process what she was going to do next. She had options.

It was too late for Plan B, but she could get an abortion.

She could have the baby but give it up for adoption.

Keep it and start her own family.

So which one was the right answer for her, right now, in this moment? Abortion made sense. Beyond her girls, she didn't have a support system. Was she really ready to be a single mom without one? Did she have the tools to do it right or would she be continuing the family curse? She'd barely gotten to a point in her life where she felt qualified to have a pet. A baby needed and deserved so much more attention and love than she was sure she knew how to give.

Then there were the logistical issues. The demands of being a small business owner weren't conducive to going it alone on the parenting route. Who would cover the flower shop when she had to go to prenatal appointments? Could she afford health insurance for the both of them? What about day care? That was easily the cost of another car payment, if not more.

Standing up, she tried to still the thoughts running through her brain faster than she could grasp and then walked over to the bathroom mirror. She lifted her shirt, looking down at her stomach. The little pudge under her belly button had been there for years, but still she expanded her abdomen to make it look bigger, rounder. That's what it could be in a few months.

But was she ready? Even with her doubts, she couldn't ignore that feeling that she was. She was staring down her thirtieth birthday, owned her own business, had an apartment, didn't have *that* much debt, and a family was pretty high up there on her want list. Most importantly of all, she *wasn't* her mother and never would be. This baby would know it was loved, had a place in the world, and was never an obligation. She couldn't fix her childhood by having this baby, but she could give this baby the childhood she'd wanted—that had to count for something.

It wouldn't be easy. Single momming it was not for the faint of heart. Then again, neither was anything else she'd managed to do in her life, including working her own way through college, starting a business, and just living life on her own in general.

She could do this.

Glancing down at her belly, she rubbed her palm over it, one soothing circle followed by another and another.

She *would* do this.

She was having this baby.

Letting out a deep breath, her lips curled upward in a smile that didn't falter until two words entered her mind: *Cole Phillips.*

How in the hell was she going to tell him?

• • •

Paint and Sip nights with Lucy, Gina, and Fallon were sacred. She wouldn't miss it, not even with her brain not taking half a breath between shooting out pregnancy factoids at her.

"Placenta" is Latin for the word "cake."

The uterus expands more than five hundred times its usual size during the course of pregnancy.

Babies drink urine in the womb.

God, her brain really needed to shut the fuck up already.

"Perfect timing, Tess." Gina slipped her arm through Tess's as they walked through the door into the studio. "I am dying for a glass of wine. It has been *a week*. The bride from Harbor City is a delight but her soon-to-be husband the accountant? Oh my God. Total nightmare. Groomzilla galore."

"Tell me everything," Tess said.

And that's all it took to get Gina off and running on this Hank guy and how high-maintenance he was. It was a brilliant move. No one told hilarious demanding-client stories like Gina, and this would get them through at least the setup for tonight's painting. She was going to tell her girls about the pregnancy and enlist their help in tracking down Cole's number so she could tell him, but she wasn't ready yet. Instead, she listened to Gina describe the ten-minute voicemail Hank had left about the difference between white shadow and eggshell mist as they sat down next to Lucy and Fallon.

"Have you seen this week's painting yet?" Lucy asked, nodding toward the front.

Larry, their instructor, stood next to a painting of a pie with a radioactive glow sitting on a windowsill with a view of a decrepit nuclear reactor. Someone must have been reading about Chernobyl or Three Mile Island.

"I don't know," Tess said. "I think including the skull and crossbones as an imprint on the pie crust is pretty genius."

"We need to get him to try some cheerier reading material just for a change of pace," Gina said as she poured four small plastic cups of red wine. "Last week was a cow being led into a slaughterhouse."

"Larry would find a way to make *Harold and the Purple Crayon* horrifying," Fallon said, accepting her cup from Gina. "The man has a gift—let him express it."

Gina made noises of agreement as she handed a second cup to Lucy and then turned to Tess, the cup filled nearly to the brim with cheap Merlot. For a second, all Tess could imagine was a little skull and crossbones etched into the plastic cup.

"I'm good," she said, waving off the drink.

Gina chuckled. "You know this high-quality product isn't available on just any grocery store shelf."

"Yeah," Lucy said, joining in on the joke. "You wouldn't want to turn this stuff down unless you're pregnant."

Tess blanched, her palm automatically going to her belly.

All three of her girls stared for a second, their jaws going slack with realization.

Tess nodded. "And I'm keeping the baby."

"You're pregnant!" Fallon practically shouted. "This is awesome."

If only it had been Gina, there would have been hope that the two words would have been whispered. With Fallon, a Hartigan right down to her feisty Irish bones, it came out as a bellow. Everyone in Paint and Sip whipped around to stare at her. She smoothed her hand over her curls, all of which were frizzing from the light snow that had just started to fall as she crossed the parking lot, and tried her best to melt into the background. It's where she liked to be. People forgot about her and, as she'd learned at a young age, it was always safer when she wasn't noticed. Being reminded of her presence had only made her relatives remember that she'd been foisted upon them in the first place. They'd start complaining loudly about the extra mouth and wondering with harsh regularity when her mother was going to come reclaim her.

That wasn't going to happen in the art studio, though. All the regulars, including her girls, were raising their cups in toast—even Larry, who almost looked like he might be smiling.

"Thanks," Tess said when they wouldn't stop staring at her as if waiting for confirmation of Fallon's exclamation. "I'll be one of the nearly forty percent of American women who are unmarried when they have babies."

All of the happy murmurings silenced, and Larry's hint of a grin disappeared as if she'd imagined it.

Way to go, Tess. Nothing like letting your awkweird show in public.

"To Tess and the forty percenters," Gina said, holding up her cup.

Years of working as a wedding coordinator and using the force of her personality to get a crowd of tipsy strangers to behave as they should must have worked its magic, because all the other painters and Larry raised their cups and then went back to getting ready for tonight's painting. Fallon, Gina, and Lucy wrapped their arms around her in a group hug that helped settle her. This feeling, the one that made her warm and content and at ease, was what she wanted the baby to grow up bathed in.

After the hug ended, Lucy held her by the shoulders and gave her the look that sent her misbehaving crisis communications clients into a flurry of I-will-never-fuck-up-again activity. "Who is the mystery man?"

"Yeah, who have you been hiding from us?" Gina asked, sitting down in front of her blank canvas, wine in hand and attention focused solely on Tess.

"I was hoping to talk to you about this later." Paint and Sip was not exactly the best location for spilling her one-night-stand pregnancy secret.

"Good luck with that." Fallon snorted and sat down on her stool. "With these two, that's not gonna happen."

The no-nonsense emergency room nurse always called it like she saw it, and she wasn't wrong. Still…

"Did you know a rhino's horn is made of hair?"

None of her girls even batted an eye. Damn it. There was something to be said for being able to throw people off their game by throwing random facts their way. It was amazing how often that worked. For someone like her who hated to people, it kept interactions blessedly contained and short.

"Nice try, Tess," Lucy said. "But we're here so often that Larry barely even shushes us anymore. Spill."

"Cole's the dad. We used three condoms, but something must have been wrong with them."

"He triple wrapped?" Fallon asked.

"At the same time?" Lucy looked up at the ceiling as if she was imagining the logistics of rolling one condom on top of another and then doing it again just to be sure. "I know he has this whole cleanliness thing, but that's just fucking weird."

"No," Tess managed to squeak out. Oh God, why was this embarrassing? These were her closest friends. They knew she had sex. "We did it three times the night before Lucy got married."

"In one night?" Gina did a quick series of quick happy claps. "No wonder you were late for hair and makeup."

"I'm impressed you were able to roll out of bed at all," Lucy said with a chuckle. "Good for you."

"Wait," Fallon said, using one of her paintbrushes as a pointer and directing it at Tess. "That was only a month ago. How can you know you're pregnant? You could just be late."

"I took tests."

"Plural?" Lucy asked.

Tess nodded. "Four of them. They were all positive."

"Then I guess after Paint and Sip, I'll go get my uncle's shotgun he left me along with the house and we go have a little chat with Cole about his intentions." Gina squared her shoulders and arranged her brushes, prepping to paint the radioactive apocalypse. "The serial number was filed off it, but I'm sure that was just a Luca family quirk and not because it was probably used in the commission of a crime like Ford says. It'll be fine."

"He doesn't need to have intentions," Tess said, the words tumbling out of her as she tried to figure out how to explain the situation to her girls so they didn't form a vigilante posse. "I'm not trying to make Cole marry me. I barely know him and, anyway, I'm not sure I even *ever* want to be married. However, there's no way I'm going to keep this baby a secret. He deserves to know he's going to have a child."

"So we go along for moral support," Lucy said.

Yeah. That was not going to happen. "I'm sure that's how he'll see it, as opposed to oh, I don't know, the torch-bearing villagers after his head."

Gina *tsk-tsk*ed. "We're not that scary."

"Yeah we are," Fallon and Lucy said at the same time.

"I appreciate it, but this is something I need to do myself. All I need is his address." She turned to Fallon, who was engaged to one of Cole's fellow Ice Knights players, and Lucy, who kept the players out of hot water. "Can either of you get that for me?"

Lucy took out her phone and opened her contacts app. "Consider it done." She hit send.

Tess's phone buzzed in her pocket alerting her that Lucy's text went through. "Thanks, you guys are the best."

"We're your best friends," Fallon said, reaching over to give her a quick hug. "It's what we do."

"Well, that and buy a million teeny tiny baby clothes," Gina said with way too much excitement.

There'd be no guessing on which one the baby's spoiler aunt would be.

Lucy swiped Tess's wine cup. "And drink your wine now that you can't."

"More wine for us," Gina said with a giggle as she snagged the cup from Lucy.

Fallon, who never messed around when it came to a competition, did an oh-look move and then just took the cup from a distracted Gina and downed it before anyone could stop her.

They were all laughing hard enough that when Larry shushed them for the beginning of class, they could barely catch a breath. That was the thing with her girls—they always made things fun, even the hard things. Her phone buzzed in her pocket, alerting her for the second time that Lucy had texted Cole's address. Now all she had to do was figure out how to tell her baby's daddy that the stork was coming to town. That would be easy, right?

Hi, we haven't talked since that dance when I told you good luck with getting back together with your ex, but we're gonna have a baby. Surprise!

Oh yeah, this was going to go over like Forever in Bloom running out of roses on Valentine's Day.

Acknowledgments

Y'all, I have the best job in the world writing happily ever afters and there is no way I could do it without the support and smarts of the good people at Entangled, specifically Liz, Jessica, Riki, Stacy, and Heather. This group of women makes the world work—even the fictional worlds. As always, I'm awed and amazed to get to work with Jenn and Sarah at Social Butterfly. These ladies know how to get things done! If you follow me online at all, you know my life would crumble without Rachel. Seriously. Shout outs to Kimberly Kincaid and Robin Covington for being my ride or dies. You two are a mess and I love you so hard. And, of course, none of this would happen without the most amazing readers in all of Romancelandia. THANK YOU for sharing the precious free time you have with my characters and me. I'm so grateful. One final thank you goes out to the Flynn family for being the absolute best—even when I'm on deadline.

Xoxo,
Avery

About the Author

Avery Flynn has three slightly wild children, loves a hockey-addicted husband, and is desperately hoping someone invents the coffee IV drip. Find out more about Avery on her website, follow her on Twitter, like her on her Facebook page, or friend her on her Facebook profile. Join her street team, The Flynnbots, on Facebook. Also, if you figure out how to send Oreos through the internet, she'll be your best friend for life.

Discover more Amara titles...

NOTHING BUT TROUBLE
a *Credence, Colorado* novel by Amy Andrews

For five years, Cecilia Morgan has played personal assistant to former NFL quarterback Wade Carter. But just when she finally gives her notice, his father's health fails, and Wade whisks her back to his hometown. CC will stay for his dad—for now—even if that means ignoring how sexy her boss is starting to look in his Wranglers. Wade can't imagine his life without his "left tackle." She's the only person who can tell him "no" and strangely, it's his favorite quality. But now they're living under the same roof and bickering like an old married couple. Suddenly, five years of fighting is starting to feel a whole lot like foreplay. What's a quarterback to do when he realizes he might be falling for his "left tackle"? Throw a Hail Mary she'll never see coming, of course.

JUST ONE OF THE GROOMSMEN
a *Getting Hitched in Dixie* novel by Cindi Madsen

Addison Murphy is the girl you grab a beer with—and now that one of her best guy friends is getting married, she'll add "groomsman" to that list, too. When Tucker Crawford returns to his small hometown, he doesn't expect to see the nice pair of bare legs sticking out from under the hood of a broken-down car. Certainly doesn't expect to feel his heart beat faster when he realizes they belong to one of his best friends. Hiding the way he feels from the guys through bachelor parties, cake tastings, and rehearsals is one thing. But he's going to need to do a lot of compromising if he's going to convince her to take a shot at forever with him—on her terms this time.

Not So Happily Ever After
a *British Bad Boys* novel by Christina Phillips

Two years ago, I accidentally, yeah maybe on purpose, crossed that line with my best friend and it ruined everything. I haven't seen him much since. But now he's standing at my door. And then he gives me that half smile, and I know I'm about to agree to do something I'm going to regret. I've got to spend two months with him now...and that's not the worst part.

69 Million Things I Hate About You
a *Winning the Billionaire* novel by Kira Archer

After Kiersten wins sixty-nine million dollars in the lotto, she has more than enough money to quit working for her impossibly demanding boss. But where's the fun in that? When billionaire Cole Harrington finds out about the office pool betting on how long it'll take him to fire his usually agreeable assistant, he decides to spice things up and see how far he can push her until she quits. But the bet sparks a new dynamic between them, and they cross that fine line between hate and love.

Made in the USA
Monee, IL
31 January 2020

21120403R00164